Anna Legat is a Wiltshire-based author, best known for her DI Gillian Marsh murder mystery series. A globetrotter and Jack-of-all-trades, Anna has been an attorney, legal adviser, a silver-service waitress, a school teacher and a librarian. She read law at the University of South Africa and Warsaw University, then gained teaching qualifications in New Zealand. She has lived in far-flung places all over the world where she delighted in people-watching and collecting precious life experiences for her stories. Anna writes, reads, lives and breathes books and can no longer tell the difference between fact and fiction.

AT
DEATH'S
DOOR

ANNA LEGAT

ACCENT

First published in 2022 by Headline Accent
An imprint of HEADLINE PUBLISHING GROUP

1

Cataloguing in Publication Data is available from the British Library

ISBN 978 1 7861 5994 6

Typeset in 10.5/13pt Bembo Std by Jouve (UK), Milton Keynes

Printed and bound in Great Britain by Clays Ltd, Elcograf S.p.A.

HEADLINE PUBLISHING GROUP
An Hachette UK Company
Carmelite House
50 Victoria Embankment
London EC4Y 0DZ

www.headline.co.uk
www.hachette.co.uk

AT
DEATH'S
DOOR

Chapter One

It was raining – an incessant drizzle, thin and misted like a giant spider's web spun over the swamps by industrious Arachne. Anaemic sunrays seeped through the clouds, giving them a metallic polish. Although the excavation site had been drained prior to the dig commencing, even this feeble precipitation was already causing trouble: the ground had turned into a soggy sponge smeared with the dirty grey icing of mud. Puddles were expanding in depth and diameter, determined to join forces and turn the dig into an underwater wonderland, Bishops Well's very own Atlantis. Now and again the wind would throw a tantrum and pull down someone's hood, give someone else a vicious slap or a lashing of water under their collar. The temperature teetered in the upper single digits. It was early November and the weather couldn't quite make up its mind whether it wanted to continue being autumnal or to boldly venture into the realm of winter.

Sam Dee was soaked to the bone. There was a leak in his left boot of which he had not been aware until now. His toes felt like slimy tadpoles wriggling in a puddle. He was cursing the day when he had agreed to join the damned Bishops Well Archaeological Association. He had done this under duress: his lovely but unrelenting neighbour, Maggie Kaye, had twisted his arm so hard that it was either joining the group or having his arm broken. If he hadn't conceded defeat there and then, she would probably have proceeded to kneecap him until he said yes.

Maggie was bristling with enthusiasm for the project. She was the driving force behind the draining of the swamp to excavate what was believed to be an ancient Celtic village. There were some scant records of the existence of a Bronze Age settlement, which the chair of the society, Cherie Hornby, had uncovered in the vaults of Bishops' church, St John the Baptist.

Maggie though relied on additional evidence, which happened to be the existence of a woman's ghost, haunting the swamps (according to Maggie, and Maggie alone). In Sam's professional opinion, and he used to be a barrister after all, Maggie's evidence would be considered circumstantial, not to mention utterly fantastical, and would be dismissed out of hand by any respectable adjudicator; though Sam wouldn't dream of telling her that. He was probably the only person with whom she had shared her imaginings. He didn't want to be unkind by trying to bring her down to earth and anchor her in the world of the living, with all its rules of common sense and rational thought.

That was his professional take on things. From a personal point of view, deep, deep down and against his better judgement, he believed her. After all, she had successfully defied reason on previous occasions, and had been proved correct. Secondly, he simply couldn't hurt her feelings. He was fond of Maggie despite her eccentricities. He had joined the Association to please her, hoping that his tokenistic act would be the end of it. But it was only the beginning, for soon he had been enlisted to get down on his knees and start digging. In bad weather. With toads jumping in and out of his pockets.

'You're doing a grand job, Samuel!'

Maggie was standing over him, beaming her wide, dimpled smile. Her yellow wellies and high-vis windbreaker seemed to bring some much-needed warmth to the hole in which he was squatting. With Maggie nearby, he no longer resented this muddy pit. On the contrary, it seemed rather cosy.

She slid into the pit and produced a hot flask. 'I thought you could do with a nice cup of coffee.'

Sam didn't have to be asked twice. He accepted the steaming

cup and drank from it in big gulps while, at the same time, warming his hands on it. He returned the empty cup to Maggie who screwed it on to the flask.

'Any finds?' he asked, not because he believed for one minute that there was anything to be found here, but because he didn't want Maggie to go away.

'Edgar and Michael found some cracked bits that look like remnants of clay pottery, and there appears to be a fragment of a wooden structure, possibly a partition of some kind, where James is digging,' Maggie enthused while Sam instantly thought of fly-tipping. 'Cherie is taking photos. We'll have them verified with Professor Fitzgerald. Vera is taking samples for carbon dating. It's happening, Samuel – this is really happening!' Another bright beam. It nearly blinded him.

'That's great, Maggie. And she – the ghost, I mean – is she still about? Even in this weather?'

Maggie peered at him with a hint of suspicion. He shouldn't be mocking her, but he couldn't quite help himself. She said, quite gravely, 'She's always here.'

'Here! Here!' James bellowed excitedly. Sam could only see his head bobbing and his arms flailing from his pit. 'Come here! Take a look at this!'

There was so much urgency in James's voice that everybody flocked to see what the hullabaloo was about.

Maggie charged out of Sam's pit but slid back right into his arms. 'Give me a leg up, Samuel!' She exhaled a hot breath smelling of chocolate into his face.

Awkwardly, Sam placed his hands on her muddied bottom and pushed, thinking that there was more to Maggie Kaye than hot air. She was one substantial lady. Her fingers skidded and she plummeted at Sam again. He tensed his shoulders to protect himself against being crushed to death. Summoning all his manly strength, he heaved her up and at last she scrambled out of the pit. She wiped her face with a muddy hand and looked down at him. 'What are you still doing in there? Come on, let's go!' Caked in dirt, the whites of her eyes flashing, she looked like one of those female mud wrestlers.

'My God!' Cherie waved her arms towards them. 'We've found human remains! It's a burial site!'

With it being an archaeological dig on a suspected burial ground, uncovering human remains seemed perfectly in order. Sam had expected a skull and a few bones, maybe a couple of artefacts, jewellery or weapons which would have been buried with their owner to accompany him or her into the afterlife. But what he saw couldn't be further from his idea of an archaeological find.

The body was exceptionally well preserved, as if it had been mummified. The skin was darkened and desiccated, patches of it missing in places. The lips were gone, exposing a macabre grin of dirt-yellowed teeth. There were no weapons, but the corpse was dressed in rotting rags impregnated with soil and mould. Perhaps they weren't rags, but a dress: a short, sleeveless tunic. There was a hint of geometrical print on it, a combination of concentric circles, squares, and triangles. There was no distinct colour to it other than hues of muddy grey.

'When I dug through to the solid wood, I thought, hell, it may be a roof beam, or some other part of a dwelling ... I lifted it to peer underneath, and there she was! In her full glory ...' James was the only one standing inside the pit – the grave – while everyone else gathered above, gaping. He looked up at them, his eyes darting from one face to the next in bewilderment. 'How did I know?'

'Know what?' Edgar Flynn asked. A clinical psychiatrist, he was good at asking open-ended questions.

'That she'd be here! I mean, look at this, I dug out the exact length and width of her tomb ... as if I knew where to find her.'

At first, Sam attributed James's strange words to the shock of discovering the body. But then, upon a closer examination, he realised: James's pit was aligned precisely with the grave. The body had been uncovered in full by removing the wooden lid. Like a well-informed gravedigger rather than an amateur archaeologist, James

Weston-Jones had hit the bull's eye when he had delineated the perimeter of his dig.

'It's the name of the game, James. You struck it lucky, that's all,' Edgar Flynn explained.

'We knew where to look,' Cherie went on the offensive. 'All the records pointed us to this area. We made an educated guess and we were rewarded, simple as that. Now, let's be careful with the remains. They are ancient, they could easily crumble in our hands … Luckily for us, it looks like they've been well preserved in the swamp. This is a typical bog body. Right … James, get out of there. I'll photograph everything every step of the way. We'll—'

'This isn't a bog body. This is a crime scene.'

It was Michael Almond. A forensic pathologist who worked for the CID in nearby Sexton's Canning, he knew what he was saying. 'We must call the police.'

'A crime scene?'

'That corpse hasn't been buried here since the Bronze Age, no way. This grave dates back to the mid-twentieth century at the most. It can't have been here much longer than fifty years. The fabric is far too well preserved, and it looks like cotton.'

Without further ado, Michael whipped out his mobile and dialled 999. He told the operator who he was and what was needed to secure the scene of crime. He had usurped full authority from Cherie, who gawked at him with dismay and the greatest of disappointment. Her prized Celtic village was no more than a crime scene!

Deep down, Sam was relieved: there'd be no more digging. At least, not for him. He would go home, have a hot shower, a double brandy, a fresh change of clothes, and spend the rest of the evening watching a good film. In future, he would think twice before agreeing to participate in his neighbour's outlandish projects, no matter how nicely she asked or how hard she twisted his arm.

She was doing it again – twisting his arm. Literally! Her fingers were clutching him tighter and tighter. Sam turned to free his arm and caught a glimpse of Maggie's face. The mud had dried on her, forming a white mask. Her eyes were rounded and her mouth gaping open, in a state of frozen shock.

'Are you all right, Maggie?'

'It's her,' she whispered, 'the ghost I've been seeing here, in the swamp. I told you about her. It *is* her!'

'We don't yet know for sure that it is a woman. All we have is a cadaver and scraps of mouldy rags.'

'Oh, it is! It's a woman. It's *the* woman! She's wearing the same dress with an imprint on it: circles, triangles. I can see it: the primary colours – vivid reds and blues and yellows, like a Cubist painting. She has black hair. Very long – all the way to her waist.'

And she is the queen of Sheba. Sam had just enough sense not to say it out loud.

Chapter Two

I should have known that she wasn't Boudicca or some other Celtic woman stranded on earth three millennia after dying. They – the dead – don't hang out amongst us – the living – for that long. If they did, the air would be thick with souls, a bit like the M5 southbound on the first day of the school holidays. No, they only pause briefly before passing on to the other side: sometimes to say goodbye, sometimes to cause mischief, and sometimes to finish unfinished business. Most of them don't linger at all – life after death seems to carry so much excitement and promise that they bounce off into it hastily. They generally move on and never look back.

I had been seeing the Swamp Lady ever since I had started seeing the dead. Whenever I wandered into Sexton's Wood I would be drawn to the swamp where, without fail, I would come across her. She would sit on a moss-covered felled tree or amble aimlessly, her feet hardly touching the ground but sometimes dipping into the murky green water, stirring it faintly like one of those long-legged water striders.

I had assumed she was a Celt. Local lore had it that a prehistoric Celtic settlement, as old as Stonehenge, existed here before slowly sinking into oblivion in the rising marshes. So, I thought the Swamp Lady was one of its inhabitants – it was an easy mistake to make.

Michael Almond had dispelled my misconceptions. He had every reason to be right – he was, after all, a forensic pathologist, bound to know a thing or two about dead bodies. Without a doubt the Swamp Lady was a modern-day woman, secretly buried in isolated marshy woodland where nobody would ever find her.

Against all the odds, *I* had found her.

Well, OK, James Weston-Jones had. But without sounding boastful, if it hadn't been for me, no one would have thought of looking for her there. I was the only one who could see her ghost prowling the swamps and it was my duty to put the poor thing to rest.

Seeing dead souls seems like such a gift – in honesty, it is nothing but a curse. I don't want to see them. I have never asked to see any of them, anyone other than my missing sister, Andrea. She went AWOL twenty-five years ago, and is presumed dead but her spirit has never showed up. Meanwhile all the others keep turning up uninvited.

I can't speak the truth about seeing the dead – people already have their doubts about me. They call me Mystic Maggie behind my back. Only my mum knows. And Samuel, my neighbour. But that's it. It will go no further. I don't want to become the proverbial village idiot – the butt of all jokes. In most people's minds, the line between the supernatural and plain lunacy is very thin. Before it all started, I would have considered someone like me a fraud and a charlatan, or at the very least, barking mad. Today, I don't know what to make of it all, but I am certain that it isn't a figment of my imagination. Those poor souls stranded on earth do exist and I can see them, but to what end, I haven't the faintest.

The police, led by DI Gillian Marsh – Michael's partner – arrived on the scene within half an hour of Michael making the call. They cordoned off the entire excavation site and erected a marquee over the Swamp Lady's grave. Michael slipped on his forensic-man overalls and dived in, in a manner of speaking. The rest of us were ushered to the outer perimeter where, for some reason, casts of our boot imprints were to be taken.

Waiting my turn, I sat on a log next to James Weston-Jones. He was still badly shaken by the experience. The fact that the body had been discovered within the boundaries of his father's estate may have had something to do with it, though personally I wouldn't have attached any weight to the location of the grave – the estate is vast. Sexton's Wood encircles it in a wide and thick belt, freely accessible to the general public, with dozens of thoroughfares zigzagging across it. It's frequented by ramblers and favoured by the homeless, and by passing gypsies as their seasonal retreat. Anyone could have buried a body there.

I told James as much.

He shook his head, rather obstinately. 'It's not that, Maggie. I still can't get over it – how did I know where to dig? It's as if I knew the grave was right there, as if I had buried her there myself.'

'Don't be ridiculous, James. You would've known if you'd buried someone – unless you had been off your head. Which is unthinkable – of course! I know you. And didn't Michael date that body to around fifty years ago? You would've been just a kid – you couldn't have buried a plastic spade in a sandpit, never mind a body! It was a pure coincidence.'

He peered at me, his black eyes grim and filled with guilt, his mahogany skin grey. 'It does sound ridiculous, doesn't it, but I went for that particular spot as if I'd known it was there . . . I was meant to find that grave. And when I looked at her, I didn't shudder, didn't get a fright . . . I wasn't surprised. Can you imagine that? Not being rattled by finding a corpse?'

I rather thought he was seriously rattled, so rattled that he couldn't see it.

'You'd expected to find something, bodies and bones included, so that wasn't a surprise,' I pointed out sagaciously but without conviction. I wished I could tell him about the Swamp Lady. Maybe he was right – maybe she had been guiding his hand. But I chose to keep quiet. The man I was talking to wasn't the James I knew. The James I knew was a rational and sophisticated man. Yes, I fancied him a little – innocently and without any sinister intentions, I hasten to add – so it mattered to me that he didn't regard me as a complete raving lunatic. Because after he came to his senses, he would look back and laugh at himself. And then, what would he make of me and my ravings about the Swamp Lady?

I didn't say a word about her. Instead, I insisted that he was in shock and not in a state to drive himself home. I offered to give him a lift. He resisted, but only briefly as I can be rather persuasive when I put my mind to it. As soon as Forensics had finished with us and our boots, I steered him towards my trusty old Hyundai and we rattled along a dirt road to the Weston-Joneses' stately home, known to us commoners as the Weston Estate.

The Weston-Joneses are one of the oldest families in the county. Their blood is bluer than blue and their pedigree dates back to the Norman Conquest. Historical chronicles have it that their family progenitor was a Breton knight who arrived on the shores of Britain with William of Normandy and fought so bravely by his side that he was later bestowed vast lands in the West Country, confiscated from some unfortunate Saxon rebel who in his turn had probably snatched them from under the feet of Celtic druids who had built the Stone Circle on Harry Wotton's farm (long before it became Henry Wotton's farm, of course).

The family's fortunes and estate have somewhat dwindled over the centuries. In recent years they have had their share of tragedy. Lord Philip's beloved younger son Joshua was murdered by a marauding terrorist – it was all over the news. Lady Weston-Jones suffered a breakdown and has been convalescing in Switzerland ever since. Lord Philip withdrew from public life. Joshua's death was a terrible blow to them, a blow from which they never recovered. Joshua was Lady Weston-Jones's only child so understandably life had lost meaning for her when he died. Lord Philip still had his older son, James, but that seemed to be of little consolation to him.

I don't have children so I couldn't even begin to imagine what they must have gone through having to bury their son. My own parents refuse to accept that Andrea may be dead despite the fact that she disappeared from our lives twenty-five years ago and hasn't been heard from since. They still tell me not to worry, that she is fine and in good health, somewhere out there in the big wide world. They believe that. I think that the acceptance of the only alternative – the only viable, realistic alternative, that she is dead – would kill them. And it wouldn't matter, not in the least, that they still had me and Will.

But who am I to judge their obstinacy? I am the same – I too am clinging on to the irrational belief that Andrea is alive, because I can't see her amongst the dead.

I had to help James out of my car – he was shattered: emotionally and physically. We trundled to the door, me supporting him, his arm draped over my shoulder. We were covered in mud and soaked to the bone. We resembled two Tommies returning home from the front-line. Gerard, the prehistoric family butler (he was already ancient when I was born), opened the door and gawped at us, silently demanding an explanation before he would let us – let me – in.

'Gerard, give us a hand,' I panted. 'James here is a bit shell-shocked. We found a corpse. It's a long story. Best we come in and I can explain everything.'

Gerard took a while to draw breath. 'I'll let Lord Philip know.' He ushered us into the sitting room.

'Tell Letitia,' James mumbled. 'Tell her to come down, please.'

'Presently, Master James.' Gerard nodded curtly and vanished. There were times when I thought he was dead too and what I was seeing was just another ghost shuffling about, bloated with hot air and haughtiness.

Letitia, James's wife, appeared first. A good-looking woman, she and James made a beautiful couple: she fair, blue-eyed, and statuesque, he athletic and bronzed. I'd heard that James's mother, the first Lady Weston-Jones, was from South Africa. He must have inherited her genes, considering that Lord Philip was stooped, with narrow hunched shoulders, and pale eyes bulging under bushy ginger brows. He reminded me of a pike.

Letitia dashed to James's side. 'What happened? Are you all right, darling?'

'Shall I pour a glass of brandy for Master James?' Gerard re-materialised out of nowhere, ready to wait on them hand and foot.

'I'll have one too.' Lord Philip entered the room.

'We could all do with something strong to drink,' I said, since none of them had bothered to offer anything to me – and I was knackered and cold, and deserved a drink more than all of them.

Gerard busied himself with the brandies, juggling the glasses on a silver tray while all the time eavesdropping as I appraised them of what had occurred at the dig and the powerful effect the discovery of the body had had on James. 'We thought we'd found a Celtic burial site and all was good and as it should be – we had our first human remains uncovered in pristine condition ... but then Michael – that's Dr Almond, he's a pathologist working for the police—'

'I know Michael Almond.'

'Well, he said it was a crime scene, and the woman – we think it is a woman, don't we, James?'

James muttered, 'I knew she'd be there.'

'Well, precisely – James dug right through into her tomb. It was uncanny,' I concurred. 'He had a shock. It turned out she couldn't have been there for more than fifty years, give or take a decade of course. Michael couldn't be sure just by looking at ... at her – her remains. But it was a woman. I should know – she's been—'

I swallowed the rest of my sentence just in time and downed the brandy Gerard presented to me on his quaint silver tray. I could tell his hands were shaking because the golden liquid in the glass was rippling. I thanked him. That was exactly what I needed: the brandy warmed me up inside and calmed my nerves.

'Oh, darling, it must've been awful for you.' Letitia threw her arms over James.

He kissed her hand. At last he was back to his senses – well, almost, because he repeated his odd mantra. 'I knew where to dig, as if I knew she was there.'

They all stared at me. I felt the weight of responsibility on my shoulders – the responsibility to put it all into perspective.

12

'Pure coincidence,' I proclaimed, 'but it shook him badly. Can I have another brandy?'

Gerard brought me another drink. His hands were now steadier.

'And that was in Bishops Swamp?' Lord Philip gazed at me with his pale, bulging eyes, sending a shiver down my spine. I always found him a little creepy, though I shouldn't really, considering that he is one of the most generous benefactors of our Archaeological Association.

'Yes. We were excavating an ancient Celtic settlement . . .'

'In Bishops Swamp? Of all places . . .' He looked incredulous.

'With your permission, sir, you'll remember that you granted us access . . . your private secretary did, come to think—Well, it's all on hold now. God knows how long it will be before the police let us go back to the dig. It's a crime scene now.'

I am not a gossip as a rule, but finding a dead body wasn't something I could keep to myself. That would be selfish. First, I had to tell my parents. There was also an ulterior motive to my impromptu visit: if the dead woman, my Swamp Lady, had been lying buried there for over fifty years then my parents might know something about her. There was no one better informed in the whole of Bishops than my dad, a retired bobby. The parish of Bishops Well used to be his patch. He'd had the oversight of the police station, then situated in Fields Pass. He had retired by the time the force was restructured and centralised, resulting in the station being transformed into a hairdresser's parlour. Dad was a walking Filofax of all noteworthy events that had occurred in the town and surrounding villages prior to 1998 – the year he had retired.

I burst in on them with the news, blabbering and spluttering, still high on adrenalin, not to mention the two brandies coursing through my veins. I relayed to them in every minute detail the location of the grave and the appearance of the dead body, bringing the latter to life by describing her vividly, her long black hair and her sleeveless dress with those strange geometric patterns which I had originally mistaken for primitive Celtic art.

'Did you know her? Did anyone looking like that ever live in Bishops? Did anyone like that go missing? You should know, Dad!'

Mum decided to derail my inquiries. 'First things first, Maggie,' she said. 'Take off your muddy anorak and hang it in the hallway. You've made a wet patch on the carpet.'

Dad sighed from above his bowl of soup. They were having dinner. I realised how hungry I was.

'Any of that soup left?'

'You can scrape some from the bottom of the pot, I imagine. Have some bread – it's fresh, still warm,' Mum told me. Mum makes her own bread. It's the best thing in the world when it's still hot.

I descended on the kitchen, emptied the pot into a bowl, and cut myself a generous slice of Mum's bread. I sat down at the table, in my usual place (I still have my usual place at the table at my parents' house – we all do: Will, me, and even now, Andrea). Mum and Dad watched me as I devoured my soup and demolished what was left of the fresh bread.

'So, Dad,' I chewed the bread and spoke at the same time, something my parents taught me never to do, 'you must know! You probably had a missing person inquiry, or something like that, when you were still on active duty …'

'I can't recall, Maggie … I can't think of it. Not right now.'

'But Dad—' I stopped and looked at him properly. He looked tired and upset, his complexion pale and his usually clean-shaven face covered in grey stubble. 'What is it, Dad?'

'It's your mum …'

'Oh, Eugene … I'm so sorry.' Mum grabbed Dad's hand, tears welling up in her eyes.

'It's not your fault, my love.' Dad tried to smile at her, but his lips went slack.

'What? What has Mum done?' I demanded, though deep down I knew. I just knew: the bastard cancer was back.

Dad said, 'We've had a routine check-up, and … It's not good … It has spread to …'

'It's just the ribs,' Mum explained to me because Dad couldn't.

14

'That's all they found, localised in the bones. They can operate – take out two bottom ribs, here on my left side.' She touched the side of her stomach and dug her fingers into it as if she were trying to push the cancer inside. 'The surgery's next week. The doctors want to, you know – nip it in the bud.'

For as long as I was with them, I kept a stiff upper lip, but the moment I got home, I broke down in tears. Everything inside me just collapsed like a house of cards. I had truly believed that the cancer had gone away, that they had discovered it before it'd had a chance to cause any real damage, before it had spread its tentacles and taken root in Mum's body. It had only been a couple of months since her first operation. Things were looking up: the chemo had been successful. Though it had wrung Mum out like a wet cloth, it had done its job of finishing off the cancer; Mum had been given the all-clear. We had been told she was in remission. But the bastard was back with a vengeance.

Only in the ribs, I kept telling myself, but it wasn't enough to put my mind at ease. I cried and cried.

Chapter Three

When Sam had abandoned London for the peace and quiet of rural Wiltshire, he had also left behind the unhealthy excitement of his high-voltage urban existence, including his Chelsea FC season ticket. With one unsavoury scandal hot on the heels of another, racism and dirty money-laundering plaguing the Premier League, Sam had no regrets about his decision. But he missed the action, the rush of adrenalin with only five minutes to the final whistle, and the camaraderie in the stands. Luckily for him, Bishops Well had its own answer to football: grassroots-level rugby. Sam had become a big fan.

It was the local derby. Bishops Well RFC were winning by three points against the favourites, Bristol Harlequins. The stands were thundering with celebrations, the supporters having come from all corners of the county despite the stormy weather. The wind howled and raced about, breaking the local speed limit of twenty miles per hour and threatening to tear people's heads off.

After Bishops' deserved victory, Sam, Michael, James, and Edgar Flynn retreated inside the clubhouse. The bar was packed and buzzing with excited fans. Alcohol-infused breath mingled with sweat and fumes from steaming coats, condensing on the windows and dripping from the mirrors. The men had a table booked in the restaurant, but there was a twenty-minute delay so they settled at the bar for a pint. Rhys, the ex-full-back who manned the bar but also worked as assistant coach for the team, looked flushed and sparkly eyed – he must have had a few already.

'A decent show, if I say so myself – don't you agree, gentlemen?' he boasted in his sing-song Welsh accent.

They all nodded and James reached out over the counter to give Rhys an almighty slap on the back. 'Well done, matey! Job well done.'

'The next round is on the house!' Rhys reciprocated the kind words. Their pint glasses clinked in the air like the three musketeers' swords.

Perhaps for the first time since his arrival in Bishops Well, in fact for the first time since his wife had died, Sam felt like at last he was home. He had found new passions here, new pursuits, new friends and neighbours – one of whom admittedly was slightly eccentric, though he wouldn't swap her for anyone else in the world. Though memories of Alice would stay with him for ever, the sharp pain of losing her had been numbed and was fading away, replaced by his new life's small blessings. Sam was beginning to find his feet again.

Their table was ready. They grabbed their pints and sat down, ordering the chef's special of steak and kidney pie and mash without so much as glancing at the menu. Nothing would beat the chef's pie.

The conversation soon swayed from the highlights of the match to the last week's events at the dig. James, usually a man of few words, was telling them about the profound effect the discovery of the body had on him. 'Last night I couldn't sleep. At least, I thought I couldn't. I was sure I was lying wide awake, but then, you see, I can't have been awake. I was dreaming.

'Well, I must have been dreaming. In that dream – obviously, it was a dream – I was running through the wood. It was all black and white. You know? Like an old black and white movie – heavily pixellated. It was unclear, fuzzy, and there was a strange perspective, as if it was filmed from the ground level.

'I was running through the undergrowth. Ferns were up to my waist. I was following someone – a man. He was walking fast, carrying a bunch of daffodils. That was the only colour in my dream – the yellow of those daffodils.

'He arrived at that place ...' James's voice trailed off a bit. He swallowed whatever was clogging his vortex. 'You know, the burial place ... I recognised it straight away. He put the flowers on the mossy ground, and sat on a felled log. And he started sobbing. I felt so, so sad for him and I spoke to him to make him feel better, I guess. I don't know what I said ... And suddenly he turned to face me, and all I could see is the scream in his face – just a huge, gaping black hole of his screaming mouth. Bloody awful!'

'After that, I just couldn't sleep a wink. I sat in bed thinking: what if it was me? If I was that man? What if I'd known about that grave all along? Could it have been me who buried her? I know it doesn't make any sense. It's driving me mad – completely out of my mind.'

'That's perfectly normal,' Edgar Flynn said, 'Your subconscious has been catching up with you. Finding the corpse and it being not what you expected traumatised every cell in your body. Your brain will need time to process it. You could compare it to an electric shock.'

'At the back of my mind I still feel like ... I don't know ... Like I was led to find her.'

'That's normal, too. You may even feel irrational guilt.'

'I do. I may come to you for some counselling,' James tried to make light of his trauma.

'No problem. I'll fit you in.'

Their pies and mash arrived, all adequately bathed in rich gravy, with only a hint of carrot and broccoli cowering on the edges of their plates. They dug in.

'What about the dead woman? Have the cops managed to establish her identity?' Sam directed his question to Michael, whose on-off girlfriend Gillian was a detective inspector with Sexton's CID. Consequently, Michael was much better informed about police secret manoeuvres than the rest of the mere mortals in Bishops Well.

'No. No leads as yet. We know she was a young female, in her early twenties, small frame, maybe five-three, Caucasian. We can estimate the death occurred around the mid-sixties. Forensics hope to narrow it down. But that's about it. No match on the database for any missing females around that time, at least not locally. I think the police are planning to extend their search to nationwide records for missing persons.'

'Sounds like a lost cause.'

'Never say never when Gillian is involved. She won't let it go cold – she'll drill in until she gets to the bottom of it. We managed to extract some DNA – the body was fairly well preserved in the bog. That's a start for Gillian. As soon as that woman gets the faintest scent, she will pursue it all the way. They don't call her Pitbull at the station for no reason.'

'Pitbull? That's not very flattering for a lady.'

'I don't think she gives a toss.'

'And how's her health?' Edgar enquired, mindful of her brush with anaemia not so long ago.

'That's something we don't discuss – not for the lack of trying on my part.' Michael shrugged his shoulders and sipped his beer, seeking solace in it.

Sam smiled rather ruefully: Gillian reminded him of Alice, the same tenacity, the same irreverence, the same *bugger-off-I've-got-serious-stuff-on-my-plate* attitude. Except that in Alice's case the attitude had been only a paper-thin façade for her debilitating insecurities, a realisation that had come to Sam too late to save her. He had been her husband – he should have seen it coming …

He followed Michael's example and drowned his sorrows in his pint.

Sam rolled home shortly before midnight, having stayed at the clubhouse until closing time. He had walked home because of the level of alcohol in his bloodstream. He was fumbling with the key, trying hard to locate the keyhole, when he was jumped on from behind by what seemed like a spectre: a white-clad hysterical woman with a crazed look in her eyes.

It was Maggie.

'She's dead, Samuel! Please, please take me to her! I must see her. Am I wrong? Maybe I'm wrong. I must be wrong! Please tell me I'm wrong!'

As usual, she wasn't making any sense, and the most sensible thing would be to send her home to sleep it off – whatever it was that was troubling her. But something made him take his jacket off and wrap it around Maggie's bare shoulders, hold her firmly in his arms, and invite her inside. It was the sheer terror in her face – she needed his help.

Chapter Four

That week had been a taut string of anxiety, each long day threaded on to that string like a rosary bead. I had tried everything: meditation and prayers alike. I attended a yoga session and spent time with friends. But nothing worked. My mind was beleaguered by anxiety.

I spent long hours sitting in a church pew at St John the Baptist's. My house, tellingly named Priest's Hole, is part of the church enclave; my garden borders the graveyard with the church's stone walls, stained-glass windows, and belfry towering over it. Arched alcoves have been chiselled into the walls of every room, where holy relics and crucifixes were kept. I now use them to display family photos or as bookshelves. I still have a wrought iron cross pressed into the blackened wood of the lintel above the front door. There are also some mysterious etchings in the exposed beams of my sitting room. They are in Latin. One day, I will have them translated. I was meaning to ask Samuel. Lawyers are supposed to be fluent in Latin, like priests.

Although I practically live on the church doorstep, I hardly ever cross it, the only exception being the annual Christmas Mass carol singing in which I partake with gusto, if limited vocal skills. Other than that, the building is a truly mysterious construct. I give it a wide berth as a matter of precaution.

My hands-off relationship with the church is a constant source of shame and remorse because of my wonderful Grandpa Bernie, who was the vicar at St John the Baptist's all his working life. Look at his granddaughter now – I'm practically a heretic!

However, in the hour of crisis I seem to gravitate towards God, so I headed for the cool interior of the tombstone-paved aisles. I skulked to the far end of a pew and sat down gingerly, gaping at the scene of the Resurrection on the window behind the altar and at the fresh white lilies nodding their heads towards me.

I tried to say a prayer for Mum, but no correct words came to me, hard as I tried to reach back to the days of Sunday school. My mind was all over the place. The cancer was taking over her body. I could not contain it – nobody could. There was no stopping the bastard and no point pleading with it. What would a prayer achieve that the doctors couldn't, I thought bitterly. My efforts to find hope were futile.

A huge wave of misery rose inside and poured out of me. I sobbed.

I felt a soft touch on my shoulder. It gave me a start. A man wearing a clerical collar, the only accent of his station in his civilian clothes, sat next to me. I recognised the new vicar, though I couldn't recall his name. He had gentle, almost beatific features but the rigid posture of a soldier. I recalled that he had been an army chaplain in his younger days. He had come to Bishops after Vicar Julian retired. That must have been at least seven – no, eight years ago. The new vicar was a busy man. He looked after several parishes, including St John's. You wouldn't see him idling about the town – you wouldn't see him much at all unless you were a churchgoer.

I swallowed back my tears and stared at him.

'I'm Laurence,' he said, 'I hope you don't mind if I sit here with you for a while.'

He didn't ask what was wrong with me or why I was crying. He must have guessed that I didn't want to talk about it with a stranger. But I couldn't say no to him sitting next to me, so I nodded, 'Of course, I don't mind. Please do.' And then I felt compelled to add, just to say something, 'I'm Maggie, I live here. I mean, at Priest's Hole – that's my house. It used to be my grandpa's.'

'Yes, I know. I knew your grandfather. I remember you. I remember you and your sister – you were teenagers ... I remember the two of you vividly. Your sister was shorter, smaller. She's a bit younger than you, isn't she?'

'Andrea – yes, she's younger. There's three years between us.'

'Yes, that's just what I thought. You came to visit your grandparents full of giggles, full of bickering and excitement, the pair of you ... You put a smile on my face – after my posting in Northern Ireland, I needed it badly, but never mind that ... I was staying with your grandparents for a few weeks. I'd been billeted with them while preparing for my new civilian life. I was about to take on my first parish – Lower Horton. Yes, yes ... I do remember the two young ladies, you and – what did you say your sister's called?'

'Andrea.'

'Yes, Andrea. And how is she? Still living in Bishops?'

'She's been gone for twenty-five years – missing.'

As soon as I said that, the weight of that fact plummeted down on me – the proverbial ton of bricks – and I could physically feel it crush my ribcage. I gasped for air, but it was thick and heavy and sticky, like tar. It choked me and I retched. 'I'm sorry,' I managed to wheeze between coughs.

'You've nothing to apologise for. Try to breathe – deep and slow.'

'And now, if that wasn't enough, it's my mum. Cancer. It came back.' And I told him everything, even though he hadn't asked.

He cupped his hands around mine, which I had rolled into two white-knuckled fists in my lap. 'I'm sorry to hear that,' he said.

'What am I to do? What's there to do?'

'Pray. I will pray for both of them, and for you. God's always around to listen.'

He heaved himself up and walked towards the altar where he lit a candle and knelt to pray. He hadn't offered me any solutions, but I felt better. The whiff of burning wax permeated the smell of old wood and dust, and lifted it somehow, taking with it my misery. I prayed without words as I still couldn't remember any.

I was bristling with all my resurrected hope as we took turns to sit with Mum, to give her a kiss and squeeze her hand for good luck before she was rolled away to the operating theatre.

'All will be just fine! Trust me, I know!' I shouted after her. She smiled and waved to us, a small flick of her wrist, and then her hand flopped down, and Mum closed her eyes. The smile stayed on her lips for as long as we could see her. I could tell she was trying hard.

Dad, Will, and I sat in the hospital corridor, waiting. We drank copious amounts of coffee from the vending machine, not because we were thirsty or in need of a pick-me-up, but because we had to do something with the time on our hands. I reiterated several times that everything would be just fine.

Will looked at me with that incredulous but benign expression that said he wanted to believe me but couldn't overlook the fact that my credibility was highly questionable. I would for ever remain his little sister with little sense. I could see the doubt in his eyes. I wished I could do more to put his mind at ease.

Dad seemed in better spirits. He had always been a glass half full person, like me. We were in agreement: if the doctors thought they could defeat Mum's cancer, who were we to doubt that? Dad and I are the optimists of the family. We believe in what the experts tell us, because they are the experts. And the experts told us that the bastard cancer was operable.

I would never be able to recall how long we waited. It could have been hours; it could have been just a few minutes. For me, it was a blur of shuffling along the corridor, punching buttons on the vending machine, and endless toilet trips.

Finally, the surgeon, Mr Devlin, emerged from the operating theatre, like a compere at the end of a play, to announce the out-come. And we were right: Dad and I. All was well.

'She's OK,' Mr Devlin said, 'You'll be able to see her when she wakes up.'

'So, the . . . is it all gone?' Will asked with atypical imprecision.

'When we opened her we found that the cancerous tissue had spread more widely than anticipated,' Dr Devlin spoke cautiously, but to us he sounded positively reassuring. 'We took everything that we could find and remove without causing any more harm.

24

The larger the affected area, the greater the risks, I'm afraid, but as I said, Irene has made it through, and she is recovering.'

That was on Wednesday. We saw Mum and spoke to her, and she – faintly, but lucidly – spoke back to us. A joyous piping voice in my head chimed away with wholehearted thanksgivings – my prayers had been answered.

On Thursday, I skipped merrily to Bishops market and bought a cake: one of Mum's favourites, coffee and walnut. In the alley just opposite Angela Cornish's bakery, I bumped into Mary Ruta and Dan Nolan. All three of us froze, startled: I because I had just caught them holding hands like a pair of love-struck teenagers, and they because they'd seen me see them. They let go of each other's hands, but it was too late.

I acted nonchalant. 'What a lovely day!' I pointed to the cloud-laden sky and we all watched a flurry of yellow leaves swirl overhead, tossed about by the wind.

'Well, if you like that sort of shenanigan,' Dan scowled, implying that he didn't.

Mary shuddered. 'Cold, isn't it?'

'I suppose,' I agreed. The weather was effectively closed as a topic. 'So, how are you? A touch of shopping, I see?' I said and, for some reason, gestured towards their hands.

Mary blushed and hid her gloved hands behind her back. 'Well, we were just ...'

I felt sorry for her. I grinned and put my finger to my lips, 'Shhh ... Don't worry, Mary, your secret's safe with me.'

Dan's head jerked towards Mary. 'Does Maggie know? That was quick!'

'Know what?' I was by now genuinely intrigued and there was no way I'd be able to let it go.

Mary raised her shoulders and tilted her head, smiling mysteriously. She pulled off her glove and there, on her fourth finger, sat a gorgeous diamond ring. 'She knows now.'

'Oh my – congratulations! You're engaged!' I shrieked. The news had just made my gloomy day so much brighter.

'Dan asked me last night.' Mary was no longer blushing – she was glowing.

'And she said yes before I even finished the sentence.' Dan was equally radiant.

I hugged them both.

Angela Cornish saw the whole spectacle from the window of her bakery. Like a shot she was out, hunched against the wind and pressing the lapels of her unbuttoned coat into her chest. 'Do I hear congratulations are in order?'

'We're getting married,' Dan said.

'Well, well, I never,' Angela cooed. 'All's well that ends well, and good people find each other in the end.'

I think she was referring to the tragic story of Dan's daughter, Leila, who died many years ago at Mary's ex's birthday party. Long story! Still, it seemed that somehow the tragedy had brought those two together against the odds.

'May I steal a peek at the ring?' Angela asked.

Mary extended her delicate, pale hand towards Angela, who grasped it in her baker-woman's strong paws. 'Awww, isn't the stone sparkly? Diamond, is it?'

'Indeed.' Dan looked proud. 'Mary deserves nothing less.'

'Lovely!'

'Thank you, Angela,' Mary said and gave another little shudder. 'It's really cold out here. Should we retreat to the Old Stables for a hot drink?'

'Why not,' I said. 'I'm visiting Mum in hospital but that's not until three. I may as well grab a cuppa and you can tell me all about your wedding plans. Come to think, I need some cheering up!'

We braved the wind and headed across the Market Square. In the café we found a quiet table in the corner and settled with a pot of tea and scones.

'I'm sorry to hear your mum's back in hospital.' Mary gazed at me sympathetically.

'I have to stay positive, for Dad,' I told her.

'That's right. You mustn't lose faith.' Dan gave my hand a friendly pat.

Before I had a chance to change the subject, Vera Hopps-Wood did it for me. She stormed into the café, saw us, and headed directly for our table. Her face was flushed red and it was evident from her puffy eyelids that she must have been crying.

'I've given him one last chance,' she informed us without any introduction. I could only guess that she was talking about her wayward husband, Henry Hopps-Wood, our local MP. His affair with his late PR officer had somehow leaked into the public domain and although Vera would have been the last to find out, find out she clearly had in the end.

Samuel and I had known for months. In fact, we had discovered it.

'That's really . . . magnanimous of you!' I praised her.

'He promised he'd never—' Vera's voice broke and she slumped on to my shoulder and wept.

'Have a good cry. It'll make you feel better,' Mary recommended.

'Not that the bastard deserves you,' Dan added, 'but well done, girl.'

When we went to visit Mum in the afternoon, I took the coffee and walnut cake to complement Dad's bunch of grapes and box of Thorntons chocolates. Will brought nothing – he had driven from London like a man possessed, without stopping for breath, never mind groceries.

Mum was weak. It hit me suddenly how small and frail she had become. Her hair had turned a lustrous silver and glowed around her face like her own saintly halo. She wasn't saying much – all she said was that she was too tired to talk.

We talked instead – well, I did. All sorts of inconsequential non-sense. I'm not sure she was listening. She had a distant, glazed-over look in her eyes, but whatever she was seeing in her mind's eyes was making her happy because a shadow of a smile flickered on her lips.

She wouldn't touch the grapes or the chocolates, or even the cake. And neither would we. It didn't feel right to have any of that without her. The box of chocolates sat virginal in its shiny plastic packaging next to the coffee and walnut cake, the cake's rich aroma fighting a losing battle against the odour of disinfectant and ill-health.

In the end, she fell asleep on us: her eyes drooped and her jaw went slack. I lowered my face towards her and felt the reassuring but faint touch of her breath on my cheek. She was alive. Of course she was. She was on the mend and mending required lots of rest.

A nurse breezed in, checked all the gadgets, and changed the bag on Mum's drip. She also told us to go home as the doctor was about to start his rounds and he didn't like families hanging about, getting under his feet and demanding answers which had more to do with divinity than medical science. She also instructed us to take the perishables with us. Mum was on an intravenous diet and would remain so beyond the cake's 'eat by' date.

Will went home to London directly from the hospital. Dad and I drove back to Bishops. We sat in the kitchen in my parents' house with a cup of tea (from a teapot, not a vending machine) and a slice of the coffee and walnut cake. We talked about Mum's lucky escape – the eternal optimists, remember?

Dad said, 'I'm so glad it's all behind us now.'

I nodded. 'I organised a divine intervention for Mum, so it's no wonder it went well.' And I told him about my chat with Vicar Laurence and how he had promised to intercede with God on Mum's behalf.

We had a second helping of the cake each. Our appetites were back on track. We agreed that I would pick Dad up tomorrow morning and we would go to see Mum – to motivate her to get better faster. What she really needed was homemade chicken soup, not a drip. Not to mention that parking costs at the hospital were extortionate.

That night I slept well – the deep and rewarding slumber of a woman at peace. I dreamt of distant times when Andrea and I were small girls and we were in my grandparents' garden at Priest's Hole, fighting over whose turn it was on the swing. Andrea was shrilling in that high-pitched voice of hers. She was calling Grandpa to 'come here and tell *her*' – that'd be me, her big sister – 'that I hate her.' Her unruly locks were bouncing against her flushed cheeks as she shook her head, vehemently refusing to let go of the swing.

Infuriated, I thrust it at her and she fell backwards, and cried.

I didn't mean to hurt her. I gaped as my little sister shrilled, 'Grandpa, Grandpa! Come here! Maggie tried to kill me!'

Grandpa stood in the doorway of my bedroom. Bizarrely, we were no longer in the garden but in my bedroom, and it was the middle of the night. I sat up in my bed. Grandpa looked a little bleached and translucent, but I knew it was him. He reached out to the little girl crying on the floor, only she wasn't crying any more.

She stopped.

She gave him her hand and hoisted herself from the floor, a bit clumsy, a bit unsteady on her feet. Her locks were still unruly and unbrushed and her little chubby face was still swollen with the pain of her fall, but she was not Andrea.

I frowned and ordered myself to wake up. I wasn't enjoying this dream. It didn't feel nostalgic any more – it felt here and now. I had to wake from it and shake it off. I didn't want it to go on.

No, it wasn't Andrea, though the resemblance was uncanny. It was the sort of resemblance that runs in the immediate family's genes. This little girl was wearing an old-fashioned pinafore over a white blouse with long sleeves. A white ribbon was trailing from her hair. Grandpa helped her wipe herself down and a few dry leaves fluttered to the floor. I couldn't hear her speak, but I could read her lips when she said, 'Thank you, Daddy.'

I screamed.

It was a resounding NO. I wasn't having this.

I wasn't dreaming it.

I was witnessing it.

I jumped out of bed. Maybe there was hope yet. Maybe we could still hold her back. Mum was not leaving us! Not yet. I ran out of the house, and stopped at the top of the driveway. I couldn't run all the way to the hospital.

My neighbour! It occurred to me that I had one. I would ask him. Samuel would take me to the hospital. And once there, by her side, I would stop her from dying.

The first thing Samuel did was to wrap me in his heavy wet jacket and take me inside his house. He asked me to repeat everything at least twice until he could make sense of it. Then he called the hospital. We waited.

They called back, having checked on Mum. She had slipped into a coma. We had to hurry.

We picked Dad up on our way to the hospital. I had to explain everything to him over and over again. He still didn't believe me. Not until we had finally made it to Mum's bedside.

A coma.

The coma is a cruel state of mind. It makes you reject everyone who loves you. You can't fight it. You can't opt out of it. It makes you give your loved ones a cold shoulder. In her coma, Mum was simply ignoring us.

But she was still there, hanging on to life. She hung in there for several hours, until Will arrived from London. Then she finally let go.

30

Chapter Five

They had been cooped up there since dawn. Sam's extremities were numb and probably ripe for amputation. In the last two hours there had been little blood circulating in his uncomfortably squeezed feet. The draught coursing through his bones was making him shiver. The incessant muttering of rain could easily pass for torture.

When James had suggested a spot of birdwatching, he had implied that they would use a purpose-built hide on the eastern confines of the Weston Estate, bordering Salisbury Plain. *Hide* was a misnomer. Sam would describe it as a dog kennel. Or a chicken cage. Or a bloody torture chamber.

He was kicking himself for succumbing to the idea of bird-watching, just like he had already kicked himself black and blue for succumbing to the idea of archaeological digs. As hard as he tried, Samuel Dee would never become a country squire. It wasn't in his genetic makeup to revel in mud, rain, and draughty barns. As he squatted, squashed like a sardine next to James, he escaped fondly into the memories of his favourite pastimes: West End theatre, Covent Garden restaurants, and infrequent recreational walks in St James's Park.

James appeared impervious to the elements. In his fisherman's overalls he was well equipped for this occasion. The trickle of rain leaking through the hole above his head was sliding off his sou'wester hat. He tore himself away from his binoculars and passed them on to Sam.

'We're still in good time for spotting one,' he whispered. 'With the clouds lying low and obscuring the sunlight, it's likely that it'll come out later in the day. But it will come out.'

He was talking about the great bustard. Sam prayed to God that the bastard bustard would hurry up.

'Patience is the name of this game,' James added.

Sam smiled faintly. He didn't want to play this game. He wanted to take his toys and go home. But instead of doing what he wanted, he obediently took the binoculars and scanned the plains for signs of life. Anything would do: an owl, a goose, a mouse, an empty crisp packet. Instead, he was confronted with the vastness of open grassland and a river ploughing through it laboriously.

And there, on the bank of the river, out of the reeds, popped a head, followed by a long neck and white plumage. Even Sam could tell that it wasn't a bustard, but it was something. A heron, he thought.

'Do you have herons in these parts?' he asked James.

'Yes, a few ... They're quite common. Focus away from the river – the bustard prefers open plains.'

The heron seemed to be looking straight at Sam; behind it, its tail was creating a firework of white feathers. Sam was mesmerised. 'Is it their mating season? Herons', I mean ... This one's strutting his feathers big time.'

James was intrigued. 'Where? Where is it?'

Sam passed him the binoculars and pointed him in the direction of the reeds where the creature stood, posturing.

James pushed the lenses to his eyes, strained his neck, and his jaw dropped to his lap. 'Blimey, Sam! That's a bloody cattle egret! You found a bloody cattle egret! I love you, matey! I love you!' He squeezed what life was left in Sam out of him in an enthusiastic embrace. 'This is an unbelievable sighting! I wouldn't believe you if I wasn't seeing it with my own eyes.'

They were celebrating the sighting of the rare egret with a glass of single malt whisky. Sam was sure the first sip had kick-started his heart, while the second got his circulation going. Sprawled in a

32

comfortable armchair in James's study, he could feel life returning to his toes and his fingertips. His back was still aching, but he welcomed the sensation. It meant that he was alive. This pleasing conclusion to a tortuous excursion into the depths of the West Country could be why people did it in the first place. The end of suffering was truly life-affirming.

James was raving about the bird. He dumped a heavy volume of the *Encyclopaedia Botanica* in Sam's lap to prove to him that the specimen they had observed on the riverbank was indeed a cattle egret. Sam didn't need convincing and was quite happy to take James's word for it. James printed the photo of the creature he had taken on his mobile. It was of poor quality and heavily pixellated but James still raved about it, animatedly drawing Sam's attention to some minuscule markings Sam simply could not see. He had quickly lost interest in the matter. A bird was a bird.

He scanned James's study, its walls lined with books, the desk littered with folders and loose papers, and crowned with a computer screen the size of a largish television set. Next to the computer were some family photographs. Sam recognised Letitia, James's wife, dressed in white, holding a bouquet of white roses. There was a picture of their two children, both fair and pale, quite unlike their father. In a small silver frame darkened with age was a black and white photograph of a beautiful woman with long dark hair, cocking her head coquettishly and looking over her shoulder with a happy smile captured in the lens of the camera. She was wearing a dress – a sleeveless tunic with geometric shapes typical of the sixties.

'Who's this?'

James picked up the photo and looked at it for a few seconds with a rueful smile. 'My mother. It's the only photograph I have of her. She left Father – and me, of course – soon after I was born. Ran away with some alleged cousin of hers, back to South Africa. Father was too proud to look for her. I think she broke his heart. He had all of her photos destroyed and cut off all contact with her family. I don't think I've ever heard him say her name. It's Helen, by the way. Her name is Helen. I have to remind myself from time to time what my mother's name is. This picture,' he handed the frame to Sam, 'I found stuck between the floorboards in my old bedroom when I was about eight. I don't know why I kept it.'

'And you never tried to find her?'

'No. Why would I? She left us. If she wanted to come back . . . It's up to her, really.'

Sam peered at the picture of James's mother with new eyes. 'Was it an affair? Between your mother and her cousin?'

'You would think so, wouldn't you? How else would I turn out the way I am – mixed race? It's not like a devious cuckoo dropped me in the family nest, hoping they wouldn't notice.' James fixed Sam with a hard look. 'You can't help but wonder – and I won't blame you for thinking this – but how else would a white mother and a white father produce a mixed race child?'

'I didn't—'

'Oh, yes, you did!' James laughed.

Yes, truth be told, the thought had crossed Sam's mind. Lord Philip was a typical specimen of Anglo-Saxon stock and it now seemed plain that James's mother was white too.

'I came to the same conclusion a while ago,' James interrupted Sam's musings. 'I couldn't be my father's son. My father must've felt the same way, though to be fair to him, he tried to . . . to love me. Um . . . So, it had to be my mother's so-called cousin. I never met him, naturally, but he was probably mixed race. He was my biological father – he had to be. As soon as I was born, that fact became painfully obvious, and they took off, my mother and the *cousin*.' James drew inverted commas with his fingers.

'Well . . . hmm . . .' Sam couldn't argue with that logic. James didn't look anything like Lord Philip, and if one considered the fact that his mother was also white . . .

'But, you see, Sam, there are things in heaven and earth, as the saying goes . . . I had a DNA test done, without my father's knowledge. And I say *my father* with clear conscience, because you know what? He *is* my father. Lord Philip Weston-Jones *is* my biological father. Go figure!'

'He is?' Sam blinked, waiting for a twist to the story.

'He is. Conclusively.'

'There you go then. He knows, I presume? You told him?'

'I only told him after Joshua died. He was so devastated, I wanted to do something, say something to ease his pain. I told him I was his son too – you know, the real McCoy, not just somebody else's spawn he loved as his own. He didn't believe me.'

James bit his lips and headed for the decanter to refill his glass. He drank the whisky in a single gulp. Only then did he offer a refill to Sam. Sam accepted. James's hand shook as he poured his glass.

'So, we had another round of DNA tests. Like I said – conclusive.'

'I see ... Interesting.'

'Yep, very interesting. Rare, but it happens: a black ancestor in your family tree generations back, long forgotten, and then some bizarre genetic variation, and here I am.'

'Here you are indeed!' Sam raised his whisky. They clinked their glasses and drank to it.

'But in those days, in the sixties,' James sobered up, 'it had to be a shock to the system.'

'You think that's why she left you – your mother?'

'She took one look at me—' There was a short but tense silence. 'She took one look at me, and ran. The shame of it. In those days, you know ... It was a scandal.'

There was no arguing with that. It would be hypocritical to deny it, that was the reality back then. Sam nodded and once again peered at the image of James's mother in the old photograph. He was looking at it with new eyes. Something was troubling him about this photo. At first, he couldn't put his finger on it. Then Maggie's words rang in his ears loud and clear.

'Do you mind if I take a photo of this?' he asked James.

'Why?'

'I just want to show it to someone.'

'Someone?'

'Maggie.'

'Maggie Kaye? Why?'

'I don't want to speak too early – I may be entirely off the mark, but please, humour me.'

'Be my guest.'

Chapter Six

The engine of the Jeep wheezed and rattled as they negotiated the increasingly unnavigable roads in the full blazing sun. The wind, when it bothered to blow, carried with it dust and the occasional foetid stench of decaying roadkill. The dust and the stink stripped her tongue and nostrils of fluid. She regretted not bringing any bottled water with her on this escapade. *Escapade* wasn't quite right – this had been a damn long journey to nowhere. She hadn't realised it would be this long and this far.

She had thought Botswana was just the size of a county and the Caprivi just a strip of land beyond it, a promenade on the banks of the Zambezi. And then, as soon as the business at hand was done and dusted, Wayne had promised, they would go and see Victoria Falls. She was beginning to think that even Victoria Falls wasn't worth all this stinking trouble.

They had landed in Johannesburg a week ago, and it had been a blast! They were staying at the Intercontinental Sandton Sun and Towers, in the presidential suite, complete with white marble floors and crystal mirrors. The chandeliers – she would swear – were made of diamonds.

She shopped until she dropped at the crisply air-conditioned, exclusive Sandton shopping mall. The sun filtered through the high domes of its glass roof and the oases of exotic rainforest plants bathed among whispering waterfalls. It felt like paradise.

The nightlife was a scream. In one of the clubs in Rosebank she had bumped into James Small, the hot rugby player she had fancied ever since she had watched him in the final of the World Cup. He had bought her a drink and scribbled his autograph on her forearm. There was still a faint residue of the permanent red marker on her skin. Wayne had had to drag her away and shove her into the black limo waiting outside because it was late and he was up early to travel to the Caprivi. A business trip.

She wanted to come, too. She wouldn't take no for an answer.

'I'm up at four thirty, gorgeous. You'll be fast asleep if I know you,' Wayne warned and passed out in bed. He had an uncanny ability to drop off at a click of his fingers and sleep blissfully right through the night. Unlike her. She took ages to drift off, her brain working overtime, ticking on and on like a bomb.

So, she hadn't gone to bed – it was no skin off her nose. It wasn't the first time she had gone without sleep for a day or two. She was young. She was strong. And she was determined to come with him. It would be an adventure.

She had a long, bubbly bath, packed her safari costume and Doc Martens in case there was any trekking across Botswana's salt water pans, of which she had heard something or other, or perhaps watched a programme about them once, keen to one day circumvent the globe on foot.

She stood on the terrace overlooking Johannesburg with all its distant buzz and twinkling lights, smoking a Marlboro Light. The cool night air slid over her skin like an ice cube. She was on top of the world, basking in luxury, light years away from the doldrums of sleepy English villages with all their creature discomforts of incessant drizzle and curtain-twitching neighbours. God, this was her first decent crack at entering paradise!

She didn't hear Wayne's wake-up call and didn't hear him creep up on her from behind, but she felt his kiss on her neck. 'You didn't come to bed, daft girl. I missed you,' he said.

'No, you didn't. You were out like a light. Anyway, there was no point in sleeping. I'm ready.'

'Ready for what, may I ask?' There was a twinkle of amusement in his eyes.

'I'm coming with you, remember? We agreed.'

'I can't remember agreeing to anything. Trust me, love, it's a long way and you'll be bored stiff. It's only mundane business. I'll be back in three days and then we can—'

'No! Please don't! Don't say no. I really, really, really want to come with you.' She threw her arms around his neck and fixed him with her cutest puppy eyes. 'I want to learn about business—'

'Not that sort of business.' He laughed. That sounded dismissive, but he didn't shake off her embrace.

'And I really, really wanted to see Africa – the real stuff out there. Come on, please …'

He succumbed. 'If you must. I suppose we could go see Victoria Falls afterwards. I've some business in Zambia – we might as well kill two birds with one stone.'

She wore black Gucci cat's eye sunglasses and a wide-brimmed straw hat. With his mane of blond hair and his square jaw, there was something colonial and distinguished about Wayne – maybe it was his posh West London accent, maybe the people he mingled with (people in high places, some, he said, as high as the government), or maybe it was his wealth, which he wielded so effortlessly and so frivolously, as if he didn't realise he had it. Wayne was a very successful businessman but first and foremost he was an old-time gentleman – he never talked about business. It would be far too vulgar.

There were twenty years between them. She loved the age difference. It thrilled her to bits to be the pretty young thing on the arm of a mature and illustrious gentleman. She had heard one of his associates call her that rather offhandedly, unaware that she was in the room at the time, but she didn't mind. It couldn't be that much of a disadvantage to be both young and pretty. Wayne's wife would kill to be young and pretty. She was an old mare.

They pulled up somewhere in no man's land between South Africa and Botswana. The only building was a dilapidated hangar on the periphery of a cracked concrete airstrip overgrown with weeds.

39

A big fat man in his mid-fifties hurried out of the hangar to greet them. He was wearing huge metallic Ray-Bans which made his face look like it was silver-plated. His face and neck were burnt by the sun to an angry shade of crimson. His khaki attire made her think he was some sort of a guerrilla fighter. That was until he presented a friendly smile and introduced himself to her, his voice high-pitched and strongly accented with the guttural Afrikaner twang.

'Hans Strydom! I don't believe I've had the pleasure?'

'My lady companion.' Wayne chose to be vague.

'Nice to meet you.' She gracefully extended her hand, expecting a gentle touch. Hans Strydom shook it as if it was a door handle.

'Good timing – we finished loading twenty minutes ago. We haven't been waiting long.'

Wayne stepped out of the Jeep and helped her down, the sort of thing he would do without thinking. It came naturally to him to be gallant.

They headed for the hangar. Inside, they found a large military truck covered with camouflage green tarpaulin. Against the back wall was a stack of cargo crates, stamped with some serial numbers, the letters SADF, and an emblem bearing blue wings and an anchor.

She was dying for a pee. 'Do you have any . . . any facilities here, Hans?' she asked, crossing her legs.

Strydom peered at Wayne for guidance.

'A bog.' Wayne grinned.

She was directed to the toilet at the back of the building, next to an office which housed an old-fashioned wireless with knobs and dials instead of buttons, and what looked like a radar screen. The toilet was clean enough, though perhaps not quite five-star quality.

When they finally embarked on the next leg of their journey, her high spirits returned. She was equipped with a few bottles of Evian. Hans Strydom joined them in the Jeep and entertained her with tales of game hunts in the wilderness of the Okavango Delta under the very noses of the gamekeepers.

Kwasi, their driver, one of the Lozi people local to the area, stopped a few times along the way: to point out a herd of elephants rubbing their bulks against tree trunks, then a bored-looking kudu grazing on yellowing grass, and finally to let her out to explore the insides of an enormous hollowed baobab containing an animal skull with curly horns – undoubtedly a manifestation of native witchcraft. She was brimming with excitement.

They were now travelling in convoy, followed by the military truck from the hangar, driven by Strydom's son, Andreas. The border crossings were easy. First, they were waved through on the Botswana-South Africa border. Then, on the crossing with Namibia, at Ngoma, they were let through by overly friendly guards, grinning at them and nodding their heads. Nobody cared to check their papers.

It was dark when they finally pulled into a deserted car park and waited for Wayne's business associates to turn up. It seemed an unorthodox venue for doing business, and she said as much. She wasn't as vacuous as she looked. After all, she was supposed to be gaining valuable work experience at Wayne's company, AfricaAid Logistics. This was after studying at the London School of Economics. She wasn't an airhead just because she had fallen head over heels for her boss.

'Aren't we nosy!' Wayne tapped the tip of her nose and laughed.

'Well, no! Not really. Just wondering. It feels a bit undercover.'

'OK, you asked,' Wayne gave in. 'You see, Kwasi here,' he nodded towards the driver who beamed back at him. 'He and his people are striving for self-determination, aren't you, Kwasi?'

'Yes, sir!' Kwasi grinned at them over his shoulder.

'And rightly so! We all have the right to be free, don't we? They want their land, the Caprivi, to become independent from Namibian rule. And I want to help them. Hans and I, and the people backing us – we want to provide logistic guidance to the Lozi, future legitimacy, so yes . . . at the moment, this is all hush-hush.'

'I see. Wow, Wayne!' She felt elevated. She had always been an avid supporter of all possible liberation movements out there in the world – on principle. She had marched and protested with her fellow students as soon as she had arrived in London. It was an honour to be part of this – supporting the struggle of the ... the ... whatever-they-were-called people, hands on! The stories she would tell her grandchildren ...

A set of bright headlights flooded the car park. The freedom fighters had arrived at last. A large truck, similar to theirs, pulled up parallel to the Jeep. Three men emerged and approached the driver's side. They shook hands with Kwasi, then one by one exchanged introductions with Wayne and Hans. She would for ever remember their names: Charles Ndala, Albius Samati, and Osbert Puteho.

Wayne stepped out of the Jeep and offered her his hand. 'Now down to the boring bits, I'm afraid. Why don't you go and stretch your legs, love? It won't take long.'

'But I want to—'

'Not this time,' he interrupted her firmly. 'They won't be comfortable with you around. Even Andreas is staying in the truck, out of earshot, because they don't know him. Off you trot. It's safe around here. And beautiful at night. Just go out there and listen to the sounds of the night – you'll be amazed. That's a good girl.'

She did as she was told, though resentfully. She wanted to be part of this. She wanted to understand how it worked. But she had learned enough about Wayne by now to know he wouldn't relent: he had that stern, focused frown on his face. On this occasion, he would have it his way.

She strolled away. She didn't have to go far to find herself surrounded by high grass and low, flat bushes, and the screams and shrills of the nocturnal creatures in the veldt. The air had cooled to a pleasingly low temperature. It smelled of animal sweat and musky soil, mingled together, pungent and raw. Suddenly she felt alone and lost in the wilderness. She stopped and looked back at the car park and the silhouettes of the six men outlined in the headlights of the vehicles. She needed the reassurance that they were still there, watching her back.

That was when Wayne fired the first shot.

She ducked. It was instinctive for her to hide. And she watched as Wayne and Hans shot the other two of their freedom fighter *associates*. She watched as Kwasi tried to wrestle Hans's gun out of his hands, Hans fought back, and Wayne stepped in to resolve that dispute by shooting Kwasi in the back of his head.

She ran in the opposite direction, into the wild African night vibrating with the sounds of hunting, fear, and death. She stood no chance. She didn't know where she was going. She heard Wayne's voice behind her. He sounded alarmed, worried. He was calling her.

She stopped running.

She turned around and began walking back into what felt like the lion's mouth. But she had no choice. She decided that she had better play the dumb blonde.

'Wayne!' she shouted.

'Here, love! I'm here.'

She ran towards him and threw herself into his arms. He smelled of gunpowder, or perhaps her senses acted on what her brain was telling her: this man had just shot three people.

'Here you are!' he embraced her.

'What happened? I thought I heard shots . . .'

'Those men – they were traitors. They attacked us – we had to defend ourselves.' He sounded calm. 'You can never tell in this game.'

He led her back to the Jeep and took the driver's seat. 'Jump in, love.'

'Kwasi?' She had to sound stupid, uninformed. She had to sound like she had seen nothing.

'He was in it with them, I'm afraid. I trusted that boy.' Wayne shook his head. 'He went for Hans. I got him in the nick of time. Hans is lucky to be alive.'

After turning off the engine Hans jumped out of the lorry the dead men had arrived in. The lights had gone off. He walked towards the Jeep. She recoiled in the back seat and avoided looking at him. Her eye briefly met Andreas's eyes. He was sitting in the lorry, rigid and pale.

She heard Hans say, 'Go ahead. I'll tidy up here ... Me and Andreas, we'll take the truck back to base.'

Wayne turned the key and the Jeep's engine began to whirr. She shut her eyes tight.

Light flooded her eyes when the flight attendant bent over her to pass a cup of coffee to her neighbour. She smiled. 'Tea or coffee?'

'I'll have tea, please. And can I have some water? My tongue feels like sandpaper.'

'Of course!' The obliging stewardess poured her tea and gave her a capsule with milk.

'How much longer?'

'We'll be landing in an hour.'

At the airport a dark figure kept a watchful distance. She knew someone would be waiting. Deep down she harboured the irrational hope that it would be Hugo, but one glance from the corner of her eye and the hope was banished from her mind.

The man who followed her from Passport Control, through luggage collection, and to the Arrivals Hall, was in his early forties, and pot-bellied (Hugo would never let himself go like that). Her minder had sleek black hair brushed back. Hugo's mane was blond and unruly. Hugo was like a lion, this man was like a chubby black Labrador.

Her new bodyguard appeared slightly disinterested: he stood a few yards behind her, arms folded on his paunch, leaning against the wall in a delinquent sort of way. She had quickly lost interest in him, especially when he had failed to help her with her gigantic suitcase. He was just shadowing her, having left good manners at home. Hugo was a gentleman. He would never have let her push her own suitcase around. She was missing him all over again, acutely and desperately.

At the Arrivals Hall, a man dashed towards her and took her in his arms. He was lean, no-nonsense: an arrow of a man. He didn't look her in the eye, but she could tell his eyes were swollen with crying or sleepless nights, or both. He hadn't changed, she thought: his stiff manner, his awkwardness at displaying emotion, and even more tragic awkwardness at trying to hide it.

'It's been ages,' she said, and kissed his cheek. Her big brother.

He grabbed her luggage, muttering something like '*yes, it has, umm …*' His voice was vibrating with all the emotion he was always so bad at concealing.

'Dad's waiting, over there.' He pointed into the blur of people pulsing behind the barrier.

But she picked Dad out instantly. He was thinner and shorter than she remembered. His hair was greyer. His skin was a size or two too big for him and it was sagging and wrinkled, but it was Dad. She hugged him and he clung to her. A heavy stale odour of cigarettes hovered around him – he had taken up smoking again. It was a long while before he regained himself. He pushed her away and looked at her with a shaky, lopsided smile. That effort left him with no strength for words.

'Dad … I am so sorry … I still can't believe it.' That about summed it all up. She didn't know what else to say.

Then her eyes met her sister's. There was no escaping that glare, hard as she tried. Her big sister marched at her like one fast and furious cannonball.

'Andrea, where the *hell* have you been?'

Chapter Seven

I had lost a mother and gained a sister in a matter of one week.

Here she stood. Andrea, my younger sister, the girl inhabiting my memories and yet absent from my life for long enough to make me doubt those memories were real. She smelt unfamiliar, wore her hair short, and spoke with an accent. But she was Andrea: the reckless little shit who took off twenty-five years ago, without a goodbye, without a forwarding address, without even a *kiss my arse*. Anything would have been better than nothing.

I stood in the Arrivals Hall, looking at that reckless little shit, fuming. Did it really have to take our mother dying for her to find her way home?

'Where the hell have you been? I was worried sick!' I was shouting at her in front of all those strangers. That was my *welcome home* greeting. People stared at me, alarmed, and that included Dad and Will. I couldn't fathom how they could have forgiven her so lightly. I couldn't.

I simply could not!

She walked slowly towards me, like in a dream, like in one of those endless dreams I had been having for years about finding my sister. When her face was just inches away from mine, I had the eerie impression that I wasn't looking at Andrea but at my own reflection in a mirror. We were so alike – we were so much like Mum, the pair of us. There was something in Andrea's eyes, in the elevation of her brows and in the specks of gold in her irises, that conjured up Mum. Andrea was damn lucky to have somehow, by coming here and by looking me in the eye, brought Mum back to me. Because otherwise, I swear, I could have killed her!

As it was, we fell into each other's arms. As we did that, everything else fell into place: she smelt right and familiar, and she felt sisterly in my embrace. I wasn't sure I could let her go for fear of her vanishing again, so I clung to her, my teeth, my eyes, and my fists locked tight.

The funeral is a blur. I remember the rain and the tears. I remember the nugget of soil in my hand disintegrating into mud as I dropped it into the grave. I remember the many bright and fragrant flowers covering the coffin like a colourful painting filling a blank canvas.

Mum loved flowers. I half expected her to join us and ask in her typical self-deprecating way, '*Are they all for me? You shouldn't have, really!*'

I can't remember seeing her there though. She didn't come to her own funeral. I could only surmise that she was already busy on the other side with Grandpa and Grandma, having a house-warming party in heaven. I couldn't blame her. Whatever it was, it was bound to be much more fun than the funeral.

Vicar Laurence proffered his deepest condolences and shook my hand. I was half expecting to hear something about Mum being in a better place, but he didn't go for the cheap and obvious. He nodded towards Andrea, who stood next to me and was weeping a deluge of tears (she was never any good at self-restraint), and said, 'At least you found your sister. A ray of sunshine on this rainy day.'

I wouldn't refer to Andrea as a ray of sunshine, rather a clap of thunder. Or a flash in the pan. Or a pain in the arse. She had a lot of questions to answer, and a lot of explaining to do, before I would be able to think of her in terms of rays of sunshine. I didn't tell Vicar Laurence any of that though. Instead I said that indeed she had returned at long last.

'God takes with one hand and gives with the other.'

Now, *that* sounded cheap and cheerful, but it was well meant. I introduced the vicar to my prodigal sister who, unlike me, recognised him in an instant, 'I remember you – you were friends with Grandpa Bernie. You gave me a bag of jelly babies.'

No, I can't remember Andrea sharing the jelly babies with me, but that doesn't surprise me in the least.

When the last of the visitors had gone, we tidied up the house. We couldn't leave it to Dad. He was sunk into the folds of the sofa, his shoulders collapsed, his chest deflated, and his jaw slack. He was watching us, his grown-up children, busying ourselves with the hoover and emptying dishes, without a trace of expression in his eyes. Along with Mum, he had lost his spark. Once sturdy and inde-structible, he looked vulnerable and weak. There was no way we were going to leave him alone. We had all decided to stay the night. Even I stayed, though I live just around the corner.

Before going to bed, Will's wife Tracey asked him if there was anything he wanted, anything at all, maybe a cup of tea, or . . . He shook his head. She kissed his forehead. It was decent of her. I didn't know my sister-in-law that well – always regarded her as an emotionally challenged, dry twig of a woman, twitchy because of her constantly blinking eyes, magnified through the lenses of her thick glasses. But she was better than that. I was grateful to her for staying with us and for being there for Dad. And for Will.

Will too needed taking in hand. He was in pieces. He hadn't said anything all day. I knew if he had tried, he would have lost it and given in to tears. Twice I saw him wobble on his feet; his knees buckled under him, and he had to grasp something – the corner of the table or the back of a chair – to regain balance. Mum's death had hit him hard, perhaps even harder than Dad.

In Will's books, Mum was dead. In mine, and Dad's, she had just moved on to her new accommodation in heaven. Dad believed in it and I knew it to be true. I had seen her wander away holding Grandpa's hand, being taken good care of. All Will had to go on was the empty black hole she had left behind. I wouldn't try to guess what Andrea was thinking. She had been gone for so long that I couldn't be sure of anything about my sister.

*

48

Andrea and I went to our old room. We had shared that room as children. It was the largest room in the house, in the converted loft under the slanting roof.

Lying wide awake in our beds with the lights off, only a faint shimmer of moonlight stealing through the gap between the curtains, we finally had our chance to catch up. Well, Andrea had her chance to answer the question I had asked her at the airport.

'I was – still am – under witness protection: new identity, new name, new country, new family. Twenty-five years ago my whole life changed in a matter of weeks.'

Twenty-five years ago, in her trademark mindless fashion, she became involved with a married man. The fact that he was married would prove the least of her worries. He was also a dangerous and well-connected criminal – an arms dealer. His name was Wayne Kew.

Of course, my daft little sister, with a pea for a brain, wasn't aware of that when she hooked up with him: a handsome, well-spoken, and stinking rich man, twenty-odd years her senior. He flew her around the globe and while she shopped in exclusive cities or sunned herself on the beaches of war-torn African republics, he traded in death. Until, one day, she witnessed him shoot dead three people in cold blood. The scales fell from her eyes and she ran for her life.

She sought refuge in the British embassy in Pretoria, and as soon as she told them her story, was placed in witness protection. She testified at his trial alongside two other kamikaze witnesses, thus putting him in prison for life – at least on paper.

He swore revenge: not in so many words, but she could see it in his steely glare as he watched her from the dock. He left her in no doubt: his life sentence would become her life sentence. Wayne Kew was a man with connections in very high places and even behind bars he wielded huge power. And he wanted Andrea's blood. He would never stop looking for her.

That was when she ceased to be Andrea Kaye and became Someone Else.

My daft little sister didn't have a clue what she had got herself into. Of course not! She had never had much sense, but managed to get away with it thanks to her lucky star. Unfortunately, her luck had run out. As soon as she'd testified behind the closed doors of Kew's trial, she had been whisked out of the country and every trace of her had been wiped from the records. Only Mum and Dad knew that she wasn't dead, but for her safety, and for the rest of us, they were supposed to act as if she was. Except, of course, they weren't very good at it, and in the privacy of our four walls they'd always maintained that all was well and she was alive. I'd thought they just couldn't accept the truth. I was wrong.

'And I've been looking for you everywhere – even among the dead,' I whispered.

'Sorry, sis . . .'

'Not as sorry as I've been. You've no bloody idea!' I had spent twenty-five years chasing chimeras, grasping at shadows on the wall and having no life of my own.

'It's been a nightmare for me, too. I tried . . . No, forget it!' I could hear her swallow and turn in her bed. She was now facing me, the faint glow of moonlight on her face. The manic expression she used to have as a naughty little girl danced in her wide open eyes. 'Did you ever think we'd be back in our old room, talking into the night?'

'Frankly? No.' I glowered at her. She was lucky she couldn't see my face.

'And yet, here we are, sis!'

'Yeah . . .'

'I know – crazy!' She sat up. Clearly, like in the old days, she could not contain herself. I remembered it would take her hours to fall asleep and she would keep me awake, babbling on, tossing and turning in her bed, her springs squeaking and my teeth on edge. She was back to her old self. 'You'll have to come with me to New Zealand and meet my family.'

'You have a family?'

'Elliot, my husband, and Jack – my little boy. Well, not so little. He's eleven. I've got his photos on my phone – hang on!' She

50

sprung out of bed and padded barefoot to her as yet unpacked suitcase. She fumbled through the contents, hurling shoes and knickers around, until she realised her phone was in her trouser pocket. And then, when she found it, she realised that the battery was dead.

'Shit! I said I'd call them as soon as I got here . . . Shit, shit, shit! They must be worried silly!'

'You've got that effect on people, I'm afraid.' I shrugged my inner shoulders. My sister was incorrigible. She would never change, never grow up. 'Go downstairs and use the landline.'

'Yes!' She pursed her lips. 'I mean, no, I can't . . . I don't know Elliot's number by heart. It's on my phone. Shit, shit, shit!'

She was pacing the room, all the lights blazing while my head spun. I sat in my bed, marvelling at how I had managed to share a room with this bundle of raging neurons all those years when we were young. It took stamina and nerves of steel to handle my sister. I felt immense sympathy for that poor guy Elliot.

'Andrea, let's turn the lights off. I am knackered, bloody knackered.'

'Me too! The flight was a killer. I'm dead tired.'

She didn't look dead or tired, but obligingly, she switched off the lights. I could hear her walk to the window, instead of her bed, knocking into something along the way and cursing. She stood in the window, her silhouette a black outline in the moonlight.

'I knew it . . . I knew it . . . Come, look down there . . .' Her voice was loaded with anxiety.

'Oh, what now?' I dragged myself out of bed against my will.

'You see?' She pointed down to a car parked on the road outside the house. 'They're here, watching me. I'm still in danger, Maggie.'

The interior of the car was lit dimly. Someone was sitting in there, well after midnight – there could only be one reason. So, Andrea was telling the truth.

I pushed her away from the window. 'We have to call the police. Now!'

'They are the police, Maggie. They're looking after me. I have a twenty-four-hour bodyguard.'

Chapter Eight

'I don't think I have to stay there for ever. I feel like a blinking refugee, like I'm waiting for some war to be over so I can go home. Except the war has been over for years and they forgot to tell me. That's how it feels to me. It's awful – bloody awful.'

'I'm sorry. But you're doing the right thing – staying safe.'

'It's been twenty-five years! All that happened – it's ancient history. Water under the bridge.'

'For you, perhaps.'

'I mean, honestly, Dad – why should I be hiding? I haven't done anything wrong. I've been hiding for so long I've forgotten who I am. I need to come back home.'

'I'd like nothing better … but think about your family over there – they are safe now. Keep them safe.'

'They'll be fine. Have you noticed? I've been under twenty-four-hour surveillance since I arrived.'

'Precisely.'

'Precisely!'

'No, you don't understand, Andrea. If they think you need round-the-clock bodyguards then, no, you're not safe.'

Heavy sigh. 'Jack needs to know his grandad. He's never known his grandma, and it's too late now.'

Silence followed her words, loaded with grief so raw that I wanted to scream at her.

'No, Dad. I'm coming home. We're coming! You'll play football with Jack and take him to Snowdonia. Everything's going to be normal. Like it should be.'

My wayward sister was making promises she wouldn't keep. That *was* normal. I knew it and Dad knew it too, so he stopped arguing with her and let her rave about Cornish pasties and clotted cream.

I stayed out of it. Tomorrow, Andrea would be tucked away on a plane heading for the green pastures of New Zealand, and we wouldn't hear from her for another twenty-five years. At least my mind was at peace. I knew she was alive, functioning like an adult somewhere out there in the world, and she even had a family – which was more than could be said for me. I had to get a life. But right that minute I had to keep stirring: the béchamel sauce was a treacherous puzzle piece in my culinary endeavour of the day. Unstirred, the sauce could easily turn lumpy.

I was doing well. I poured my perfectly smooth sauce between the layers of steaming pasta and minced beef, just as the recipe said. I marvelled at the love I had for my sister. Lasagne was her favourite. I wanted her to have it before she went back to New Zealand's lamb and kumara.

Alice turned up in my kitchen and hovered by the window, heralding the arrival of Samuel. He was on his way to mine, though I didn't remember inviting him to dinner. Still, I fetched another plate and a set of cutlery, and set up another place at the table.

'Who's that for?'

'Samuel.'

Andrea eyeballed me for an elaboration.

'My neighbour – Samuel. You met him.'

'Oh yes, him! I didn't know he was coming.'

'Neither did I,' I told her.

She looked at me awkwardly, then at Dad.

Dad said, 'Maggie knows things no one else does. Don't ask, it's complicated.' I could see a spark of mischief quivering in Dad's eyes and even though, as was his old habit, he was having fun at my

53

expense, I was delighted. He was getting back to his old self. Pulling my leg was the best way he knew to show affection.

There was a knock on the door.

'That'd be Samuel then,' Dad said, unnecessarily. Of course it was Samuel.

He stood on my doorstep, soaked to the bone, looking apologetic. 'I'm sorry to be dropping in on you unexpectedly, but I've got something I must—'

'Come in, Samuel. Perfect timing.'

He took off his muddy boots and proceeded to the dining room, as I instructed him. He left wet footprints on the floor. Where on earth had he been, I wondered, bog snorkelling?

'Do you want a towel?'

'No, thanks. It looks worse than it is. We've been birdwatching. I dried up a bit at James's but then had to walk in the rain. Never mind that, I just wanted to show you something.'

'Sit down,' I waved him to his place at the table. 'The dinner's ready in twenty minutes.'

'I don't want to intrude ...' he mumbled.

'You're not,' Dad said, winking, 'Maggie's been expecting you.'

Samuel peered at me, uncertain about the joke.

'Alice,' I said quietly, and he nodded his understanding. As I mentioned, Samuel knows about me and the dead. There's very little one can keep secret from one's neighbours.

He sat down and took out his mobile. He slid his thumb across the screen impatiently, it wasn't having any of his wet-fingered handling. 'I want you to look at this photo. It's James's mother ... Hang on ... It's black and white and a bit grainy, but ... yes, here it is. Have a look.' He passed me his phone.

I couldn't believe my eyes. She was looking right at me, over her shoulder, her long dark hair obscuring some of the unmistakable geometric shapes printed on her dress. Despite the photo being in monochrome, I knew the circles were yellow and blue, and the triangles red.

'It's her, Samuel! It's definitely her! It's the Swamp Lady!'

We peered at each other, triumphant. We had identified the body!

Dad's voice broke into our moment of glory. 'Helen? You're talking about Helen?'

'James Weston-Jones's mother. Was her name Helen?' I asked.

'Yes, it was. Show us that photo.' Dad turned Samuel's phone in his hands, and nodded. 'Right you are. It's Helen.'

'She is the dead woman James found in the swamp. No doubt about it.'

'Are you sure?'

I couldn't quite tell him about seeing her spirit wandering the swamps for years. 'Yes, quite sure, Dad.'

'But ... didn't she ... I mean, she ran off with that—'

Dad stopped himself from finishing his sentence with an expletive. I can always tell when he swallows a curse before it comes out of his mouth. His face goes red. Mum had trained him well to *mind his language in front of the children*. He composed himself, though something hard stole into his eyes.

'Helen ran off with her lover ... her cousin, he called himself, but everyone knew he was up to no good. A ladies' man, damned bastard!' I don't think he even noticed the profanities this time. 'Karl sodding van Niekerk ... Messing with all our girls' heads, he was! He had us all fooled ... made us think they eloped together. We were happy to see the back of him. Didn't stop to think—'

'Do you think he killed her?'

'I wouldn't put it past him,' Dad spat. 'He was a right cunning bastard. Bastard, I tell you!'

Chapter Nine

Gillian Marsh visited Michael Almond often, arriving late in the evening for a touch of cosy companionship and leaving early in the morning to return to her crime scenes. Samuel and I had been watching the street corner where Michael lived from the bay window of the Rook's Nest, the better of Bishops Well's two public houses, which was full to the brim. Apart from getting pickled, the patrons were busy placing illegal bets on the game of darts going on in the back room. Stakes were high – it was the county qualifier. The landlord, Terrence Truelove, commonly known as TT (though not to his face), and his voluptuous wife, Sandra, were run off their feet, dashing between the back room and the bar, taking orders and delivering trays of liquor. The spectators couldn't afford to come up to the bar to order their drinks – they wouldn't dream of missing the game. So the bartenders took it upon themselves to courier endless rounds of beer and wine. Considering that the bar area sat on the ground level and the back room was in a dungeon-like basement, some twenty stairs below, poor Terrence and Sandra were running a marathon. Sandra's ample bosom was glistening with sweat. I felt for her.

'Do you need a hand?' I offered. My offer was partly altruistic, partly selfish. I had been sitting idly for a while. I could do with stretching my legs.

Sandra peered at me and managed a smile of gratitude. She blew her fringe out of her eyes and wiped her brow with a hanky she retrieved from somewhere in her bra. 'You're all right, Maggie, thanks all the same. Can I get you something?'

'We're fine.' I raised my glass to her.

'Come on, love,' TT prompted his wife, 'you keep standing here, the beer will go stale.'

'Give me a break, Terry!' Sandra growled. 'I 'aven't sat down since five!'

They headed for the games room, bickering along the way.

We returned to our strategic planning conversation. We now had the privacy of an empty bar area as everyone's presence was required in the back room. Samuel was lecturing me as we waited for DI Marsh's blue Vauxhall.

'Let me do the talking, Maggie. If we mention the spirit of the Lady of the Swamp, DI Marsh will probably show us the door.'

'I had no intention of mentioning any spirits to her. She wouldn't understand. What do you take me for, Samuel? I'm not a complete numpty!'

'I never said you were. No, not a complete one – not by far.' He tried his best to reassure me but was failing miserably, digging a bigger hole under his feet.

I gave him a hard glare. 'Stop there. It's fine. I'll let you do the talking.'

'If she turns up tonight.'

'If she doesn't, we'll have to go to Sexton's tomorrow and report our suspicions.'

His prompt retreat into his pint told me that he didn't consider that a viable option. But he was gentleman enough not to say it out loud. At face value, I had to agree: it was an outrageous idea to assume the body from the swamp belonged to the previous Lady Weston-Jones who, by everyone's account, had eloped to Africa with her Casanova cousin. It was also common knowledge that His Lordship had subsequently divorced her *in absentia* on the grounds of abandonment. It hadn't been something he wished to advertise to the world – he has a big aristocratic ego after all – so he'd engaged a firm of solicitors in London. Still, word had got out, but only in a low whisper. No one in their right mind – definitely not our good friend, Chief Superintendent Alec Scarfe, Marsh's boss – would care to stick their noses into the private affairs of the Weston-Joneses without just cause. My hunch didn't qualify as anything remotely resembling a just cause. We had to handle this with sensitivity – of course, I knew that!

I sipped my martini thoughtfully. In all honesty, I don't like martinis except for the olive on the toothpick. I probably chose it because it made me feel like James Bond on a secret assignment. I have always associated martinis with spies. Samuel was enjoying his pint oblivious to the fact that I had always associated beer with football hooliganism. Of course, Samuel is nothing like a football hooligan.

A familiar blue Vauxhall turned into the narrow road under our surveillance. We finished our drinks and hurried across the Market Square. The tower clock, which is fifteen minutes late due to the abysmal lack of maintenance, struck nine. DI Marsh worked long hours.

Our knock on the door was answered with a low growl and the sounds of muffled commotion inside. After a minute or two, Michael opened the door, pushing his girlfriend's Alsatian back with his knee. He – Michael, not the Alsatian – struggled to hide his dismay to see visitors on his doorstep well after civilised visiting hours. He knew straight away why we were there.

He gestured towards the lounge. 'You've got business with Gillian? Come in.'

'Thank you, Michael,' I said. 'We won't be long.'

Samuel mumbled something apologetic.

As we entered the room, we found DI Marsh doing up the last button of her top.

'Sorry,' Samuel repeated himself.

'Bad timing,' I expanded.

'Take a seat,' she said drily. 'To what do I owe the pleasure of your company?'

Samuel took a seat. The Alsatian settled at Gillian's feet and gave me the evil eye. So I sat down too. Michael offered us something to drink, which we both tactfully declined.

I said, 'The body we found at the dig—'

'Oh, that one!' she exclaimed, as if there were hundreds of other bodies scattered around the county. Maybe there were, who knows? DI Marsh comes across as a very busy, unapproachable type. I have no idea how she ever solves any crimes – she certainly doesn't inspire trust and confidence in potential witnesses.

Nevertheless, I pressed on, 'It belongs to Lady Helen Weston-Jones.'

'And how did you reach this conclusion?'

I opened my mouth to let her know when I felt Samuel's hand grip my forearm. He looked at me pleadingly and I remembered I was supposed to leave the talking to him. I pursed my lips and let him speak. It took a lot of self-restraint, but I managed.

Samuel said, 'We recognised the clothing. It was a pure coincidence. I saw the previous Lady Weston-Jones's photo when visiting James this morning. She was wearing a short dress with a geometrical imprint. It seemed familiar. I ran it by Maggie and she distinctly remembered—'

'I did!' I nodded, 'The blue, red and yellow patterns, quite distinct.'

'Blue, red, and yellow?'

Samuel cleared his throat and took over, 'They may've been blue and yellow . . . or not. But the pattern is quite – it's the same. Maggie had a good look at the body when it was found, and – you know – the shreds of fabric . . . She recognised it straight away when I showed her the photo.'

'Can I see it?'

Samuel showed the photograph on his mobile to DI Marsh. She tilted her head doubtfully and frowned.

I pounced towards them and stabbed my finger at the dress, 'You see, circles and triangles.'

'I can see those in the photo, yes.'

'The same ones as on the dead woman's dress.'

'There was hardly any dress to speak of.'

'Enough to see the pattern if you look hard enough,' I insisted.

Michael joined us in examining the image on Samuel's phone.

He made a few non-committal grunts, but nodded in the end. 'Perhaps.'

'It's worth checking it out. You've nothing to lose,' I told them, in case they didn't yet realise that I was absolutely, a hundred per cent right. 'All you have to do is to take DNA samples from James. She was his mother.'

'If it is her. This could well turn into a wild goose chase ... Scarfe won't like it.' DI Marsh was addressing Michael. I could detect some hesitation. She had not rejected our idea out of hand.

Samuel put on his best ex-lawyer's hat. 'You have been looking at missing persons, have you not? Helen Weston-Jones went missing in the early sixties. It was assumed she had gone back to South Africa, but it wasn't positively verified. James has never heard from his mother. Lord Philip has never heard from her – and never really looked for her. He may have had his solicitors advertise for witnesses as to her whereabouts, but that was a mere formality to complete the divorce. It isn't beyond the realm of possibility that she never made it to South Africa and was instead buried in the swamp, is it?'

I agreed. 'I say you find that cousin of hers, Karl van Niekerk, and ask him. They supposedly eloped together.'

'First things first,' DI Marsh said, 'we have to confirm that she is who you say she is. If James Weston-Jones cooperates by giving his DNA sample—'

'Oh, he will!' I told her.

I was delighted. She believed us!

Chapter Ten

Her bodyguard with the sleek black hair saw her off at the airport, following her all the way to passport control. When she stared at him pointedly, so that he knew she was aware of him, he smiled and nodded curtly. He then turned and walked away with his hands in his pockets, glad that his mission was over without a single incident.

Andrea scanned the rows of seats in the Arrivals Hall, the faces, the shapes and sizes of people there. Hugo would be older, maybe bald, or skinnier, or stooped and grey – she took that into account. Still, he was not there. She presented her passport and her ticket and proceeded to board.

The air on the plane was dry and cold; it made Andrea's lips chap. She wrapped herself in her cardigan and sipped slowly from a glass of red wine, remembering the same plane trip twenty-five years earlier. To her left a young Asian man was sitting, reading a book.

Twenty-five years ago it had been a middle-aged gentleman keen to make conversation, except that she couldn't bring herself to utter a word back to him. That man next to her should have been Hugo. They had led her to believe that. Though no one at any time had said Hugo would be accompanying her, it had not occurred to her that he wouldn't. It would be unimaginable . . . But that's what it was, whether she could imagine it or not: he wasn't with her. He had gone from her life as suddenly as he had come into it. A fly-by-night.

Outside, clouds formed a cotton wool bundle giving out a false sense of warmth and security. You could dive into that fluff, eyes shut tight, arms outstretched like the wings of an aeroplane, only you wouldn't glide – you would plunge to certain death. *It's all illusions.* Andrea smiled ruefully at the thought of returning to the safe haven of Aotearoa.

Did she need that safe refuge any more? Had she ever needed it? The trip, the first trip back home in twenty-five years, had proven that she was no longer in danger. No one had come after her; perhaps no one had ever been after her. An overzealous bureaucrat had sent her to the far end of the world, had turned her life inside out and torn from her heart everything that she held dear. For no reason. She'd had nothing to run from.

It was time to go back home – her real home. It was no good crying over spilt milk. Her life – without her family, without her past, without Hugo, without her own name – was a river of spilt milk. No use crying over it. Everything was about to change.

She had seven hours to kill in Kuala Lumpur. She booked into an airport hotel and took a sleeping tablet with plenty of water. The tropical humid heat was beginning to disperse in the heavily air-conditioned room. She called the reception desk and asked for a wake-up call at six. She drew the blinds and turned off the lights. Lying on the bed, Andrea was staring into the black of the night, to where the ceiling would turn up by daytime. Her head felt heavy, her thoughts were chaotic tatters. The sleeping pill was reluctant to take effect. Her brain was working overtime, anxious to find itself in this alien place and relax.

The hotel room, the artificial coolness of it with the heat breathing just beneath it and the oppressive darkness, was too much for her to handle. She sat up. Searched for the water bottle on the bedside table. Her fingers found it and knocked it off. She swore.

Then she allowed herself to cry.

She sobbed loudly and without restraint. She should have let the tears out before, at home where Dad and Maggie, and even Will, could have done something, said something to make her feel better. Here, in this hotel room, she was on her own. Crying like a baby.

62

Mum came at last. Her hand stroked Andrea's hair. Mum's hands were unmistakable: they were always warm but callused, the hardened skin around her nails catching in Andrea's hair. Mum was sitting next to her with her feet curled under her bottom. Andrea lowered her head into her mother's lap.

'There's nothing in the world like the smell of your hair,' Mum said, burying her nose in her daughter's curls. 'It's not quite camomile, nor wild berries ... it's ... it's—'

She, on the other hand, smelt of cinnamon and sometimes, vanilla. Mum's scent would invariably conjure up images of cake baking: she would be working the dough with her swift, strong hands, Andrea and Maggie pilfering it and eating it raw when she wasn't looking; the heat from the oven would spill all over the kitchen, and the whiff of the sweet, exotic spices would overwhelm all senses.

At last Andrea relaxed and let herself drift into sleep.

The other man she had already met – he was her *case officer* and he would remain just that, a nameless Home Office official. Names were superfluous, identities dispensable. All those officers she had met so far blurred into one anonymous Necessary Evil in her Kafkaesque world. Clones. Her eyes didn't linger on Hugo for long either. He was one of them. Here today, gone tomorrow.

The three of them sat in her impersonal, angular hotel room: she perched birdlike on the edge of a huge double bed, her knees drawn together defensively. The two men sat in deep chairs at the opposite ends of a coffee table: the case officer pushing his chin forward, Hugo slumped, his right foot on his left knee. In the dim yellow light of a bedside lamp their silhouettes were blurred.

At that time Andrea's brain did not register Hugo's square shoulders and large hands with well-defined knots of knuckles. She would not marvel at his intensely blue eyes, determined and steadfast. Already, at thirty-something, his shock of thick hair had begun greying at the temples, but she did not notice that either. His jaw was strong and as square as his shoulders; his nose was straight with a thick bridge separating equally thick eyebrows. He was wearing washed-out blue jeans and a pullover – civilian gear, inconspicuous and non-threatening. He had made an effort to be average and unmemorable.

'You will be Mr and Mrs Grousser,' the case officer pronounced. 'Even to each other, Christopher Grousser, Chris for short, and Andrea Grousser. No children, no pets – it's easier that way, less to remember.'

Only then did she really look at Hugo and pay attention.

'Hi, Chris,' she said.

He offered her a business-like smile.

'You can trust Chris unconditionally, he's one of our best. He doesn't make mistakes,' the case officer continued self-assuredly, as if his word stood above any doubt or reproach, as if he himself could be trusted unconditionally.

She had only met him a few days earlier. He had told her she would be looked after and had nothing to fear. What he had failed to say was that her life was about to be torn to shreds; that her past would be wrung out of her.

She nodded. 'Great to know.'

'Would you like a drink? I could do with one myself.' Hugo got up and headed for the mini fridge. 'Evian, tonic water, lemonade ... Maybe something stronger? A glass of wine?'

She shook her head. 'No, just water.'

'Good choice.' He handed her a small bottle of Evian then flicked open a can of Heineken.

'How about Mr ...' She searched for the other man's name in vain, eyeing him helplessly.

'I don't drink,' he informed her, shooting Hugo a scolding look.

'He doesn't,' Hugo shrugged his shoulders. 'I'm surprised he breathes.'

Andrea couldn't help a smile. She liked his blasé manner. She liked him. 'Actually, I could have a small glass of wine. Red.'

The case officer regarded them both critically as they sipped their beverages, unperturbed by the circumstances that had brought

64

them together. He went on with his briefing, bombarding her with details she would not remember.

She was beginning to enjoy herself: the whole surreal oddity of her situation, the conspiracy and secrecy, the code words, made-up identities, Her Majesty's undercover personnel, and the adrenaline rush – until he uttered his last sentence.

'And under no circumstances, of course, will you be able to contact your family or friends.'

Chapter Eleven

Elliot stood big and clumsy behind a gigantic bouquet. His shirt was crisp and his shoes smug with polish. He smelled of Boss. As Andrea approached, he thrust the flowers at her and tried to kiss her over the prickly leaves and rustling cellophane. His face stretched into a forced smile while his eyes examined Andrea with concern, if not suspicion.

Her eyes stung with dehydration due to the high altitude and the red wine she had drunk. Her skin felt like sandpaper and there was a stale taste in her mouth. She kissed him back, and again the kiss ended up vacuously in mid air.

'You made it home, at last.'

Her first instinct was to contradict him: home was twelve thousand miles away. But then guilt kicked in. The mess she was in wasn't Elliot's fault.

'Where is Jack?' she croaked.

'At home, with my mum. He can't wait ... He missed you stupid.'

'Me too.'

'And I missed you, a lot ...'

'Yes.'

They reached his car in the short stay car park. He threw her luggage into the boot and opened the passenger door for her. As soon as they were seated, he asked, 'Are you OK?'

'Absolutely. Just tired – a long flight and all that …'

She switched on the car radio. The news was on. Anything would do – anything to pollute the silence and block his questions. God, she had a lot of questions to answer! Their whole life together had been built on a lie.

The car slid over the Harbour Bridge and came to a halt in an orderly line of stationary traffic. Beneath them, stretching into the distance, was the impossibly turquoise ocean merging on the horizon with the azure of the cloudless sky. It was so perfect that it bordered on artificial. Andrea was immune to its appeal. She was already missing the iron clouds and dirty shades of grey blowing over the Northern Hemisphere.

On the hills hung glass and wood villas designed to absorb light and the views that lay at their feet. There were no dark, stone cold corners in those houses, no shadows and no secrets, no cellars with boarded-up doors, no past.

Andrea and Elliot's home was one of them, a neat, eco-friendly weatherboard house bordering mangroves spread over a wide estuary. The air smelt of seaweed and wet wood. The mangroves were inaccessible – nice to look at but beyond reach.

Their closest neighbours were a childless older couple who were very guarded. Andrea knew their names and nothing else. A happy family of five, the Watsons, lived two houses down the road. Jack played rugby with their boys. On occasions, Andrea and Elliot would be invited to a barbecue there. Mrs Watson – Vicky – was an untidy flabby thirty-something with an abundance of freckles and even more to say. She drawled in the typical broad Kiwi way and would invariably get orgasmic over new baking recipes, which she cruelly tested on her unsuspecting visitors. Mr Watson – John – was only ever capable of talking nuances of rugby, which meant Andrea had absolutely no idea what he was on about. He did however get along with Elliot, usually over a few bottles of Carlsberg.

And that, in short, was the jolly world Andrea was being driven back to in her husband's navy blue Toyota Hilux.

Heavily jetlagged, she lowered the back of her seat and let her head drop back on to the headrest. She drifted away within seconds.

'I can make a fantastic egg on toast,' was the first thing Chris Grousser said to Andrea Grousser as they entered the house. Their home was a suburban semi with a private garden. It had tinted windows, the glass reinforced by a crisscross of fine mesh. There was a pagoda at the far end of the garden, crowning a narrow footpath. The house was spotlessly clean and tidy, the impression being it had never been inhabited, but it comprised everything your average tenant would need: a kettle, a set of decent stainless steel cutlery, sensible crockery, toilet paper, the lot.

They duly introduced themselves to their neighbours. The house to the left appeared empty. Across the road was a school: full of children's voices and laughter.

Hugo's egg on toast was fantastic. They ate it awkwardly and in perfect silence – their first night together as husband and wife. Andrea felt his eyes on her. They slid furtively from her lips to her neck, meandering curiously over her breasts and lifting rapidly to meet her eyes as she confronted him with a questioning glance.

'Do you like your job?' she asked. 'All those different identities?'

'I don't get confused as to who I am. My briefing was clear. I am here to protect a Crown witness. I know my purpose and I know my place. Though sometimes,' there was a shift of light in his eyes as he suddenly smirked, 'sometimes I feel like one hell of a Robin Hood.'

'You do?'

'Fight the bad guys and take care of the poor and righteous, that's what I do. The dream job if you ask me.'

'Dangerous.'

'I like *dangerous*. It makes me feel alive.'

The more she learned about him, the more she liked him. There was a perpetual conflict to him: the boy who played with toy soldiers and the soldier who had long suppressed the boy inside him.

Every time the boy would peer over the unguarded flanks, the soldier would pull him back with a tight fist. His self-discipline was rigorous, made of iron. It was his second nature.

He didn't tell her anything about himself yet managed to extract from her every intimate detail of her life: her family – Mum and Dad of course, her big brother Will, her bonkers sister Maggie, her friend Hannah and their wild adventures behind Wotton's barn, and her now long-forgotten boyfriend Matthew who had taken off with Hannah and broke her heart for five minutes.

And finally, Wayne Kew.

She had drunk most of the wine and was pretty much sozzled by bedtime. He took her to their bedroom. The bed was wide and luxuriantly soft when she sat on it. Against all common sense, she hoped that he would be sharing the bed with her.

'I will sleep in the spare bedroom,' he said.

'Of course, absolutely!' she exclaimed with a vehement nod as if his announcement was exactly the sort of reassurance she needed. He looked at her in an asexual, paternal way, then quickly swept the bedroom for any threats.

'Good night.'

She was surprised that he didn't salute.

For the next ten months, they had lived together, sentenced to each other's company day in and day out, holding polite conversations lovingly embellished with endless cups of tea. She would laugh at his dry as pepper jokes. He would accept an unmanly share of the household chores. They would endure each other's irritating habits, brushing by each other between their respective bedrooms, exchanging ritual *good mornings* and *goodnights*. Almost unnoticeably they had got to know each other intimately.

Ten months into their cohabitation, he told her she would be giving her testimony the following week.

'When it's all over I'll invite you out for coffee in the real world.' She beamed at the notion of walking arm in arm with him in the street, taking a table under an umbrella, and watching life go by. It seemed like a natural progression. She didn't quite say it but after the coffee, she imagined, they would get back home – their home, this home – and go to bed. Together. It felt right.

'It is never quite all over.' His eyes shone with dispassionate, ice blue inscrutability. 'Once you see death happen in front of you, the corpses become alive inside your head. You'll never forget. I can't. And Kew – he won't let you forget, even from his prison cell. It'll never be all over.'

The QC for the Defence had fat lips, the bottom one hanging down in a grimace of contempt, and a double chin spilling out of his collar. His wig sat on his head slightly askew. He had asked her lots of irrelevant questions aimed at confusing and frightening her. But she was not frightened or confused, not in the least. This must have been highly annoying to him, for he glared at her angrily and the contempt in his protruding lower lip travelled to his eyes.

She was equally calm and confident answering John's questions. He was the barrister for the Prosecution. They had rehearsed questions and answers ad nauseam. What she had witnessed had been reduced to a simple script. It no longer seemed to belong to her as her own memory.

It was only when he asked her to point out to the Court the man she had seen shooting the three victims in cold blood, her eyes met Wayne's and her composure wavered. Up to that point she had not looked in the direction of the accused even though subconsciously she knew where he was sitting.

'Yes,' she said in a small voice, 'it was him.'

'Are you absolutely sure? Take a good look, we can't risk convicting the wrong man.' John prolonged the moment unnecessarily.

Obligingly, Andrea focused her eyes on Wayne. His eyes were unforgiving. There was a warning in them: reconsider, retract and stay alive …

She couldn't do it. It was too late.

Chapter Twelve

Jack screamed from the door and ran to throw himself at her with the impact of a runaway steam train.

'Sixteen days you were gone, I counted!' Jack informed her, a frown of resentment forming on his forehead. 'Did you get me anything?'

There was nothing in her bags for Jack. She had to be quick on her feet or he would never forgive her. She put on her best woman-of-mystery face. 'Oh yes ... Something you can't touch. Or eat ... I have a plan!'

His face crumpled. He didn't like the sound of it.

'How would you like it if you were to travel all around the world to meet your grandad?'

Jack's face bristled with excitement. 'When are we going?'

'Very soon. I just need to make some arrangements.'

Elliot's jaw tightened. His face flushed red. Andrea couldn't remember the last time she had seen him so rattled.

When she came out of the shower, Elliot was waiting. He was sitting on the bed, his hands sliding up and down his thighs.

'We need to talk about it, Andrea.'

'About what?'

'About what!' He was angry – no doubt about that. Elliot had never been angry as long as she had known him. His fury took her by surprise. 'I don't even know who you are! You told me your parents were dead! You said you'd left no close relatives in the

UK . . . It was all a big fat lie. About what! That's rich! How about: who the fuck are you? Is Andrea even your real name?'

She had to tell him – only the bare bones of it, only what he needed to know to understand the lies. No names, no details, nothing that he could go and research online. It was for his own good – to protect him and Jack.

'For the last twenty-five years I have been in witness protection, Elliot. They gave me a new identity and set me up here, in New Zealand. The man I had testified against was a powerful – very powerful – criminal. I had to become someone else, cut out from my life everyone close to me so he couldn't find me . . . It wasn't much fun, believe me! And I didn't lie to you! I lied *for* you. And for Jack. Do you understand?'

She could see his Adam's apple move as he spoke haltingly, 'Were you involved in—'

'No. How could you even think that? No, I wasn't involved in any of his dealings. I had no idea, not until I saw him kill people. I witnessed him murder people – do you understand? I can't tell you any more than that. Please, let's leave it at that.'

'You could've told me. You could've trusted me.'

'I do trust you, but this isn't about trust. It's about protection. Because I . . . because I love you and because I love Jack.' She was fighting a losing battle against the surge of emotion in her chest.

'God, I missed you,' Elliot whispered and pulled her towards him. He kissed her with the fervour and greed of a man on his first date. And he made love to her as if she were a woman he had just met and fallen in love with at first sight.

Before falling asleep, she pushed damp streaks of hair from her face and stared into the night searching for something else. Someone else.

While Elliot was snoring softly in bed, Andrea got up and tip-toed to the window. She opened it to feel the fresh breeze dry her face. She stood there motionless and quiet, remembering the other man and feeling guilt creep up on her like a thief in the night.

Chapter Thirteen

Now that the mystery of the bog body was as good as solved, I decided to concentrate all my efforts on putting my family back together – well, what was left of it. I hadn't spent the last twenty-five years searching for my sister in this world and the next, fraternising with the dead and their restless spirits, and – who knows – maybe with the devil himself, in order to let her go now that I had found her.

A month had passed since Andrea had gone back to New Zealand. I was missing her. Our mother was gone and there was a huge gap in our lives, in humble Bishops Well – a gap that only Andrea could fill. I resolved to bring her back. Andrea and I had to be there for each other, just like when we were kids. We also had to be there for Dad. I could see that he was beginning to fall apart.

I had invited him for meals: lunches and dinners. It was an open invitation. He couldn't possibly cater for himself. I wasn't sure whether he could boil an egg without breaking the pot. I couldn't remember a single occasion from my childhood when Dad had cooked a meal. Without Mum, he was bound to starve himself to death and not care a jot.

In reply to my invitation, he had turned up for lunch, once. He had sat at the kitchen table with me, staring at his plate. I tried to entertain him with conversation, but he didn't seem to hear me, never mind listening to a word I was saying. An hour into his silence, he got up.

'I'd better be going. Irene will be wondering where I am.' He gestured towards his untouched salad Niçoise. 'Thanks for the quiche, Maggie. It was lovely. Who would've thought you could . . . um . . . cook . . . Full of surprises! Yes!' He nodded. 'Well done!'

His bizarre words left me speechless.

I had spent a whole week worrying sick about him. He hadn't come back, even though I would call him every morning to let him know what I'd be serving for lunch and dinner. I had raked my memory for his favourite dishes: hearty stews, pork chops, roast beef – you name it. I ended up eating it all by myself. My waist couldn't take it any more. But more to the point, I couldn't carry on pretending that nothing was amiss. Dad was beginning to lose his mind, and even more alarmingly – his will to live.

I had to do something to take his mind off losing Mum. It was a daunting task. I had spent the whole night mulling over it. Finally, by five o'clock in the morning, I had a solution: Dad needed a change of air.

I scrambled out of bed, pulled my everyday jumper and joggers over my pyjamas, and headed for Dad's place. It was a cold and wet morning – the day hadn't yet broken through the night. It was still pitch black. Only when I stepped into a puddle and felt the slimy touch of mud on my feet did I realise that I wasn't wearing any shoes. I often sleep in my woolly socks on cold nights – it's one of my very few creature comforts. In the end, I live alone and don't really need to look sexy in bed. Anyhow, I had forgotten to put my shoes on. I too was losing my mind, and my will to live.

I found Dad asleep in a chair – he hadn't even bothered to go to bed. I shook him by the shoulder. He opened his eyes, peered at me, baffled and confused.

'Irene?'

'No, Dad. It's me, Maggie.' I had to swallow back tears. 'Your daughter – Maggie.'

'I know that!' He glowered at me indignantly.

'Listen, Dad, I think you and I – we really ought to visit Andrea in New Zealand. You should meet your grandson, don't you think?'

His eyes cleared and twinkled. 'Jack?'

'Yes, Jack!' I was relieved. His mind wasn't gone, not entirely.

'That'd be nice, wouldn't it?'

'It bloody well would,' I concurred. 'We'll just have to travel to New Zealand. I'll let Andrea know. What do you think?'

'That'd be nice,' he repeated.

It wasn't yet six o'clock in the morning, so I gathered it was early evening in New Zealand – a perfect time for a social call. I dialled Andrea's mobile number after I worked out all the intricacies of international dial codes.

'Hello?'

Every cell of my body performed a joyous little somersault when I heard her voice. I think I was still disbelieving that she was alive and well, and hearing her voice was like the greatest of the least expected surprises.

'Hello there, stranger . . . It's your big sister.'

'Maggie!'

'That'd be me.'

'Is everything OK at . . . home?'

'Tip-top, tip-top,' I chimed. 'Actually, better than that. Dad and I have come up with a plan. We're dying to meet Jack, and Elliot, of course, so we thought we should pay you a little visit.'

'What, here? Now?' To my chagrin, she sounded alarmed.

'Well, yes, now . . . It's the middle of summer over there. We could do with a nice break from torrential rain. What do you say? Would you have a spare bedroom?'

There was a long, ominous silence at her end. For a second I thought we may have been disconnected. Then I heard a child's voice in the background.

'Mummy, who's that?'

'No one,' I heard her muffled reply. She hadn't quite succeeded at covering the receiver with her hand. My heart sank to the bottom of my stomach.

'Maggie,' she spoke, 'now isn't a good time. Listen, why don't we come over – me and Jack. Leave it with me. I'll make arrangements, and I'll call you.'

75

The tone of her voice was such that I couldn't bring myself to ask why. I put the phone down and turned to face Dad, offering him a stupid, big grin.

'Right,' said I, 'so, we got the ball rolling ... And while we wait, let's have breakfast.'

Chapter Fourteen

It had been years since she had last dialled the number they had given to her *for an emergency*. Her only emergency had been to speak to Hugo. She had rung that number repeatedly after arriving in New Zealand, and the same male voice at the other end would calmly and repeatedly tell her that Hugo could not be contacted via that number and that she should bear in mind that the number was only to be used *for an emergency*.

Eventually, she had stopped calling.

Years later, she had met Elliot and consigned Hugo to the past. With time, she had been able to replace her childhood and family back home through her carefully constructed domesticity with Elliot and Jack. Everything had worked fine – until her mum's death.

Now that Andrea's past had been brought back from the dead, and she had made a promise to Jack to meet his grandfather, she dialled the emergency number.

They had called her right back. As always, in a matter of seconds her phone would ring and that same male voice would be on the other end. However many of them there were, they all sounded the same: clones of undisputed authority, each with a stiff upper lip.

'Hello, Andrea. Is everything all right?' the clone asked in his clipped Queen's English.

She braced herself and blurted out, 'I'm just letting you know – I am not asking, just letting you know, do you understand? – I'm going back home ... So that you know.'

'Going back where precisely?'

'Home. Back home. My husband and son are coming with me. We'll be staying with my father in Bishops Well – for your records.'

'Bear with me, please …' He gulped, the line clicked and there was a long silence.

She was sitting on the balcony overlooking the bay. The wind had stirred ripples across the estuary. They were bouncing about where the sunrays hit the surface of water. In other places, the shadows of tree ferns kept things calm and grim. Andrea's eyes swept vacantly over the bay and travelled back to the living room where Jack was watching telly. The sliding doors were pulled shut – Andrea didn't want Jack to hear her conversation. He looked up from the TV screen and beamed at her. She gave him the thumbs up.

The line clicked again. For the very first time, the clone's voice carried a tinge of anxiety, 'This isn't a good time to come back, Andrea. Wayne Kew has been released from custody on compassionate grounds, and …' Another gulp. 'And at the moment we don't know where he is. He may be after you – especially after your recent trip to the UK. This isn't a good time.'

'This is as good a time as any. If Wayne wants to find me, he'll find me wherever I am—'

'If you stay there, he won't find you. You are safe where you are, but we can't guarantee your safety if you return to the UK.'

'I am going home, and—' She spoke before she had a chance to think, 'And you lot owe me protection.'

Andrea knew she sounded childish and petulant, and totally naïve, but she had made up her mind.

'The anonymity of your life in New Zealand gives you just that. It is the best protection we can afford to give you.'

'This isn't protection. It's exile. I'm sick and tired … Hugo promised I'd be looked after. I believed him.'

'Hugo?'

'Aniston.'

Puzzled silence. Perhaps she should not have said his real name – she was not supposed to know it.

'Major Aniston is no longer in active service. It's totally out of the question. We don't have the resources to provide you with twenty-four-hour protection. You must understand, that was only at the time of the trial. Now your only protection is the distance and your anonymity.'

'I will be going back.'

'It'll be at your own risk.'

'Fine.'

'I strongly suggest you reconsider. Think of your family—'

'Why don't you just fuck off!' She slammed the phone down.

She ran back to the living room and gave Jack a big cuddle.

'Mummy loves you very, very much! She'll never let anything bad happen to you.'

'OK,' Jack mumbled, none too pleased. 'Can you get out the way of the TV, Mum? I want to see the ending.'

Back at the semi, Hugo offered her a glass of double malt and she gulped it in one go. Heat rippled through her veins. Her cheeks pumped with colour. Hugo drank nothing. From his posture and painfully tightened facial muscles she could tell he was tense and alert.

'That bastard will never forget what you did today. He'll hunt you down,' he said. 'Someone should've damn well explained to you the dangers of testifying against him.'

'I had to. Was there a choice?'

'There's always a choice.'

'I saw it in his eyes,' she admitted and instantly felt a current of cold chill slide down her spine. 'He scared the living daylights out of me today.'

Hugo put his hand on hers and squeezed. It was deliberate and firm. 'I told you it'd never be over. But I will look after you, I always bloody well will. Now I don't have a choice.' His grip tightened. She could feel his eyes drilling into her face. There had been a quiver inside her, an onset of panic and fear but now it was gone. Wayne had ceased to exist.

'Thank you.'

He looked at her intently and inhaled to say something, but reconsidered. He had said enough as it was, more than enough. He let her hand go.

That night, Andrea lay in bed, wondering. Would he knock on her bedroom door or just burst in, hungry for her, wild with desire? He did neither. She calmed down by telling herself what an idiot she had been. Hugo wasn't coming. Why the hell would he! He was only her guard, assigned to her by a higher authority. She had to get a grip.

In the days that followed in lazy, uneventful succession, Andrea's relationship with her minder had regained clarity and professional distance. They would still eat together and sit next to each other on the sofa to watch TV, they would laugh at each other's jokes and would talk about the small, insignificant things in life. But he no longer allowed himself to touch her hand. She never again caught him watching her when she wasn't looking.

That May, Wayne's conviction was secured and a custodial sentence imposed. Two months later his appeal was disallowed. Hugo told her about it in an impersonal tone.

'Does that mean I am free to go?'

'I have not been released from duty. They can't be too sure of what he may do next.'

'Wayne?'

He nodded.

'But what can he do? He's in prison.'

He laughed. It was a humourless laughter. 'He can do a great deal of damage, if he wants to. And he will want to harm you. He'll have you tracked down and—' Hugo scrutinised her face with scorching intensity as if ensuring she understood what he was saying. 'We'll look into forging a permanent new identity for you. A new name, new address.'

'So I won't be Andrea Grousser. I'll be someone else? And you? You won't be Christopher Grousser.'

'I never was Christopher Grousser. My name is Hugo.'

*

80

It was after midnight when the telephone rang. Andrea had been lying in bed awake, but she didn't stir to answer the phone.

Elliot woke with a start. 'Who the hell – at this hour?'

She looked away. 'Leave it, they'll go away. Wrong number. Let's sleep.'

'It may be important – it could be Mum.' He yawned, threw off the duvet and shuffled downstairs to get the phone.

A minute later he was back, baffled and suspicious. 'It is for you. Someone called Hugo. A Pommy? Sounds like it. Who's he? He said, an old friend ... Is he?'

She was gone in a flash, grabbed the receiver and put it to her ear. Silence. She couldn't hear him – her heart was pounding too loud.

'Hugo?' she heard herself say.

'Andrea.'

She had to sit down on the step. 'Yes?'

'Andrea, I've been contacted by your case officer. He asked me to explain a few things.' He sounded formal and impersonal.

A sharp needle stung her in the chest, but she refused to acknowledge the pain. It was obvious that Hugo was being watched – on a loudspeaker, somewhere in a stuffy, wood-panelled office, watched by her *case officer*, their conversation being recorded for future reference. He could not speak freely.

'I've been asked to explain to you the danger you will be putting yourself into if you come here now—'

'But you'll protect me.'

'I'm retired.'

'But you said—'

'You must think of your safety – yours and your family's safety first. That's what I would do if I were you. I cannot protect you.'

'OK,' she said weakly. It was time to put the phone down, but she couldn't bring herself to do that. Neither could he, she realised. He was still at the other end, as silent as she was, but still there.

'OK,' she repeated, rather hopelessly.

'OK – you'll stay there?'

'Yes.'

She put down the phone gently, conscious of the finality of her gesture and the finality of her concession. She held it down, then, irrationally, she picked it up again and lifted it to her ear, 'Hugo?'

He was gone. A long flat signal brought her back to reality. She hung up.

Elliot was standing on the landing, his arms dangling aimlessly by his sides. From below, his frame, shrouded in shadows, looked hostile. It gave Andrea a fright.

'Who is that guy?' His voice was husky.

'That was the Home Office,' she said vaguely and moved up a few steps towards him.

'It sounded much more personal than that. Who is he to you?'

She stopped halfway up the stairs and, squinting with the landing light shining into her eyes, tried to see his face but it was obscured in semi-darkness. She could hear his shallow breathing. She said, calm honesty in her voice, 'He's no one to me.'

Elliot shifted his feet and a floorboard squealed faintly, 'Then what does he want with you now? Why has he called you?' His voice was thinning with rising anxiety.

'To dissuade me from going back.'

There was a long pause, but he wasn't moving and neither was she.

'Has he succeeded?'

'Yes, I think he did. To hell with it! Let's go back to bed. You shouldn't have answered the phone.'

Chapter Fifteen

Christmas came and went without me noticing. For the first time in my life, I couldn't be bothered to put up a tree. If it hadn't been for my dear neighbour, Dad and I would have missed out on Christmas altogether. Samuel however had invited us for Christmas dinner and his mother Deirdre had outdone herself on the turkey and stuffing front. For a couple of hours it felt as if Mum had come back to us. But soon the illusion was gone and Dad and I went back to our state of bewilderment and unrelenting grief.

All in all, it had taken me three long months to swim back to the surface and re-emerge in the land of the living. I was still reeling from Mum's death, and even more so from finding and once again losing Andrea. She had not got back to me with details of her flight back home. She had gone under the radar. Again. At least she was alive, if otherwise detained on the other side of the world. On the run from the criminal underworld. My poor brain had been struggling to take it all in, so I resolved to leave it (the problem, not my brain) in the unfinished business bucket and seek human contact.

Fortuitously, I received a phone call from Bishops Ace Academy (the fancy new title for our secondary school) asking me to supply for two weeks, possibly more. One of their English teachers had taken to their sick bed on the grounds of a mental breakdown. I should have taken heed from that nugget of information, but didn't. It was my lack of experience. I usually supply at Bishops Lord Weston's CE Primary, which is light years away from the black hole of the secondary school. Little people present problems proportionate to their size; teenagers blow everything out of proportion, particularly their egos.

In the first two days, everything went smoothly with the Year Ten class I had taken on. They had been revising *An Inspector Calls* when I joined them. We started by looking at the class divide in inter-war Britain, and then drew parallels with modern day society, pausing briefly to consider the feudal hierarchy of Bishops Well, with Lord Weston-Jones perched on top of the ladder and the rest of us languishing at the bottom. When we moved to the Suffragettes the following day, I noticed a young man at the back of the class lean forward, press his forehead to the table, and wrap his arms around his head. He had gone to sleep in the middle of my lesson.

I should have left him to get on with his nap. Instead, unwisely, I addressed him.

'Thomas, am I boring you?'

'Yeah, you fucking are.'

Which was truthful, if rather rude.

My pride severely tested, I made a point of allocating to him three fat adverse behaviour points, which judging by his already high score would lead to detention. I didn't care. He owed me respect and if he wasn't offering it voluntarily I was determined to extract it from him by force. That was my second big mistake. Thomas had different ideas. Showing me respect, even under duress, wasn't one of them.

His first response was to not turn up for my lessons. He missed two in a row. Without him and his antics, the lessons were a breeze. We covered capitalism, socialism, and went as far as anarchy. I should have rejoiced. But something possessed me to report Thomas for internal truancy.

On Friday, Thomas was back in class: in body but not in (good) spirit, and armed with several disclaimers attached to his return. He walked in late, slammed the door behind him for effect, and rolled his backpack on the floor. He didn't follow his backpack, but paused to gaze at me.

'I'm here. You'd better tick me off on the register.' If looks could kill, I would be lying on the floor in my final spasms.

'Welcome back, Thomas,' I tried to rise above the provocation and be jolly. 'Why don't you take your seat?'

'Why don't you fuck off, Miss?' Thomas retorted and the whole class shook with collective laughter. Thomas, however, took his seat and promptly went to sleep.

The Thomas issue bothered me and I had to deal with it – with him – if I were to continue teaching this class for another week, or perhaps longer, while their teacher was recovering his or her wits upon their sick bed. I approached the school's pastoral lead, Ivo Murphy. Ivo had been head-hunted by Bishops Ace Academy after their exclusion rates had risen to such unprecedented levels that more of their students were hanging around outside the local Co-op than sitting behind their school desks in term time. This was the result of Little Ogburn Comprehensive being put into special measures and most of the disadvantaged kids from there being transferred to Bishops Ace with the objective of affording them a quality education. Ivo and his wife Megan had moved to Bishops Well and he had begun to perform his magic of seducing the disenchanted youth back to school. Apparently, he was worth every penny the school had paid him to relocate from Bristol.

Ivo is a man in his prime, with the smouldering good looks of a paratrooper with a degree in rocket science. His body is lean, toned, and perfectly proportioned. He wears Harry Potter spectacles and the wizard boy's innocent expression with ease. I would fancy him if he wasn't so young. And married, of course, though that never stopped me from fancying James. Back to Ivo. He has a degree in child psychology and knows how to handle slippery little shits like Thomas Moore. He listened to my predicament, nodded his empathy and said, 'Do no harm—'

'I try not to, though – God is my witness – I've reached the end of my tether!'

'No, no. *Do no harm* is Thomas's rule. Thomas hates rules so he has only one. We agreed on it after we'd trialled a dozen others. So that's

Thomas's rule. He does you no harm as long as you do the same. Just don't invade his space and you'll find he is as good as gold.'

'But he's sleeping in my class!'

'Doing you no harm whatsoever ...'

'He swears.'

'Only in self-defence. Like I said, don't invade his space and he won't swear. Just let sleeping dogs lie – literally,' Ivo concluded and took himself out of the staffroom, whistling the bouncy tune from *Bridge Over the River Kwai,* and dragging behind him a faint ghost of a girl, no older than sixteen – whoever she had been to him in life, she clung on to Ivo firmly in death. Presumably, one of the students that he hadn't been able to save. There's always the odd one.

I wasn't going to poke my nose into that but looked to Cherie Hornby for a clarification regarding Ivo's advice. Apart from being the chair of Bishops' Archaeological Association, she also teaches history at Bishops Ace Academy.

'Ivo is a bit on the nutty side, but that man is pure magic! He performs miracles with those kids.' She pondered it for a second longer, and added, 'I suppose you have to be nuts to do his job.'

'You have to be nuts to do our job, too.'

'True, but he knows what he's talking about, unlike you, Maggie. You are an amateur. Not good enough in this day and age.'

'Am I that out of touch?'

'I'm afraid so. Nowadays, schools are battlefields and we teachers have to behave like generals – strategize to outmanoeuvre the mob, plan ahead of them, keep them in line, take them by surprise. You have to know what you're doing, or you're cannon fodder.'

Military metaphors are Cherie's forte. She is an expert in military history, specialising in the Napoleonic Wars. But even with that in mind, she sounded rather ominous to me. For a second, I was sure I smelt gunpowder.

I shuddered.

She ended on a high note, 'Just do as he says. You'll be fine.'

'OK, I'll let the sleeping Moore lie – literally.' I shrugged. 'I feel like something strong before I face him though.'

'Coffee is the strongest you get here.'

'Then coffee will have to do.'

I headed for the cupboard to requisition a chipped mug with the school logo. As I was spooning in sugar, Cherie produced her lunchbox, where in little compartments she had tactically placed a neat ham sandwich with no crust, a middle-sized apple, and some pasta salad. The spirit of her dear departed mother gazed at her daughter with approval. The spirit of my mum was nowhere to be seen, not even by me, which was a blessing on this occasion. Mum wouldn't be amused by my dietary routines, or rather the stark absence of them. She used to bemoan my eating habits.

My stomach rumbled. I had forgotten to bring lunch. I don't even own a lunchbox. Whenever I start preparing lunch for the next day, I end up eating it the night before. If I somehow manage not to devour it, I usually forget it in the fridge anyway. I had given up on the idea of packed lunches a long time ago. Now I regretted it. I needed regular sustenance to complete this teaching assignment.

I plunged an extra two teaspoons of sugar into my coffee and stirred with vigour. Mum was probably turning in her grave.

'So, how are you feeling? I haven't seen you in weeks.'

'I was just lying low, licking my wounds, I guess.'

'And now?'

'I'm here, aren't I?'

Cherie nodded her understanding. 'You know, when my mum's dementia got the better of her, I'd have moments when I'd grieve for her as if she were dead. It was easier, I guess, when she actually—'

This time I nodded my understanding. I didn't want to trudge on into the subject of grief. I had been keeping it at arm's length and wasn't going to give in to it now. I sipped my syrupy coffee. It was vile.

'So, what have I missed?' I had failed to attend at least five of our AA meetings. The only person I had seen on and off during that time was my lovely – but poorly stocked on local gossip – neighbour Samuel. I would usually spot him on his patio, a cup of coffee in hand. But even with him I had usually avoided direct interaction, on account of my pyjamas, bad hair, and stale breath. I was starved of information.

'Oh yes! You haven't heard! So, Michael has been keeping us abreast with developments – you know, about the body from the dig?'

My ears pricked.

'You'll never believe it but it's James's mother!'

'Yes, I know that.'

Cherie looked at me, disappointed. 'Who told you?'

'I told them! I told DI Marsh.'

She peered at me quizzically, but didn't verbalise her obvious thought, *and how the hell did you know?* She stabbed a piece of macaroni from her pasta salad and shoved it in her mouth.

'Anything else?'

'It depends on what you already know.' A squeak of resentment ground between Cherie's teeth.

'That's all I knew.'

'In that case, you wouldn't know that the cops have tracked down the woman's cousin in South Africa – Karl van Niekerk is his name. He left at about the same time as she'd gone missing, so you can imagine, he'd be the prime suspect: killed her and ran ...'

'Yes, it makes perfect sense.'

'But, you see, with no evidence whatsoever, they couldn't pin it on him, hard as they tried. I believe DI Marsh went all the way to Johannesburg to interview him, but came back empty-handed. Michael says they're still looking for the slightest trace of forensic evidence to link that Van Niekerk chap to the woman's grave. It's an open case.'

'Hmmm ...' I mused, 'if he had nothing to hide and no arrest to fear, wouldn't he be on the first plane over here to find out who had killed his cousin? I would! I'd want to know how she died, and why ... And besides, how come he never bothered to contact her in the last fifty-odd years? Have you wondered that? There's only one explanation – because he knew she was dead. Guilty as sin, if you ask me!'

The bell went. I finished my coffee and dragged my feet back to the classroom to face Thomas Moore. When I arrived there, he was already in his seat at the back of the classroom, sleeping. He looked peaceful and harmless, like a newborn baby.

Chapter Sixteen

Sadly for Andrea, Elliot didn't believe her. His mother moved in with them a week later. Judging by the size of her luggage, Heather had every intention of staying indefinitely. Her dour face was even more determined and inscrutable than usual. The bob of her grey hair seemed set in concrete. Her whole face seemed set in concrete. She was the last person Andrea wished to entertain.

She stayed out of Heather's way as much as possible, but the house was full of Heather: her voice, her bossiness, the smells of her cooking, her opinions. It was on a Sunday morning that, after a sleepless night, Andrea had a lie-in and only rose at noon. The aromas of Heather's Sunday roast were already present. Pots were being banged and the tap hissed with activity, but above all of that towered Heather's voice, 'She can go to hell as far as I'm concerned, but she isn't taking you and Jack with her. Over my dead body!'

The murmur of Elliot's reply was swallowed by a creaking cupboard door.

'And you trust her? You're more naïve than I thought! How can you possibly trust her about anything – anything at all! You don't know anything about her. She lied to you, Elliot – all she did was lie, and you think you can take her word? Don't be daft! Pass me that tea towel.'

Andrea descended the stairs on tiptoe and flattened her back against the wall in the hallway.

Elliot said, 'You're too harsh, Mum. She—'

'God give me strength!' A pot was smashed on to the hob. 'For all you know she could be booking plane tickets for herself and Jack under whatever bloody name she can dream up! I'm not losing you or Jack to her. She'll go, take Jack with her, and we won't hear from her again. Would you even know where to look for them?'

'I want to ask her where her father—'

'And she'll tell you?'

'Well, yes . . .'

'Well, no! We're holding on to Jack's passport and you'll be applying for an urgent injunction.'

'That's a bit drastic, Mum.'

'Do you want to hang on to your son?'

'I do. And I also want to hang on to my wife. I need to show her some trust.'

'Is she even your wife? Are you even legally married to her? She's been parading under a false name since the day you met. You may've married a serial killer for all you know!'

'Now you're being bloody-minded.'

'Mind your language, young man, and get on with the carrots. They won't peel themselves!'

Andrea felt an irresistible urge to swoop on the woman and crash one of those pots against her head, over and over again until the last spark of light fled from her eyes. It took a while to compose herself. Casually, she ambled into the kitchen, yawned and asked, 'Is there anything I can help with? Potatoes? Brussels sprouts?' She took a knife from the rack.

Heather and Elliot gaped at her, trying to read her face, dying to know how much she had heard of Heather's diatribe.

'Hello, darling.' Elliot got up and kissed her on the cheek. 'Did you sleep well?'

'Like a baby. Where's Jack?'

'At the Watsons'.'

She smiled. As long as she played ball, she still had her boy and her husband. Heather couldn't do anything about it – as long as Andrea stayed put. Her past and her family back in the UK had been lost to her the moment she entered the witness protection programme. All she had left were memories, and she had to be content with that.

There was a noise in the middle of the night, an unidentifiable but distinct noise: the scream of shattered glass. Andrea sat up in bed, startled. The pounding of her heart was louder than the sounds coming from downstairs. Only a few seconds passed between the jangling of broken glass and Hugo bursting into her bedroom with a wild look in his eyes. Yet to her, it seemed an eternity. She was sitting up, paralysed.

'Get under the bed! Now!' he wheezed at her. There was a gun in his hand. To her inexpert eye it was the same weapon Wayne had used to kill those three African men. Her gaze froze on the gun.

Hugo grabbed her by the shoulder, his fingers cutting into her skin, and dragged her off the bed. 'Climb under! Don't leave this room.'

He was gone.

She pulled herself to her feet, and followed him. She couldn't stay behind. She was too scared. What if he didn't come back? What if it wouldn't be him? She could not take the chance of waiting to find out.

She stepped gingerly down the stairs, her lips white with fear, her hands cold. She couldn't tell what she was touching in the dark as she slithered her way down into the kitchen.

There was another thud. A cry, like that of a child. Her eyes began to adjust to the night. She could see Hugo's silhouette, his square shoulders tense and alert. A ragged stack of broken glass towered over a carnage of shards. They screeched in protest as Hugo's feet ground them into the floor. Hugo gasped, and swore; a shadow jumped off the wall. A deafening clap of gunshot erupted, followed by an even more deafening silence.

It was Hugo's gun that had been fired – only his gun, Andrea realised. The shadow of his hand moved slowly to the light switch. Brightness hit her in the eyes, blinding her for a split second.

'Oh, fuck!' he muttered.

At last, she saw the cat. It was a very large tabby, its tummy sprawled on the kitchen worktop, its back paws stretched, front ones oddly out of alignment. It was dead.

Hugo had shot a cat.

She lifted her gaze towards him. He was beginning to steady his breathing. There was something dark and primeval in his face; his lips were curled, baring his teeth; his pupils were enlarged, spilling their blackness over the usual cool blue of his eyes. His hand was clutching the gun in a steady grip. There was no hesitation in that grip, only determination, an instinct to kill. He pointed the gun at her and lowered it in the same fraction of a second.

'What are you doing here – fuck's sake!' he hissed at her angrily. 'I told you to climb under the bed, why couldn't you fucking well listen!'

'You shot a cat.'

It wasn't quite the answer he expected. 'You do as I tell you! Do you understand!' He was clutching her arms tightly and shaking her back and forth.

Her head felt loose on her shoulders, ready to come off. 'Please . . . don't. It hurts.'

'I told you!' he shouted, and pulled her close, his hands releasing her shoulders and travelling frantically to her face, cupping it, squeezing, his fingers brushing the hair off her forehead, his lips sinking into hers.

'I told you . . .' His breath was hot. 'I told you to hide.' He was kissing her – all over her face, her neck, her hair. His passion was permeating her, shooting right through her skin and into the pit of her stomach. Her whole body tingled, then tumbled, heaved itself up and sank again. She was falling with him into the madness of that passion.

He scooped her off the ground and carried her out of the kitchen, up the stairs, along the hallway, and into his bedroom. He laid her on his narrow bed, his face only inches away from hers.

'I love you, do you get it? I can't lose you . . .'

Chapter Seventeen

St John the Baptist's was full to the brim. Mourners from all ends of the world had flocked to pay belated last respects to Lady Helen Weston-Jones, née de Klerk. That included the incumbent Lady Weston-Jones, who had flown in from Switzerland for the first time in nearly three years. Lady Helen's brother, Jan de Klerk, and his wife, were also present, as were their children – both middle-aged men accompanied by their partners. They had travelled from Australia for the funeral of the aunt they had never met when she was alive.

Karl van Niekerk was there too. He had come to England for the first time in over fifty years.

Helen's family were a handsome lot, all tall and upright, fit and full of vigour despite the jetlag and their advanced years. Good looks were in their genetic make-up. Karl van Niekerk was a deserving member of that exclusive club. He might have been in his late seventies and grey as a pigeon, but there was something strong and distinguished about his face and his posture. His complexion was weather-beaten by years of exposure to the merciless African sun. His pale grey eyes were alert and quick. He sat, proud and inscrutable, with the rest of Helen's blood relatives in the front pew on the left-hand side of the aisle.

The front pew on the right was occupied by the Weston-Joneses: Lord Philip and his wife, and further along, James, Letitia and their two children, brought back from their boarding school in Berkshire. James's late brother's widow, Pru, was there too. She had travelled from France, where she had moved after Joshua's untimely death at the hand of that infamous Afghan terrorist. She, too, like a few other in-laws of the Weston-Jones clan, seemed to have severed her ties with the family as soon as she could. Rumour had it that Lord Philip wasn't the easiest man to be around.

That unverified rumour was imparted by Maggie to Samuel without any solicitation on his part, minutes before the service had started. During the first reading, she also felt compelled to inform him that Helen's spirit, the Swamp Lady as Maggie continued to call her, had elected to sit with her kith and kin in the pew on the left. That too was an unverified piece of information.

'Isn't that interesting?' she pondered in a stage whisper which forced a few heads to turn and several lips to hiss admonishment at her.

Maggie was unrepentant, for she went on to add, 'What puzzles me is Karl van Niekerk ... The nerve to come back! You know, I never thought—'

She was shushed by Vicar Laurence, who ostentatiously cleared his throat and glared at her before returning to the business at hand at the altar.

'Sorry!' Maggie mouthed at him. She was one of those women who always had to have the last word, Sam mused quietly and with mild amusement.

On Maggie's insistence, he'd had to arrive in the church half an hour before the service was due to start. Maggie wanted to take a good look at everyone, particularly at Karl van Niekerk. Though reluctant at first (Sam disliked churches and all other manifestations of religion), he had to admit she was right on one account. The first rows of pews had been reserved for family, friends, and all manner of aristocratic relations of the Weston-Joneses. That left just a couple of rows at the back and, beyond that, standing room only, with onlookers and even members of the local press spilling out into the churchyard. Arriving as early as they had, Maggie and Sam had secured two spaces in the last pew. They were sitting in the company of like-minded individuals who had the foresight to arrive early: Cherie Hornby and Les Foreman (the headmaster of Bishops

Ace Academy), Vera Hopps-Wood accompanied by Henry (he wouldn't miss the opportunity to be seen mingling with the highest echelons of society), Parish Clerk George Easterbrook as well as the entire body of Bishops Well Parish Council. Even the reclusive horror writer, Daryl Luntz, had joined the mourners, although he, a newcomer to Bishops, couldn't have known the Westons from Adam. He arrived with his secretary, Hannah. At least she was an established and verifiable Bishopian. In fact, she had hung around with Maggie and Andrea when they were young. She was now married to Matthew Lithgow, but he was nowhere to be seen. Matthew wasn't given to ceremonies and hierarchies, and rumour had it that he didn't approve of Hannah's employer.

Helen's body would join the ranks of the Weston-Jones forebears, whose tombstones were embedded in the church's walls and floor slabs, going back to the early sixteenth century. There was a family vault in the cellar of the church where the late Lady Weston-Jones would rest. So, there would be no burial as such among the mere mortals (Maggie insisted they were actually the mere *immortals*) whose earthly remains shared the communal space of the outdoor cemetery.

After the service, an outpouring of condolences was bestowed upon both the Weston-Joneses and the De Klerks. Maggie grabbed Samuel's hand and began forcing her way towards the front.

'I must know what's said between them,' she explained her manoeuvres. 'Who says what … It's vital to our investigation.'

Sam wasn't sure what investigation, though he had a sneaky suspicion that Maggie had embarked on a spot of sleuthing, not quite yet satiated with their earlier joint triumph of identifying the body.

They pressed rudely ahead, but the crowds were thick and everyone seemed to have the same idea as Maggie – albeit about getting to the head of the queue with their commiserations, not eavesdropping. By the time they were within earshot of the two grieving families, Lord Philip was shaking hands with Jan de Klerk, saying, 'Please do come to the house for a drink and a few nibbles. In fact, I insist you stay with us as our guests.'

Mrs De Klerk smiled faintly and dared to resist, 'Oh, we're comfortable where we are. The hotel is—'

'I do insist. Please.'

Jan de Klerk thanked Lord Philip, who then went to shake hands and extend the same invitation to the two sons and their wives, while Lady Weston-Jones embraced Mrs de Klerk without words.

Sam noted that the cordialities came to an abrupt halt when it came to Karl van Niekerk. Neither he nor Lord Philip offered to shake hands with the other. Van Niekerk looked sternly at Weston-Jones from the sidelines. Weston-Jones gave van Niekerk a perfunctory glance in return, but it didn't escape Sam that there was a twitch of a muscle in the lord's jaw. He could almost hear the grinding of his teeth. There was anger, or deep suspicion, between the two men. And that was *interesting*.

Maggie snaked her arm around Sam's. 'Let's go, then. Shall we take your car?'

'Where are we going?'

'The Weston estate. For a drink and nibbles.'

'Isn't that just the family—'

'And friends. We're friends. James's friends. We have every right to be there. And we owe it to James, of course.'

Somehow, through trickery and sheer pushiness, Maggie managed to weasel her way into the close proximity of the De Klerks. Sam felt obliged to follow her, especially because the one drink for which they had arrived had, in Maggie's case, transformed into three shameless martinis. Sam had to make sure that no more would follow.

'It was a beautiful service!' Maggie enthused. 'I'm Maggie Kaye.' She thrust her hand at Jan de Klerk. 'And this is Samuel Dee. We are friends – family friends. James's friends, really. I've known James all my life. Samuel, not so long. He's only moved to Bishops … hmm … a year or so ago. A newcomer, really, but a good friend nonetheless.'

Jan de Klerk, his hand entwined with Maggie's in her lethal grip, looked like he was dying to say something – anything to stop the strange woman from blabbering everyone into their early graves. He was holding his breath, his face growing redder by the second, readying himself in vain to reply to Maggie's introductions.

Sam intervened, 'My condolences.' He wrestled the poor man's hand away from Maggie.

'Thank you,' De Klerk exhaled and clutched Sam's hand as if it was a lifebelt.

'It must feel awful to find out – all these years later – about your sister!' Maggie was relentless.

'It was a shock, yes.'

'A terrible, terrible shock!' Mrs De Klerk added. She had the sweet innocent face of an amiable old lady who had been sheltered all her life from shock. 'We thought Helen was alive and well, living in luxury . . . a lady of the manor . . . She had married into nobility, after all! We never, not for one minute, we never thought that she was—My dear poor Helen! That she was rotting in a hole in the ground . . . Never!' Mrs De Klerk covered her mouth with an elegant hand that had never experienced a day of domestic chores. She appeared genuinely shaken – as violently as Maggie's third martini.

Maggie put aside her empty glass. At last, she wasn't looking to replace it with a full one. Her attention was on the De Klerks.

'But what I can't understand,' she began, 'is how on earth you could make that utterly stupid assumption . . . You didn't hear from her, not a word in over fifty years! Weren't you concerned about the . . . the lack of contact? She was your sister, for crying out loud, and you didn't bother to try to get in touch – and, *and* you weren't alarmed by her silence! That's just not normal!'

'How could we have been so naïve, Jan!' Mrs De Klerk gave in to tears.

Sam feared that Jan de Klerk was about to give Maggie a slap and he, Sam, would have to defend her. She deserved it – the slap. But de Klerk was evidently a man of peace – and his wife was in pieces. He embraced her and kissed the top of her head. A tear was glistening in his eye, too.

His son came to the rescue. 'You see, my parents thought Aunt Helen had given us the snub. They thought she didn't wish to hear from us, that we were too lowly for her in-laws. *Plebs*, isn't that the term you use in this country?'

Maggie blinked.

'Yes,' Jan looked at her from above his weeping wife's head, 'I had a bad feeling about Helen marrying into blue blood and moving over here ... I'd tried to convince her to change her mind, but she wouldn't hear of it. She was in love.'

'It makes people do crazy things – love,' Maggie nodded thoughtfully. Sam was relieved to see that she was calmer now, at last entering the more tranquil phase of her alcoholic daze. It was time to guide her home.

But she had one more card up her sleeve. 'So how does Karl van Niekerk come into this?'

'At the time, we – our parents and I – we decided to ask Karl to go with Helen to England – to keep an eye on her.'

'Though she hated the idea, didn't she, Jan?' Mrs De Klerk spoke.

'It grew on her ... She liked Karl. They grew up together, as kids, you know ... So she accepted it. After a while. But ... But when Karl came back and said she didn't need him – want him there – here ... she wouldn't talk to him any more, or see him ... Well, we gave up. She gave birth to a son – she was a mother, mother to the heir apparent. Karl was just a nuisance ... We just – we were just too proud – proud and stubborn! We thought she didn't want to be reminded of her humble roots. So be it, we thought. We got on with our lives.'

'We made a mistake. All of us. Your mum and dad, and Karl, and you and me too,' Mrs De Klerk listed all the suspects, gazing around her guiltily. 'I've been thinking about it – it was probably post-natal depression, her attitude to Karl, her mood ... I should've known something wasn't right.' She was on the verge of tears all over again.

Sam dreaded tears. He said quickly, 'I see Mr van Niekerk – Karl – isn't here.'

'No,' Jan nodded. 'He's an angry man. Angry with himself, I think. He can't forgive himself for not ... not sticking around.'

'He's angry with the Weston-Joneses, Jan. They should've told us she was missing. They said nothing – all these years, nothing.'

Maggie waddled in on their recriminations to rub some salt into the wound of their guilt, 'Ah! You can't blame them. They all thought that Helen had gone away with Karl!'

Chapter Eighteen

While all of the De Klerks accepted Lord Philip's hospitality and moved into the east wing of Weston for the remainder of their stay, Karl van Niekerk continued to rent a room above the Rook's Nest in the centre of Bishops Well. Fortunately for him, the influx of tourists inspired by our Celtic dig had motivated Terrence Truelove to convert the loft into three guestrooms and rake in some cash, much needed for re-thatching the roof. Karl van Niekerk had become one of the first loft guests. Consequently, I took up residence in the pub below. My intention was to shadow Van Niekerk and see where that would take me. As far as I was concerned, he had a lot of questions to answer. I couldn't understand why he wasn't in police custody, answering those questions:

When was the last time he saw Helen?

What was the nature of their relationship?

How did they part ways?

Why had he not attempted to contact her in fifty-odd years?

Was he aware of the fact that she was dead?

And the most important one: did he kill her?

I am not saying that I would expect him to answer those questions truthfully, especially if he was guilty as anticipated, but I wanted to put those questions to him and see his face when he answered them.

I took my usual position by the bay window straight after school on Wednesday afternoon, armed with a glass of orange juice. Since those three dry martinis last Saturday, I had been feeling wretched:

dehydrated and nauseous. Clearly, martinis didn't agree with me; I wasn't Bond material. Well, not James Bond material, but I still stood a chance as a Bond girl. I hoped. Bond girls don't drink those dreadful martinis. They are wholesome. They drink orange juice. I was drinking orange juice and making resolutions to lay off the liquor for a while.

The Rook's Nest wasn't the most suitable place to adhere to such resolutions. It was enveloped in a yeasty whiff of beer and by flammable cider fumes, with an occasional accent of more potent beverages punctuating the air like sloshed exclamation marks. Still, I was focusing on staying true to my sobriety while waiting for Van Niekerk to emerge.

While I was watching out for him, a man by the bar was watching me. A couple of times I had caught him leering at me. I thought I knew everyone in Bishops, but this individual was a total stranger, although he acted like he owned the place. I sent repelling vibes his way, but he was too sozzled to get the message. He picked up his pint and toddled towards me. He had an unsteady stride, staggering with his feet wide apart like a drunken sailor. His head was clean-shaven (or he was as bald as an egg), but to compensate for the lack of hair on top of his head he had an impressive red beard sprouting from his temples to a couple of inches below his collarbone. I only had a moment to contemplate what he would look like if tipped upside down – his beard would make a decent mop of hair, shoulder length – when he slumped on to a chair at my table, and said, 'Fancy a drink, love?'

'No thanks. I've got one,' I replied politely and raised my glass to prove my point.

'What is it?'

'Orange juice.'

'Orange juice?' He thundered with laughter, allowing me to discern a golden tooth in the top-left of his mouth. 'How about something stronger, love? It's on me.'

'No, thanks. I'm trying not to.'

'Playing 'ard to get? I been watching you … three days in a row you been sitting 'ere on yer own, wanting company.'

'I enjoy my own company, thank you.'

'Mine ain't good enough for you?' A twist of menace stole into his eyes that were glazing over with alcoholic stupor.

Karl van Niekerk emerged from upstairs to save me.

'Sorry, I must go! Nice talking to you!'

In sensible khaki shorts and walking boots, a small rucksack on his back, Van Niekerk was dressed for a hike. I wasn't. I don't know what possessed me to wear brand new sandals with wedge heels and a skimpy, body-hugging dress that was riding up my hips. That single jolly ray of sunshine that had graced Bishops' sky this morning, the first ray in two months, was probably to blame. My dress code – or more to the point, my rather suggestive state of undress – may have been the reason for attracting the attention of Redbeard. He probably thought I was on the prowl. My reputation was in tatters.

As much as I found that idea horrifying, I had no time to indulge in introspection. My prey was fast-moving, despite his age. I picked up pace, tottering behind him with a mad look in my eyes. I could not afford to lose him, but I also could not afford to let him discover that he was being followed. I would run several steps forward and then dive into a narrow alley or a doorway whenever he paused for breath. He knew his way around the town and he knew exactly where he was going. We were making steady progress eastward – towards Sexton's Wood.

We stopped at the bakery. He entered. I waited outside, watching him have a lengthy chat with Angela Cornish. Funnily enough, he bought a Cornish pasty, and began eating it there and then while chatting to Angela.

My stomach rumbled – I do love a Cornish pasty, but I had to arm myself with patience. Angela is known for her sociable nature and she does have a lot to say to anyone willing to listen. Clearly, Karl van Niekerk was willing. Angela's pink cheeks glowed with excitement as she was doubtlessly relaying to him every major – and minor – event in Bishops since he had left town all those years ago. He had finished his pasty and purchased a bottle of water. I squatted on the pavement outside the bakery and tried to pull the hem of my flimsy dress over my knees. In vain. I waited and waited. My legs went to sleep, but I stayed awake – just.

An eternity later we were on the move again. Van Niekerk headed straight for the Weston estate. He knew his way there and used a shortcut across the paddocks to get to the back entrance by the outbuildings. I zigzagged between bushes and hedgerows, trying to remain invisible. I was successful on the whole, apart from one near miss where I tripped on a jutting root, fell, and yelped in pain. Van Niekerk paused, glanced over his shoulder, and scanned the fields. Since I was already lying on the ground face down, I flattened my body against the grass, using the root as a shield.

After a few seconds of holding my breath, I dared to lift my head. Van Niekerk was continuing on his way towards the estate. He hadn't spotted me after all. I scrambled to my feet and followed him, expecting that he was planning to pay the Weston-Joneses an unannounced visit. But I was wrong. He swung by the outbuildings but he did not enter. He stood by the wall for a long while, just looking at the house in the distance. He took a few sips from his water bottle. The inside of my mouth was dry. I resolved that next time I would come better prepared for shadowing suspects. Bringing provisions and dressing appropriately topped my list.

My calves were itching – I had wandered into a patch of nettles. My only consolation was the fact – or an old wives' tale – that nettle stings were good for one's circulation. Judging by the number of angry red bumps bubbling on my legs my circulation was going strong and fast.

My musings were interrupted: the suspect was on the move again. I went down to a squat to conceal my presence. A nettle brushed my cheek like an electric eel. The idea occurred to me that I should abandon my ill-conceived surveillance, go home and change into something suitable. I dismissed that thought.

Van Niekerk circumvented the Weston estate, heading again in the direction of Sexton's Wood. I had to navigate open fields, zigzagging between boulders and stray sheep, to finally traverse the paddock full of frisky bullocks. I crossed it warily on my haunches, and remained intact.

I was relieved when I reached the relative safety of the wood. The undergrowth was still soggy after weeks of rain so no cracked twig would betray my presence. I was hot on Van Niekerk's heels. And I was in no doubt where he was leading me: to the swamp.

The police tape – what was left of it – was still there, marking the scene of crime. Was it his crime, I wondered. He wasn't going to tell me. He found the grave amongst all the other excavation pits with ease, but that proved little. The grave was clearly demarcated. He stood over it and gazed inside. Then he sat on a log near the grave, held his head in his hands, his elbows propped on his knees. And he stayed like that.

She was there, too – the Lady of the Swamp. Helen. I knew she liked that log. I would often find her there on my excursions into the swamp. She would amble about in the woods or sit on that very log. Karl van Niekerk didn't have a clue his long-lost cousin was sitting right next to him. Her face, as always, was expressionless – gripped by the same nebulous stillness. She, too, wasn't going to tell me anything. It seemed like the two of them were unaware of each other.

I lingered around for what seemed like a lifetime, and nothing, but *nothing*, happened. Van Niekerk did not venture into a loud confession or any other form of audible monologue that would give me some answers. Neither did he pull out a spade and start digging up more bodies. He just sat there, still and silent as a stone.

A mosquito buzzed over my head. I was hidden in a shady bush – the mosquitoes were bound to come. And one of the bastards had found me. It sat on my bare arm. I swiped at the bloodsucker and it buzzed off. But only to tell his mates about this fresh piece of meat squatting in the undergrowth ready for the taking. Soon, a whole squadron of the bastards began its synchronised dance, circling around me like vultures over a dying antelope. Then, they descended. It felt like a coordinated attack was taking place against my face and shoulders: one on my cheek, another one on my ear, and one, I was sure, had tunnelled directly into the artery on my neck. I killed the latter. Half a gallon of my blood spilled out of it as I squashed its bloated body. But more came to take its place in the formation. I had to run.

I left Van Niekerk and Helen on the log and hit the road back home, waving my arms and slapping myself on my face and head like a woman possessed.

I stumbled home on my bare feet (the sandals and their wedge heels were too much to handle), feeling hot and bothered. And itchy.

Samuel popped out of his house as I was retrieving my key from under the pot plant. He came over to help me lift it. I don't know why he does it – I am perfectly capable of elevating a middle-sized terracotta pot!

'My God, Maggie, are you all right!' He was staring at me with alarm. I realised I may have got a bit ruffled in the wood, and my lips were probably cracked due to dehydration and my hair may have acquired a few dry twigs, or maybe even a whole bird's nest.

'Perfectly fine,' I croaked. 'Just been out in the wood – hiking.'

I picked up the key and unlocked the door. As much as I like Samuel, I didn't want his company. All I wanted was to shed my clothes and scratch myself to death. And take a cold shower.

'But it's your face, Maggie. It looks like you've got chickenpox or measles. You must have it checked. You look – scary!'

'Oh, thanks.'

'I don't mean ... I mean. I'll drop you at the surgery.'

'No, Samuel. It's the bloody nettles, I'm sure.'

'Nettles?'

'I got stranded in nettles. That's all.'

'You did? How tall were they? It's your face—'

'And the mosquitoes finished the job. Don't ask. I need a cold compress.' I pushed him aside and slammed the door in his face. I just couldn't act in a civilised manner for a minute longer.

Once behind closed doors, I did as I had planned. I tore off my dress and dug my nails into my skin.

At first it felt like salvation, but then the itching returned with a vengeance. I jumped into the cold shower. The first blast of icy water almost gave me a cardiac arrest, but soon the relief came. I stood under the stream of soothing cool water for a long, long time.

When I finally gave up and came out of the shower, I looked in the mirror. OK, so it did look like chickenpox. My cheek was throbbing. The only solution now was a calming cup of tea with a Jaffa Cake. An entire box of Jaffa Cakes. I had to use diversion to take my mind off the itchy rash. I sat naked in the kitchen with a mug of steaming tea in hand and a box of Jaffas in front of me. The first Jaffa didn't touch the sides. I just dropped it down my throat. But as I calmed down, I relished the second one a bit more, and the third one paved the way for the fourth, and the fourth was a culinary masterpiece that called for seconds – or fifths, as was the case on that occasion.

I wasn't impressed to see Karl van Niekerk standing in *my* driveway. He was the cause of all my unspeakable suffering. And what was he doing here? Why was he watching me? Had he followed me here? Was it payback? I wasn't afraid of him. I didn't care if he had seen me follow him. I was happy to go out and confront him, all guns blazing!

I stormed out of the kitchen, realising just in the nick of time that I was covered in nothing but a rash. I grabbed an apron – the first item of apparel to hand – and tied it around my waist. That covered my front. My coat was on the stand. I availed myself of it, and burst out of the house.

'I can see you, you know!' I shouted as I marched towards my suspect. 'You've been watching my house! I demand to know why!'

At the same time, alerted to the rumpus, Samuel ran out too, covering my rear.

'Can I help you, sir?' He was much more polite than me, but then he didn't have to reckon with itchy blisters, courtesy of the intruder.

The intruder didn't seem to hear either of us. He gazed at me as if he were mesmerised by my good looks.

'Irene? My God, you look just like Irene ...'

Chapter Nineteen

'Irene was my mother, but I bet you knew that!' Maggie shouted at the man, unnecessarily. Unless, of course, she knew he was deaf and required this level of amplification.

Sam winced in discomfort. He disliked loud noises. He was however too intrigued to go back to his house and barricade himself behind the thick walls. He had recognised Karl van Niekerk and wanted to know more – for example, what had brought him to Priest's Hole.

'She used to live here,' Van Niekerk said.

'Course she did. It was my grandparents' house. And why are you here, may I ask? Because if you have a problem with me following you ... well, I wasn't! I was having a stroll in the wood. It's a free country – we can all go where we please. As long as we aren't trespassing, which I wasn't! So, there!'

Van Niekerk was apparently indeed hard of hearing for he did not rise to Maggie's challenge – he did not seem to hear it. 'So, she moved out? Of course! After she got married, I suppose. A beautiful girl like Irene ... Where to? Was it somewhere local? I wish I could see her, have a chat – catch up. I wish—'

'You can't. Mum is dead. She died ...'

Maggie's voice shrivelled to a tiny whimper. Her face dropped and even her chickenpox rash went pale. Sam couldn't help himself – he wrapped a protective arm over Maggie's shoulder and gave her a comforting squeeze.

Van Niekerk reacted most curiously: he too went as white as a sheet, seemed to stumble and steadied himself against the wall. 'Dear God, not Irene too ... She wrote ... Oh, dear, dear girl—' That was all he managed to say before his breathing turned to gasps and he clutched his chest.

'Are you all right, sir?' Sam abandoned Maggie and reached out to offer the man an arm to lean on.

'Yes, yes ... it's the old ticker ...' he wheezed. 'I've had a long walk—'

'You can say that again! It nearly killed me and I'm half your age!' Maggie exclaimed bizarrely. Sam was used to her odd commentaries and let it pass unchallenged.

'I just need to take my tablets – in my pocket—' Van Niekerk's weight was now entirely pushed against Sam.

'Come inside. We'll get you some water. This way, Samuel. Let's go to mine.' It was Maggie's first graceful utterance of the day.

Inside the house, Van Niekerk swallowed his tablet and rapidly recovered his breath. Soon reinforcements arrived in the shape of Jaffa Cakes and a pot of tea with all the usual trimmings. Maggie served it while still wearing her coat. Her rash was back in angry red evidence, but her mood had mellowed. Sam was still considering forcing the issue of seeing the GP – it wasn't natural to wear a winter coat on a warm spring day, and the rash looked ominous.

'So, you knew Mum?' Maggie poured the tea and handed a cup to Van Niekerk.

'Oh yes ... She was a pretty lass. Pretty as a button. You look just like her, my dear.'

Sam observed Maggie's face transform from tense to very pleased indeed. That dimpled smile of hers sprung up and reached for her eyes, and sort of tickled them so that she blinked several times in the most endearing way. Her face – nettle rash notwithstanding – was a picture!

'We were all so young then. Every Saturday, there was a dance at the back of the fire station. It was a big room with springy wooden floors. Girls were all pretty and giggly, in those beautiful knee-length dresses, flashing their net stockings, pouting their plum red lips . . . And Irene – she was a stunner, she was.'

Van Niekerk was smiling to his memories, a twinkle of youthful pluck in his eye. Sam remembered Maggie's father referring to Van Niekerk as *a ladies' man*. He could now see why. The man must have been quite a stallion in his youth. And now he was charming the pants off Maggie.

Literally, as it would soon become all too apparent . . .

'Yes, Mum was a looker,' Maggie said dreamily. 'I've got some old photo albums here. They used to belong to Grandpa Bernie – he was an avid photographer. I kind of inherited them with everything else in the house—'

'There'd be some photos of Irene there, I'm sure. I wouldn't mind to have a look for old times' sake.'

'I can't remember the last time I looked at them. Why not! Hang on, they're in the cupboard under the bookshelf. I'll fetch them.' And that was where Maggie, excited and keen to share her mum's memories with her old, long-lost friend, shed her winter coat.

It all became clear to Sam: the reason why she had been hanging on to it. She was wearing nothing under that coat but an apron. And as much as that apron just about covered her lady's modesty in front, it had little to offer at the back, nothing really but a pair of tied-up straps that dangled over her bottom. It was a handsome and ample bottom, admittedly – something to rest one's eyes on. It rippled pleasantly as Maggie crossed the room to the bookshelf and bent down to retrieve the photo album.

Sam's and Van Niekerk's eyes widened as they both observed the scene. Sam then took swift action: he jumped to his feet and stood between Maggie and Van Niekerk, facing the old man and forcing his sight away from the bare bottom on display.

Van Niekerk gazed at Sam, amusement quivering between them, threatening to erupt in an explosion of laughter.

Sam held his nerve. He said, still facing away from Maggie, 'Would you like me to pass you your coat, Maggie?'

He then heard a heartfelt, 'Oh, fucking hell!' and the sound of bare feet padding out of the room and away.

'That was ...' Sam started, but had no idea how to finish.

'It was something.' Van Niekerk helped him.

It took a good twenty minutes for Maggie to return to the sitting room, where Sam and Karl awaited her with bated breath. While waiting, the two had taken the liberty to properly introduce themselves to each other and were now on a first name basis. She came back wearing a thick tracksuit. Sam had expected full body armour, so he was relieved.

'Right,' she said courageously, 'where were we?'

'The photos?'

'Oh yes!'

With a couple of photo albums in hand, she sat on the sofa between Karl and Sam, and embarked on a trip down memory lane, blabbering without a pause for breath for a good hour. It was quite cathartic for her to at last talk about her mum without resorting to sadness, and also to put the incident of the bare bottom *behind* her.

'So, this is Mum when she was a baby ...' She pointed to a small, yellowed photograph. 'That was her christening. Look at the gown! It was all Honiton lace, you know? And that's Grandma. I can't remember her, to be honest. I was only very small when she died.' Maggie turned a few pages. 'This! Look at this! I don't think I ever saw this picture ... They were on a holiday – it looks like Weston-super-Mare. The old pier, isn't it, before it burned down?'

She did not give either Sam or Karl a chance to reply. 'Yes, it is. Look at her! Her hair was all blond and curly. Mine goes blond in the summer months – it's the sun. Oh my! She did put on weight when she was a teenager! But it suits her, doesn't it?'

Neither Sam nor Karl managed to confirm or deny. There was no time as Maggie babbled on.

'It does! Ahhh ... the dress! I know what you were talking about. Those dresses were a scream in the sixties. Just like the one Helen

111

wore ... Your cousin, Helen? You do remember, don't you?' This time Maggie took a break from her incessant talking to look at Van Niekerk. She added pointedly, 'You do recognise the style, don't you? The geometric pattern of blocked colours, just like Helen's dress. Hers had those circles and triangles, yes? You must remember that particular dress. She wore it when she died ...'

Sam might have been mistaken thinking that Karl had disarmed Maggie entirely. She wasn't quite as charmed as he had thought. She was more cunning than Sam had given her credit for.

'Yes,' Karl spoke slowly, weighing his words carefully. 'Yes, I do. In fact, that was the dress she was wearing when I saw her last.'

'That was the dress she was buried in.' Maggie fixed him with a penetrating glare.

'Is that right?'

'Yes.'

'She liked that dress a lot. She wore it all the time. It looked great on her, even after she gave birth ...'

Maggie sighed and pursed her lips tight. 'And that was about the time when you left, wasn't it? Without a word! You just walked away, never looked back. You didn't care to get in touch! While she was lying cold in her grave ... Forgive me for thinking this, but I do think you knew she was dead and that there was no point, no point at all to get in touch – because she couldn't possibly get back to you! And I think that you and her – you were in a relationship and when James was born, she rejected you ... and you killed her!'

'That's not true!' both Sam and Karl shouted at the same time.

Puzzled, Karl looked to Sam for an elaboration. Sam felt he had to oblige him and also to put Maggie straight before she caused the poor man another cardiac arrest. He said, 'There was nothing sexual between Karl and Helen. They were cousins. For crying out loud, Maggie, James is Lord Philip's biological son. He took a DNA test. No doubt about it! Can you please stop spreading—'

'I wasn't spreading anything,' Maggie said in a dignified, but slightly shaky tone. 'I was just asking Mr van Niekerk a question.'

'It sounded like an accusation to me.'

'It's OK. I understand. The police asked me similar questions.' Karl sounded philosophical about it.

'And?' Maggie pressed on.

'And what?'

'And what did you tell them?'

'The truth. After James was born, Helen had grown distant. It was Philip, I'm sure. People blame post-natal depression. Claptrap! In those days, women were stronger. They didn't get post-natal depression.'

'Ha!' Maggie quipped and went quiet.

Sam shook his head. Karl and his views were typical of his generation. Karl harboured convictions similar to those of Sam's mother. The elderly had no use for political correctness. And they let it rip.

Karl continued, 'It was Philip – he made her. He wanted her all to himself. He forced her to cut ties with her family. And that included me. The last time I saw her, she implored me to go, to leave her be. She said her happiness, her family's happiness hinged on that. She said I was a *bad influence*, that I was disrupting their *harmony*. Those weren't even her own words! The Helen I knew wouldn't use words like that! He was behind it! I was angry ... I told her to her face how stupid she was, how she'd come to regret it and would be running back home, but I was done here. I was done with her. I left! I should've stayed—' A stray tear rolled down his face. He wiped it.

'I'm sorry.' Maggie looked contrite.

An uneasy silence stole into the room.

Karl broke it. 'Right, that's out of the way now. Can we look at the pictures?'

Maggie was only too keen to carry on. She turned another page in the album. 'That's Mum at her wedding.'

'Looking smashing! And who's the groom?'

'My dad – Eugene.'

'Oh, let me see ... Do I know him? Eugene ... Is it Eugene Kaye? He used to live in that Tudor lodge house?'

113

'Yes, that's Dad!' Maggie beamed.

'Yes, I recognise his face now. I remember him.'

'He remembers you!'

'Everyone remembers me.'

Maggie pointed to the photo of her mother with a baby in her lap. 'And that's Mum with Will.'

'So that's her son, William? Your brother?'

'Yep, my big brother, Will. There's a few years between us. Then there's me, and finally, Andrea — our wayward little sister. She lives in New Zealand of all places, but that's a long story.'

'So, that's the Kaye clan?'

'That's us.'

'You look just like your mother. But I already said that, didn't I?'

'Yes, you did. Andrea and I both take after Mum. I don't have her recent photo, but the last one of the whole family together — that'd be at Will's wedding ...' Maggie thumbed through the second album she had fetched from the bookshelf. She found the right page and passed the album to Karl. 'Here we are, the Kayes in full force. So that's obviously Will and his wife. Her name is Tracey. She's all right. She takes her time to grow on you, but I've come to like her. Especially after Andrea took off without a forwarding address. That's a long story, and I don't think I'm supposed to talk about it. So ... that's Mum and Dad. And that's Andrea. She looks even more like Mum than me, don't you think?'

Karl didn't answer. He was totally absorbed in the photos. He turned the page to look at more pictures from the wedding, some random group shots, others posed in the studio and in the garden of the estate where the wedding reception was held.

'Well, there you go then.' Maggie snatched the album out of his hands, visibly disconcerted about the way the old man ignored her running commentary. She closed it.

Karl stood up. 'Thank you for sharing all of this with me. It was lovely to meet Irene's girl ...'

'Nice to meet you, too,' Maggie was delightfully civil. 'You're most welcome to pop over again before you leave.'

'Oh, I'd really like to visit Irene's grave. I always wanted to pay my respects while I was here, even if it is to be the last respects, sadly.'

'Mum is buried in the cemetery, St John the Baptist's – just over the wall. It's the grave under that large cedar.'

'I'll find it. Thank you, Maggie.'

Sam saw Karl out and returned to the sitting room. He didn't know what possessed him, but he took one look at Maggie ensconced in her heavy duty fleece tracksuit, and said, 'Aren't you a bit overdressed for this time of year?'

She shot him a fiery glance, and barked, 'Don't go there!'

Chapter Twenty

It was the last day of term before the Easter holiday. My temporary assignment was at an end. The day was warm and sunny, and I had the same feeling that a caterpillar has when it is about to break out of its cocoon and turn into a butterfly. I was looking forward to flying away from Bishops Ace Academy and heading for my recently neglected garden to pollinate the flowers. My mind had already flown ahead of me.

After the assembly led by Vicar Laurence, we had gathered in the staffroom for some cakes and a glass of wine. I couldn't say no to the cakes though I rejected the wine out of hand. I was still drying out.

I couldn't believe that I had lasted so long teaching in this school. Two weeks had transformed into a full term in no time. The English teacher who I was covering for had given up on teaching and handed in his notice. Apparently, he was going to take up work at Tesco, stacking shelves. Good on him, I thought, there was more to life than educating Thomas Moore.

And this was where Thomas proved me wrong.

I was munching on a fairy cake, listening to the headteacher exulting about the joys and rewards of shaping young people's minds, which would in turn shape this planet's future. The headteacher, Les Foreman, is an active member of the Green Party, and a total environmental fanatic. Rumour has it that he occasionally indulges in unruly and disorderly behaviour by joining in Extinction Rebellion rallies dressed as a banana. His inspired speech was interrupted by a knock on the door.

'Enter!' hollered the PE teacher, a man with his voice as large as his muscles.

Thomas Moore's head appeared. 'Miss Kaye here?'

'Thomas?' My blood ran cold. I was struck by the idea that Master Moore had prepared a cruel parting shot for me. Knifing teachers had become quite popular in some circles. I feared the worst.

'Here, for you! To say soz for being a fucking shit.' Thomas Moore handed to me – a flower . . .

OK, so it wasn't quite a bouquet of roses, and it certainly had not been paid for. It was a twig of white lilac brutally and crudely torn off a bush, judging by the roughed-up stem. It wasn't pretty, but it was the thought that mattered. I had been given a flower by a young man. That was much more than just doing no harm. It was an effort on his part. It was a positive endeavour!

'Well, thank you, Thomas,' my voice trembled with emotion. 'You shouldn't have . . .'

'Nah, just found it lying on the road . . . You all right, Miss? You'll look after it. I seen your garden.'

In any other circumstances, I would be mortified to learn that a student knew where I lived. But not this time. I felt a fuzziness settle in my stomach.

Thomas exited the staffroom. The scent of lilac filled my nostrils, and I sneezed. And sneezed a couple of times more until my eyes watered.

'Blimey.' Ivo Murphy looked equally moved. 'I never got a flower from him!'

'You're a bloke,' Cherie reminded him.

'That might be it. Still, a bottle of wine wouldn't have gone amiss.'

'Alas, you can't find them lying on the road, unless they're empty of course. Still, it's the thought that matters.'

'That's what I mean,' Les interjected, brimming with enthusiasm, 'we shaped a young man's mind. Pat on the back, everyone.'

From the school, we headed directly to the old village hall for the meeting of the Bishops Well Archaeological Association. By *we*, I mean Cherie, Ivo, and me. Ivo had decided to give it a go and join us. Cherie had been harassing him about it since he'd arrived in Bishops. Cherie doesn't take no for an answer, so I imagine it must have felt like a mental bloodbath each time Ivo said no to another one of her offers. Finally, he had no choice but to say yes.

All the long-standing members had turned up for the occasion: Vera Hopps-Wood, Mary Ruta, Vanessa Scarfe (Alec's wife), Edgar Flynn, Michael Almond, and Samuel ... Even James Weston-Jones was there. It was vital that we were in full force. We have a special initiation ritual for admitting new members.

Apart from securing a direct debit for the society's monthly fee against their bank account, we also record their name and full particulars in the Membership Book, an entry which has to be countersigned by every existing member. To a random passer-by we must look like a demented religious cult. It wouldn't be that far from the truth. I am surprised that we haven't yet thought of drawing blood from new applicants with a silver dagger, blending it with our own in a golden chalice, and then drinking it. That'd be fun, and it would add gravity to the initiation proceedings.

As it were, Ivo got away with it lightly by simply parting with his bank details and shaking hands with all of us. Cherie delivered a welcome speech, which even by Cherie's standards was very dry and unwelcoming. It sounded more like a victory speech to the subjugated: *you came, you saw – we conquered*.

After that, we returned to the order of the day. The second item on the agenda was the resumption of the excavation works in Bishops Swamp.

'We'll have to redouble our efforts now that we're heading towards summer,' Cherie informed us. 'All of us, as one. We've had a long pause – it was unavoidable – but we can return to the site now. I've had it authorised by the police. They're finished there. Right, so – I hope nobody's going away this summer and I can count on everyone pulling their weight?'

James shifted shiftily in his chair and expelled a little groan.

'Are you going away, James?'

'No, it's not that, Cherie. Well, Letitia and the boys have gone to France, and I was going to join them for a while . . . But it's not that. It's something else.'

'Well, what is it? Spit it out, man!'

'It's my father. He doesn't want the dig to go on. He says it's my mother's final resting place, and it shouldn't be disturbed any more than it already has been. I am sorry.'

'Your mother's final resting place is in the church's catacombs! The Swamp is the location of an ancient Celtic settlement!'

'It's just the . . . the spiritual thing for Father – It's where my mother lay for years. It's like an open wound—'

'We cannot become over-sentimental! He needs to get over himself. This is *history* we're talking about. *Ancient* history, at that!'

I was feeling sorry for poor James, but I understood Cherie's point of view. The dig had to go on. I said, 'How about we get the vicar to bless the place?'

'Bless it? The dig?'

'Not the dig, as such. Helen's grave. She'd been buried there, in not-so-sacred soil, you know? We could get Vicar Laurence to – well – bless it! And then, when it's all blessed and proper, we can get on with the digging.'

'How's blessing the soil going to make Lord Philip change his mind?' Samuel is a logical man, I understand that, but logic wasn't called for on this occasion. Not everything has to make sense in life.

'Oh, Samuel, can't you see? It'll be a symbolic gesture – releasing the lady's spirit from that . . . that *location*.'

Samuel squinted.

Before I could query that squint, my phone rang. All I remember clearly was the first sentence, 'Am I speaking to Margaret Kaye?'

Everything else is a blur. I think I blacked out. When I came to, I found myself in Samuel's car. We were on the motorway, going pretty fast. He gave me a sideways glance.

'We're nearly there,' he told me.

'Where? Where are we going?'

Chapter Twenty-one

The weeks that followed Heather's arrival were filled with . . . more Heather. She had agreed (*agreed* being a misnomer, Andrea thought – Heather's arrival was a wilful imposition) to stay with them for a while. She would take care of the house, the cooking, the washing, the daily chores, everything a self-respecting housewife would generally be expected to devote herself to.

Barricaded in the spare bedroom upstairs, Andrea had begun a slow process of disintegration. She slept most of the time. When she was awake she would stare vaguely towards the ceiling, lost in the fluidity of her thoughts which, despite her efforts, would not crystallise. She no longer knew what she wanted. Nothing further had been said about moving to the UK. She dared not even think about it.

With time, she had developed a fear of leaving the safety of her bedroom. With a racing heart she would listen for footsteps on the landing, approaching the door and pausing ominously outside. The voices downstairs grinded in her head: her family talking about the events of the day, shreds of news blasting from the TV, good mornings and goodnights. They seemed surreal. She would hide deeper and deeper inside herself and cover her ears. But despite that, she could still hear Heather chatting over the fence to the elderly neighbours next door and informing them casually that Andrea had suffered a breakdown. A spot of gossip-mongering had generated an opportunity for Heather to make waves in the neighbourhood and set up alliances. She was already on a first-name basis with the most private residents in the street.

So that was it: everything sorted out, all loose ends neatly tied up. A breakdown. Everything as clear as mud.

This morning – she had worked out that this was a morning because she had just woken up and the sun was low on the horizon when she glimpsed it from behind the closed curtains – she had heard sounds of a rushed commotion downstairs. Jack was being told to put on his hiking boots. Heather wondered out loud if she had remembered to bring her walking poles. Elliot was fumbling in the storage cupboard under the stairs. Then they all got into the car and drove off. Silence rang in Andrea's ears.

She had waited in the bedroom for a few moments, just in case it had been a ruse and they had all come back to take her by surprise. Twenty minutes later she peeled off her pyjamas, had a soul-and-body cleansing shower, and got dressed. She was desperate for air.

The beach was deserted. The lazy tide kept lapping against the slippery green rock. The sun was hovering over the line of the horizon, a bit too heavy to rise properly. The air was saturated with salt and the pungent scent of seaweed. A large piece of bone-white driftwood lay half buried on a small patch of grainy, dark sand. Having walked for more than an hour, Andrea took refuge in the cavernous shelter the driftwood provided. She pulled her knees to her chin and wrapped her arms over her legs. The wind had picked up, tugging at her hair.

She gazed into the ocean, towards home. Her mind was by no means clear. Disjointed memories swooped on her. She tried to fight them off, thinking of her family here and now – the daily bread of togetherness, the unspoken certainty of it, the continuity, the reliance, the security. Why would anyone want to destroy it? Especially Andrea.

The bay was deserted. It was a well-kept secret. Only the locals knew about it, and very few came here anyway. Sometimes she felt like she owned it. It reminded her of the glade in Sexton's Wood: remote and hidden from prying eyes on the other side of the swamp. It was her refuge as a child. Even Maggie knew nothing about it, and Maggie knew everything else.

But Andrea had shown it to Hugo. It was that one and only time when she had brought him to Sexton's Wood. It was after the trial and shortly before she was sent packing to New Zealand. Hugo had offered to take her there after she had told him about it.

It went against every rule in the book: coming so close to her parents' home, compromising her safety and theirs, disappearing from the radar with no backup and no trail, yet he did it. He could see she needed to draw strength from somewhere and it wasn't within her to find it. He already knew it would be her last time at home before leaving for the unknown and that she may never see it again. He wanted to make her happy. And he wanted to see it for himself.

Hugo drove to the edge of the forest and parked in a small lay-by. Before that, they had passed through Bishops and she had pointed out her home to him, in passing, without stopping.

The sight of her home stirred something inside her. The driveway alone was paved with memories. Laughing, she recalled the day when she had grazed her knee on that driveway, falling off her bike after Dad removed the stabilisers. The knee had bled and she had cried rivers of tears. The next day – the grazed knee a distant memory – she had got on her bike and conquered the precarious driveway, and the road beyond.

They followed a single file path through the wood. It was the peak of summer, the greenery was dazzling, the heat of sweating trees and buzzing insects overwhelming. They walked in silence until they found themselves in her glade. It was rippling with knee-high grass.

'This is my kingdom. Do you like it?' Andrea turned to face him.

He swept the place with his eyes, inhaled deeply through his nose, taking in all the scents. 'It's peaceful. It's a perfect place,' he said. 'It'd be a perfect place to die.'

'Let's not talk about dying.'

'Let's not.'

He reached for her and caressed her bare arms with his

hands – large, strong man's hands. Those hands were used to holding weapons, not caressing a woman's skin. Yet his touch was
soft and gentle. And tentative. She felt his fingers trembling. She
steadied them with her own hands. They kissed. And they made
love. And after that they fell asleep in her glade, in the rippling high
grass ...

The tide had come in, the water almost touching the large piece of
driftwood where Andrea was sheltering. She got to her feet, shook
off the sand and walked back home.

She was hoping to sneak back unnoticed, but they were already
back from their hiking excursion. Jack was the only one happy to
see her.

'Mum! Where have you been? We just came back from Taupo. I
was allowed to go in. Granny said it was OK.'

He was hugging her and shouting into her ear, his warm breath
spilling over her cheek. It was a great sensation. She realised how
much she had missed him.

'That's very decent of Granny. I would've made you wear
armbands.'

'It was only shallow there – up to my knees!'

'That man, Hugo, called when you were gone.' It was Elliot. His
voice sounded deep and hostile.

'They shouldn't be calling here,' Heather added. 'It's simply not—'

'What did he say?'

'He said it was urgent. He said to call back on *the usual number*.'

Andrea pulled Jack's arms away from her neck and stood up. She
went to the phone and dialled the emergency number. It was
answered after the first ring, as usual.

'Hugo?'

'Andrea, I have bad news for you ...'

It was one of the clones, pronouncing his vowels in their trademark clipped Queen's English. It wasn't Hugo. He had called and
then let somebody else do the talking. Coward.

The clone was saying something, carrying on. She had not been listening.

'Sorry, I couldn't hear you,' she said at last. 'Can you say that again, please?'

'It's your father, Andrea. I'm afraid he passed away yesterday.'

They all came to see her off at the airport. Jack had understood that he would not be coming with her, even though she had promised before ... He stood with his head hung on his chest and an *I'm-being-brave-against-my-will* scowl on his face.

Elliot squeezed her shoulders and kissed her on the side of her head. He repeated for the millionth time how sorry he was.

Andrea looked him straight in the eye. 'I should've been there for him – after Mum ... I shouldn't have left so soon after.'

Elliot hunched under the accusation, but Heather stood there unmoved, her lips pursed tight, holding back what she was dying to blurt out – that this was another hoax, another lie.

'Have a safe flight,' she said instead.

Andrea took her bag from Elliot, hugged Jack, and joined the queue.

Chapter Twenty-two

I had a dread-imbued sense of déjà vu: here we were again, at the airport, watching Andrea emerge through the sliding doors of the Arrivals Hall. She was wearing the same clothes as last time and pulling behind her the same check suitcase. She looked as tired and as thin as before, unsure of herself and scared. And as she had done in November, again today she did not recognise us at first, sweeping her eyes past us. Will took the initiative to go to her. He waved. She saw him and her face cracked into a smile.

We were all there, plus Samuel who had insisted on driving me to the airport for some reason.

But less Dad, of course.

I say *less Dad* but this only applies until the point of Andrea's arrival. Because Dad was tagging along with her. There he was, clinging to her in the crowd of passengers, not letting her out of his sight for one second, passing through other people and their luggage as if they were wide-open doors. He was in his prime, the age he had been when I was about seven or eight. That was when Dad had been at his best, his strongest, invincible and absolutely indispensable to the two of us.

'So that's where you've been,' I whispered to him, but he didn't say anything back to me to either confirm or deny it.

I felt a little dejected, I must admit. I know it's selfish to think of myself first, and I know if anyone needs looking after it is my trouble-plagued sister, but I felt abandoned and unloved.

Dad had not waited for me.

By the time I had made it to his hospital bed, he was gone – in every possible way. His spirit had not bothered to linger around for one minute longer to say goodbye to me. I had spent the entire night wide awake, waiting for him to pay me a visit, just to sit on the edge of my bed and keep me company until I got my head around him dying so suddenly and without any warning. I had only wanted to know that he was still around. But he wasn't.

At last I knew why he had been in so much of a hurry to leave. He had gone to be by Andrea's side. That tiny niggle of jealousy was chewing away at the corners of my mind as I watched Andrea – with Dad glued to her side – run to me with tears streaming out of her eyes. When her face was only inches away from mine, I discovered how ravaged she actually looked.

It wasn't just because of the jetlag. It was something deeper and more permanent than that: her eyes had sunk and lost their spark, and black circles had formed below them like old bruises. Andrea looked wretched and ill. I could tell now why Dad had to run to be by her side.

'Oh, Andrea!' I pulled her into my arms. She was skin and bone. I could feel her protruding shoulder blades and the rings of her ribs. 'What happened to you?'

'I don't know what you mean,' she said, but she was lying. I always know when my little sister lies. She lies a lot, but in her case practice doesn't make perfect.

From the airport we came to my place. I insisted. After Dad's death, our family home was a cold, empty shell. I wasn't ready to enter it. All I would feel would be the bitter disappointment that Mum and Dad weren't there. Not even in spirit.

Deirdre, Samuel's mother, was waiting for us with sandwiches on the table and tea brewing. She had come the day after Dad died, purportedly on a random visit, but I had my suspicions. Samuel had summoned her to help look after me, I was convinced of that. He had been all over me during the previous few days, making sure I got up in the morning, had my breakfast, drank my tea (and tea only), and put my feet up. There were moments – I could swear – when my feet simply never touched the ground. I think he might have confused me with a woman in the last trimester of pregnancy. Deirdre, I suspected, had been deployed as a mother figure for the motherless – and now fatherless me.

As soon as we arrived, she directed Samuel to take Andrea's suitcase up to the second bedroom.

'You'll be staying here, dear,' she informed Andrea. 'I changed the sheets for you and got out fresh towels. Have something to eat, and then you need to hit the sack and get some rest. I'll make sure they're all quiet down here.'

Andrea thanked her sheepishly. Obediently, we all did as we were told – we sat down, ate the sandwiches, and drank our tea. Will and Tracey had left soon after. They were driving back to London, collecting the kids from Tracey's parents in Reading on the way. Deirdre and Samuel took themselves to the kitchen to wash up and put away the crockery. It was just Andrea and me left in the room. Dozens of questions were screaming to come out but I had kept them at bay until we were alone. Now at last, I would find out what was wrong with her . . .

There was a knock on the door. I wasn't expecting anyone else.

'It's probably Jehovah's Witnesses,' I speculated, as it was Sunday and they usually prowled on Sundays. 'I'll blow them away.'

I was surprised to find Gillian Marsh and her sergeant on my doorstep. I couldn't quite remember his name, though I had met him before.

He said, 'Good evening, ma'am. I'm DS Webber and this is—'

'Yes, I know Ms Marsh—'

'*DI* Marsh, Sexton's Canning CID,' she interjected, her feathers ruffled.

'Yes, I know that.' I was already irritated by the intrusion, even more so for being lectured and for her pulling rank. I knew who she was. I would not be bowing down to her official capacity.

'We are sorry to intrude but we need to talk to you, and to your sister. I believe she's here with you.' DS Webber sounded more placatory.

'Yes . . .'

'And will she be staying at yours?'

'I certainly think so. Why?'

'We've been asked to make arrangements for her protection.'

I invited them in. I felt any resistance would be futile against DI Marsh.

'The police,' I introduced them to Andrea. I gestured to them to make themselves comfortable on the sofa, though I didn't really mean it.

'You were watching the house the last time I was here,' Andrea addressed DS Webber.

He smiled. 'That's correct, ma'am.'

'Thanks, I guess.'

'Just doing my job.'

'So,' DI Marsh interrupted in her customary fashion, 'we've been assigned to keep an eye on you until you leave. That'd be soon after the funeral, I suspect.'

'I haven't decided yet.'

'I was told my men would only be needed until the funeral, but you mustn't worry about that.'

'I'm not. I'll leave when I leave.'

DI Marsh glared at my sister. She was not used to meeting her equals in the department of being stubborn and obnoxious. 'Of course, you will. Until you do, you should expect to see DS Webber, DC Whittaker, or DC Macfadyen following you around. Don't be alarmed. You already know DS Webber. I want to show you pictures of DC Whittaker and DC Macfadyen so you're familiar with their faces.' Marsh showed Andrea images on her mobile phone. 'If you see any other people – strangers, anyone you don't know, shadowing you or behaving oddly, you must immediately contact us. Myself on this number,' she handed her business card to Andrea, 'or call *the usual number.*'

Andrea nodded. She slid the card into her trouser pocket without looking at it.

'OK then!' I concluded. 'Thank you very much for coming to let us know.' I stood up to show them the door.

They remained seated.

'There's one more thing. We're treating your father's death as suspicious. We'd like to ask you a few questions, especially you, Miss Kaye.'

'But it was a heart attack,' I said weakly. Automatically, I looked towards Dad who, naturally, was here with us, next to Andrea. I wished I could demand some answers from him. I wished he could – would – talk to me. But he was just gazing at his feet, either oblivious to my silent cry for help or deliberately avoiding it.

'Yes, it was, but what caused the heart attack will need to be investigated. You see, your father wasn't alone when he suffered the seizure.'

'What are you saying?'

'The emergency services were called from your father's landline. An ambulance was requested.'

'Could it not have been Dad making the call?'

'We don't believe so. We listened to the recording. Someone's gone to a lot of trouble to disguise their voice.'

'What did they say? I mean how did they—'

'All that the caller said was that Mr Kaye had collapsed. And they gave the address. They didn't answer any questions by the operator. When the paramedics arrived they found your father alone in the lounge and the phone was off the hook in the hallway.'

'But ... but how did they? What did they do to—'

'To cause the heart attack? Shock, fear, panic ... He could've been threatened, interrogated ... That's what we'll be trying to find out.' DI Marsh said it matter-of-factly while my heart was beating at the speed of a jumbo jet plunging to earth. I remembered Deirdre's helpful diagnosis that Dad had died of a broken heart, that he could not go on without Mum and died to be reunited with her. I liked that explanation. It had made it easier to accept Dad's death. But this! This was preposterous!

'Who would want to hurt Dad? Or threaten, or interrogate him?'

'I wanted to ask you if he had any enemies.'

'No, he didn't! Dad was a well-respected and loved man. Everyone loved Dad, everyone—'

'It's me,' Andrea whispered, sheer horror stamped on her gaunt face. 'I have enemies . . . It's Wayne. It's him.'

After the detectives left, I returned to the sitting room and stared at Andrea, studying her face contorted with guilt and pain, trying to remind myself who this woman was.

She was the reason – the cause of Dad's death. For the first time I wanted her out of my life. For the first time, I wished she had actually died all those years ago. For the first time, I wished I didn't have a sister. I was gripped by terrible anger. I couldn't control it, as hard as I tried, but I could hide it. I bit my lip and said, 'They could be wrong.'

Andrea looked up towards me. She shook her head. 'I'm so, so sorry! They warned me I'd put everyone in danger if I came back. And I didn't listen. I never listen, Maggie! Wayne is out of prison . . . I am so, so sorry!'

'Well, there's no use beating yourself up . . . It's too late to dwell on it. Why don't you go upstairs and get some sleep—'

She got up. 'I can't stay here with you. I would never forgive myself if something happened to you too! I'll stay in the house.'

'Don't be silly! Who would want to bother with me—'

But she was silly. She charged upstairs to fetch her suitcase. She dragged it downstairs. She hugged me and cried on my shoulder and apologised again about Dad.

'Andrea, you don't have to do this. I want you to stay. Dad would want you to stay here with me. I can't let you go there, on your own.'

'I'll be fine. More to the point – you'll be fine.'

I let her go. Dad, of course, followed her. I shut the door and slumped to the floor. I had no strength in my legs to get up.

Samuel picked me from the floor and guided me back into the

sitting room. Deirdre was standing in the middle of the room, a look of utter incomprehension in her eyes.

'What happened just now?'

Samuel forced me to sit down and sat next to me.

'What's going on, Maggie? Please tell me. I want to be able to help.'

'I'm not supposed to talk about it,' I declined to speak, and then I told them everything. About Wayne Kew. The murders he had committed. About the witness protection Andrea had been under for the last twenty-five years. About the suspicions surrounding Dad's death.

I felt better when I had finished. Samuel was rubbing my back, saying that he wouldn't let anything bad happen to me, promising we would get to the bottom of it together. It was sweet of him – probably only words, but I did feel better.

Then Deirdre said something really important. Well, firstly she offered me more tea, which I refused point blank. Only then did she part with this nugget of wisdom: 'What puzzles me is that he called an ambulance . . . You say this Kew character is a cold-blooded gangster. Why would he call an ambulance?'

Chapter Twenty-three

Sam was determined to keep an eye on Maggie. She was in shock, having lost both her parents in quick succession. She needed a friend. And, according to his mother, she also needed to be fed and watered, and surrounded by people. Sam remembered vividly that after Alice's death he ate just enough to sustain himself and craved nothing more than solitude. He could not bear people poking at his pain. But he was a man, a different species altogether when emotions were at play. He had bottled up his emotions and hidden them in a dark cellar where they would mature into vintage desolation. He couldn't let that happen to Maggie.

He had requisitioned his mother's professional services and she had ordered plenty of food and company for his grieving neighbour. At nine o'clock sharp, Sam was dispatched next door to invite Maggie, as well as Andrea, to a dinner of cottage pie and treacle tart for six thirty that evening. His mother had commenced operations in the kitchen at the crack of dawn.

Sam crossed the driveway to Maggie's door, tipping his virtual hat to DS Webber who was sitting in an unmarked car on the road outside Priest's Hole. Andrea must have come to her senses and returned overnight to stay with Maggie after all. DS Webber mouthed a silent 'good morning'. His car may have been unmarked but it was conspicuous in its splendid isolation. Perhaps the purpose was to deter potential assassins rather than to operate undercover, Sam speculated.

He knocked on the door and waited. Maggie appeared in her

bedroom window a few minutes later. She peered down at Sam with a bleary eye.

'It's open!' she croaked.

So much for extra vigilance, Sam moaned under his breath. He would have to remind Maggie to lock the doors in future. The woman was incorrigibly reckless.

He went in, heading straight for the kitchen where he put the kettle on. Maggie descended from her bedroom a minute later, still enveloped in sleep, her eyelids droopy and her left cheek presenting a detailed imprint of her wristwatch. The cords of her dressing gown were dragging behind her, one longer than the other. Under the flaps of the gown, her nightdress was crumpled, thus distorting the imprint of the once smiley teddy bear on her chest who now looked heart-wrenchingly sad. Sam wished he had the guts to hug and kiss her better.

'I've put the kettle on,' he said instead. 'Mother wants you – you and Andrea – to come to dinner. She's cooking. She won't take no for an answer.'

Maggie slumped on the sofa with a heavy groan. 'I couldn't sleep,' she said. 'I can't even think of eating.'

She wasn't herself at all, that much was obvious.

'You'll have to.'

The kettle whistled in the kitchen.

'Right,' Sam sprang into action. 'I'll make tea. I think I'll offer some to DS Webber. He's sitting outside. He's probably been there for the best part of the night.'

'DS Webber?' Maggie stared as if she was trying to figure out who DS Webber was.

A vigorous knock on the door prevented Sam from explaining it to her. 'That's probably him, wanting to use the loo. I'll get the door.'

It wasn't DS Webber. It was James Weston-Jones. He wasn't likely to have come all this way to avail himself of the facilities. There had to be another reason for his visit.

'Sam, hi!' James was as surprised to see Sam as Sam was surprised to see him. 'Is Maggie in?'

133

'Yeah, come in. I was just making tea.'

James pushed past him into the sitting room. He did exactly what Sam only wished he could do. He strode to Maggie, pulled her into his arms and held her snugly ensconced there, muttering, 'Oh, Maggie, Maggie . . . I don't know what to say . . . My dear, dear friend . . .'

'You don't have to say anything,' Maggie muttered back under his armpit. 'What's there to say?' Her voice was quavering, on the brink of breaking to pieces.

James was only too happy to lend her his shoulder to cry on. Sam gazed, consumed by self-loathing. Why wasn't he capable of simple human affection like that?

'Thank you for coming, James,' Maggie said as soon as she recovered her composure.

'I'm sorry it's taken so long. I should've been here for you like you were there for me, but,' he sighed heavily, 'you've no idea! Things at home have got out of hand – totally out of hand . . . I only came to apologise, really. I won't be here for your father's – for the funeral, I'm so sorry! But I do have to leave or I'll go barmy. I'm leaving tomorrow, going to join Letitia and the boys in France. I can't stay here, not now, not until this whole mess has been cleared up!' He was looking positively tortured.

'What mess? I miss everything,' Maggie mumbled.

'What happened, James?' Sam sat down, forgetting all about the kettle and the tea.

'My father!'

'Is he all right?'

'Well, it's all relative, isn't it? He's in rude health, but . . .' James rubbed his temples in a frantic, circular motion. 'It's something else – something much worse. He's been interviewed under caution about my mother's death . . . *Under caution*, you know what that means! He'd be arrested if he wasn't Lord Philip! I can't cope with this – it's beyond me . . . my father a suspect in my mother's murder . . .'

Both Sam and Maggie sat in gobsmacked silence, mouths gaping.

'I can't look at him and not think, *Did you kill my mother?* I'm doubting him. I don't know what to think any more!' He threw his arms in the air. 'I must leave and clear my head. I must be with my family . . . If my father . . . No, I can't!'

Seeing his torment, Sam attempted to put things into perspective. He donned his old lawyer's hat and asked, 'Did the police produce any evidence, or are they just fishing?'

'Evidence?' The word seemed to bewilder and inflame James even more. 'It turns out my mother did not run away with Karl. It turns out she never left the estate. It turns out she was buried in our very backyard. It turns out only Father—'

'That's not evidence. That's speculation.'

'I know what you're trying to do, Sam. You're a good friend, but there's doubt in my mind and it's eating me alive!'

'Poor, poor you, James!' Maggie cried.

'I'm leaving today. I just wanted to offer my apologies. I won't be back for your dad's funeral, but I'll be thinking of you.' Another heartfelt hug followed, and then James tore himself away from Maggie, and left. The front door slammed angrily behind him, then all went quiet.

'Well . . . there . . .' Sam stumbled to break the stupefied silence. 'I hope he's wrong. For his sanity's sake.'

'I can't believe it. It's too awful to imagine.'

'Um . . . I'll make that tea then. Would you like to call Andrea down? She could do with a—'

'Andrea? She isn't here. Surely you remember, Sam! She was hell bent on going to stay on her own at our parents'.'

'So what's DS Webber doing outside on the road here? I thought he was watching her back.'

'Good grief!' Maggie wailed. 'No one's told him! She's there all by herself! A sitting duck!'

Chapter Twenty-four

It was good to be home. Andrea slumped on the bright lime sofa and took in her surroundings. Everything was exactly as she remembered it: the creaky parquet, the intricately patterned Persian carpets, and Dad's rubber plant forming shadows on the net curtains. Only now the plant was thrice its original size and the carpets were threadbare, their corners eaten by bugs. On the mantelpiece stood the cheap and tacky souvenirs Andrea and Maggie would bring home from school trips. Mum had kept them all, even the ugly plastic seagull from Blackpool despite its thermometer tube being broken.

From the sideboard Andrea pulled out a drawer full of old family photographs. That drawer had always been filled with photos. Ever since she could remember new pictures were added to the messy collection: school photos, holiday snaps from the seaside, weddings of various relatives.

She carried the treasure drawer up to her and Maggie's old bedroom in the roof trusses. She tipped its contents on to the floor. Yellowed photographs fluttered out and settled on the carpet. There were so many of them, each a little memory-butterfly. She began shuffling through them, gorging on images of the past, willing them to become reality again. They resurrected smells and sensations she had long buried at the back of her mind. Those freeze-frames were slowly coming back to life. She and Maggie in Grandpa Bernie's garden: Andrea flying high on the swing, Maggie waiting her turn wearing a sullen face. She, Maggie, and Will rolling down the slope of the paddock with Mr Wotton's sheep scattering away in panic. It wasn't a good photo, the images blurred, but it had been wicked fun! A photograph of her and Maggie sitting atop the huge bulk of one of the sarsen stones in the Stone Circle brought back memories of their time travel games. Andrea smiled. There was she sitting on Dad's lap, his hand wrapped protectively over her small body. Another photograph captured a moment of distress: what had Mum been saying to her in that patient, soothing tone of hers as she stood bent over a wailing Maggie? Were those tears over a graze on her knee or some monumental injustice Maggie had suffered? Where was she at the time? Why would Dad take a photo of that moment?

Andrea stretched on the floor and looked up at the sturdy rafters. She fantasised about filling this house – her home – with life again. Jack would love it here. He would love romping in Sexton's Wood, bothering the sheep in Mr Wotton's paddock, playing hide and seek in the Stone Circle, jumping in puddles, and making friends with the local kids. If only Elliot allowed that. If only Heather—

But Heather wouldn't, and she would probably be right. Every instinct told Andrea that this wouldn't be a safe place for Jack. Yet even though anxiety swirled inside her gut, she rejected it. She didn't act on instincts – she acted on impulses. And this would be such a grand new beginning! Jack and Elliot would get to know the real Andrea, and they would come to love her as she was.

She must have fallen asleep when something startled her awake. She had the distinct sensation that someone had passed near and a foot had trodden on the photos scattered around her – a few of them were dented and crunched. But there was no one. The room was dimly lit by the lamp with a deep yellow shade. Corners and crevices under the rafters were blocking light. Andrea sat up and looked for the source of that very faint intimation of activity she had detected.

She saw her dad. He stood there, only a couple of metres away.

She knew it was Dad though his features were obscured and he didn't speak. There was an air of absolute, perfect calm around him, radiating out, reaching towards Andrea arrested on the floor in disbelief.

She told herself that she was dreaming and none of it was really happening, but she followed him as he turned and headed towards the wall. The photographs underfoot slid as she stepped on them. She twisted her ankle and almost fell.

That wall wasn't quite room height. The rafters stooped there to just over a metre. There was a storage room behind that wall. A little door leading there had lost its handle ages ago, but there was a hole where the handle used to be. Mum used to keep junk in that space.

Dad went through that door and was gone.

Andrea hooked her index finger into the hole and pulled the door open. It resisted slightly as it scraped open. She peered inside – irrationally. Dad could not possibly be there. And he wasn't.

What was there, as could be expected, was the junk: an old radio dating back to the sixties, a few misshapen cushions, a duvet rolled and trussed up with string, a couple of notebooks, and a few shoe-boxes containing anything but shoes. One of those boxes drew Andrea's attention. It was wrapped in gift paper with a faded floral pattern and bound with a knotted pink ribbon. The ribbon was tattered and frayed, which testified to it having been frequently tied and untied. Andrea picked the box up and painstakingly undid the knots. She lifted the lid to find a few brown notepads, a bundle of unopened letters, and a few envelopes with foreign stamps and slit-open sides. She examined one of the stamps. It was from the Republic of South Africa.

She opened the letter. It was written on plain paper in faded blue ink, in fluent joined handwriting.

My dearest Irene, my Love, the letter read, You will never know how sorry I am about leaving without a word. I could lie and say my mother had taken ill and I had to rush, but I won't do that. The truth is that I had to go and couldn't stay there a day longer. The truth is I was resolved to never contact you – to disappear.

It had taken me two months of torment to realise I was a fool. I can't live without you. I need you. I need you here by my side.

I have come into some money and was able to buy a house.

We have a huge house – five bedrooms all in all, a guest cottage, and servants' quarters. The house comes with a swimming pool (that's me in the picture by the pool in our garden).

You would love it here!

What I meant to say was – you WILL love it here because you must come. I will pay your sea fare. Just say YES.

Lord, I miss you!

Write back the moment you read this letter. Tell me when you can travel, but do hurry. I can't wait for ever!

Don't even look at other men. Just the thought of it makes my skin crawl.

All my love,
Yours,
Karl

Andrea checked the date of the letter. It was a bit faint, but she could just read the date: the April before Mum and Dad had married. Karl predated Dad by a smidgeon. He was Mum's first love. It was quite some discovery.

Andrea reached for the second letter in the small bunch of those that had been opened. It was dated four months after the first one.

My dearest Irene, my Love,

I can't wait any longer for your reply. I suspect my letter got lost in the post. I thought I had better write again.

I can see why you wouldn't write back. I understand. But believe me, when you get here, I will explain everything face to face. It isn't simple and I can't do it without looking you in the eye. But rest assured, I have never lied to you. And I won't start now. Just come over and I will tell you the truth. You will understand I couldn't stay in that place any longer.

I sent you a photograph of me but now I can't be too sure if you received it and didn't care, or maybe it never reached you. I pray for the latter.

Surely, you haven't started seeing someone else?

I know you wouldn't.

I miss you badly.

When you come you will see how good life is here. You will wallow in luxury. People will wait on you. I will bring heaven down to earth for you.

Just come.

There is a big gaping hole in me and I won't be happy until we are reunited.

Write the moment you get this letter. I wish those ships were faster carrying my letters to you, and more importantly yours to me. Days drag without you, months without you are beyond endurable.

Love,
Yours,
Karl

Four more letters were sent that year, all in the same vein of pleading and yearning, and remorse. There was also a Christmas card with illegible writing, letters and words smudged across as if someone had wiped the ink off before it dried. Perhaps it had been smudged later, after the letter had been received and tears shed over it.

After that Christmas Mum had stopped opening Karl's letters. They lay there, pristine and sealed, unwanted. Andrea opened and read each of them. They each had the same message: they begged for a reply, all depicting the pain and disbelief of a crumbling heart. Before Andrea's eyes unfolded the story of unrequited love. Why had Mum not responded, if only to take the man out of his misery and tell him she didn't love him? It was cruel of her to stay silent.

There was a change of tone in the letter Karl sent in October the following year:

Irene,

I have given up. You do not reply. I have no more strength to pester you, for it does feel to me that I am nothing but pestering you. It is time to stop. I shall do just that.

I feel acute heartache when I think of you, and I think of you all the time. I try to stop myself from thinking. The thought of you seeing someone else, just the possibility of it, would kill me.

I am heartbroken, and believe me, I know the meaning of 'heartbroken' — I can feel the crunching in my ribcage and I can feel the ripping pain.

I have been living on the edge of sanity, expecting a letter from you — every day. And every day my heart would contract a little bit tighter, until now, until it can take no more, until it got broken at last.

There will be no more letters from me and no more pain in my ribcage. I will try to forget you. I won't allow myself to think of you ever again.

I wish you well. I have so much more to say to you, but I will only say, farewell.

Karl.

There was one more letter that had not been opened. Despite Karl's vow to the contrary, he wrote again:

Dearest Irene, my Love,

It has been two months. My last letter is about to reach you any day now, maybe it already has. I wish I could claim it back so that you never get a chance to open it. But there is nothing I can do. You will open and read it and you will be hurt by my rushed words, words I didn't mean.

I was desperate, lost my mind. I purged my madness in that letter, but it wasn't me speaking — it was my despair. But I can't take you out of my mind and I know you can't do it either. Whatever it is that is stopping you from writing to me, it is not that you don't love me. I can feel it.

I will keep writing until you answer.

Please forgive me my outburst. Destroy that tempestuous letter I sent you. Take it out of your mind.

Please forgive me. Write back as soon as you can.

All my love,
Yours for ever,
Karl.

Andrea returned the letter to its envelope. She came to the window. Sunlight shone through and illuminated specks of dust quivering in the air. She wondered about Dad. When did he find out about that man, Karl? Did he know him? Was Dad the one who had come between Karl and Mum? Was he the one who had stopped Mum from responding to the other man's love letters?

The unopened letters and the fact that they had been kept hidden in the attic where Mum stored her old junk pointed to her keeping Karl a secret from Dad.

Dad would have destroyed the letters. Mum clearly could not bring herself to do that, though she chose Dad over the other man . . . Neither of them was here any more to tell the story.

The dog next door barked. It was a yappy thing, she had discovered during her last stay; once it started it just would not shut up. She peered out of the window. The dog was standing erect with his front paws on the gate, hollering at a man on the other side of the road, in front of a crumbling section of the wall overgrown with thistles and poison ivy. Behind the derelict wall was Mr Wotton's paddock.

Clearly annoyed by the dog, the man was hurrying away towards a car parked several yards down the road. It was a black BMW, tipping precariously over the roadside ditch.

There was something familiar about the man. At first, she thought it was one of her minders. DI Marsh had shown her their photos . . . Except that she had shown her their faces. Andrea was looking at the man's back, his stride, his body language. That was where the familiarity lay – in his demeanour, in his square-shouldered posture.

'Hugo?' The name whispered itself in her head, a shy, wistful guess.

Hugo had changed in those last twenty years: his hair was now cropped unusually short for him – just a grey stubble; he was much slimmer, his frame almost hollow, and he was more fluid in his movements. The clothes that he was wearing, dark suit trousers and a pale blue silk shirt, weren't quite his trademark attire. It looked expensive. He must have gone up in the world.

She flung the window open to call out to him.

Before she did, he stopped, turned around, and scowled at the barking dog. Seeing his face at last, she stepped back, mortified, but it was too late. He was looking right at her. Yes, he was bound to seem familiar.

He was Wayne Kew.

Chapter Twenty-five

We bundled into DS Webber's car and drove, sirens blazing, to my parents' house, where Andrea could be in mortal danger, or already dead. DS Webber was on the radio talking to an operator, demanding to know why the bloody hell he hadn't been informed. I could have mentioned that the fault lay with me – I hadn't informed them in the first place – but I let the operator take the blame. Besides, we had arrived. DS Webber sprang out of the car and couldn't have heard what I had to say even if I had decided to say it.

Andrea was alive and in one piece as far as I could see. We found her in the loft bedroom. I was out of breath by the time I climbed the second flight of stairs. I really ought to do something about my fitness level. Get a dog, for example.

DS Webber was the first one on the scene. Samuel and I pushed in shortly after. We found Andrea in a right state. She was slumped on the floor under the window, mumbling incomprehensibly under her breath and shaking her mobile phone.

I knelt next to her and grabbed her by her shoulders. 'Andrea! What's wrong? Talk to me!'

'Call the police ... I'm trying to call 999! It won't do it! It's broken ...'

I looked at her phone. It was dead. Her mobile was always out of charge.

'The battery is dead.'

'Call the police!'

DS Webber stepped in. 'Andrea, I am the police. Remember me?'

She gazed at him with a scowl, but recognised him. 'Where were you!'

It would be a long story if she really wanted an answer. I felt a pang of guilt prickle my chest, but bravely I took in breath to begin the explanation.

She wouldn't let me. She shouted, 'Wayne! He was here!'

'In the house?' Samuel asked.

'No. Outside. Right there! I saw him!' She waved towards the window.

'How long ago was that?' It was Samuel again. DS Webber appeared seriously confounded, probably kicking the shit out of himself for letting the fugitive through his fingers.

'Seconds! Seconds before you arrived.'

'Was he on foot?'

'He had a car. Yes, a car. A black BMW. He parked in the lay-by – by the ditch opposite the Martens'.'

Samuel addressed DS Webber, 'Detective?', but he didn't have to say any more. DS Webber had finished kicking himself and was on the phone calling on all units to look out for a black BMW in the immediate five-mile radius of Bishops Well.

'We'll find him,' he informed us.

To me it sounded more like wishful thinking than a statement of fact, but I kept that observation to myself. Andrea was already beside herself with sheer panic. I decided to reassure her, so I said loudly, 'You'd better find him! I want to look Dad's killer in the eye. And I want to see him pay.'

It had taken two cups of tea and a brandy to calm Andrea. The brandy was for me – Andrea was on antidepressants and alcohol was out of the question. The more I was learning about my sister, the more worried I was becoming. She may have been putting a brave face on a bad game but the fact was that life hadn't been that kind to her. She was a bundle of nerves. She deserved better. I wish I could get my hands on that Wayne character. I wouldn't hesitate to wring his neck. I was feeling rather bellicose, even more so because I was so helpless. Everything was out of my hands. Dad's spirit was lingering about, but he wasn't doing much to assist.

I was grateful to Samuel. He threw a blanket around Andrea. She was shivering and complaining of the cold though the temperature outside was already hitting the low twenties. Of course, it was the shock. I had another brandy.

Samuel asked Andrea where she kept her mobile charger. He found it somewhere totally different to where she said and plugged her phone into the wall. 'You must remember to keep your phone charged at all times.'

'I will now,' she squeaked.

'They'll probably catch him today.'

'Yes,' DS Webber concurred. His radio phone was constantly crackling on low volume. 'A clever and callous crook, Mr Kew,' he spoke over the noises, 'he used your father's death to flush Andrea out—'

'What do you mean he *used* Dad's death? He *caused* it!'

'If they don't catch him, he'll be back,' Andrea said. 'I know Wayne. He doesn't give up. And right now he has nothing to lose.'

'Being caught is a risk.'

'Not for Wayne. He doesn't care, I don't think. Before I came back, I was told he had terminal cancer. That's why they let him out – on compassionate grounds. But instead of dying in the comfort of his home, he went under the radar. They warned me not to come. They said he'd be after me. They were right. That's the Wayne I know. He's going to use whatever time he's got left to settle old scores. I am at the top of his list. I saw it in his eyes at the trial.'

My blood ran cold when she said that – so casually, so typically Andrea! 'You must come back to mine. I won't—'

'No, Maggie. Absolutely not. I told you and I'm not changing my mind. I'm not putting you in danger.'

'But he might not know about me! You will be safe—'

Andrea laughed bitterly. 'By now Wayne knows everything there's to know about you. I said no.'

Little shit of a sister! I could throttle her with my bare hands. She wouldn't be helped. She wouldn't listen. She was her old petulant self and I would have to forever be worried sick about her. I sighed so heavily that I felt a vacuum hurt my lungs.

DS Webber said, 'We'll be reinforcing the men on the ground while the search for Kew goes on. There'll be two undercover officers watching outside day and night. It won't be long. But I agree with Mrs Chapman—'

Who the hell is Mrs Chapman? The urgent query shot across my mind until I realised that he must be referring to Andrea.

'The fewer civilians put at risk the better. Here, in this empty house, we can contain the situation better than if Mrs Chapman moved in with you.'

I rolled my eyes and cursed the man inwardly. He hadn't been much help so far, I thought. Gillian Marsh's intervention was called for. As much as I disliked the bossy little madam, I would value her taking Andrea in hand. And she would. And she wouldn't dither.

Miraculously, it was at that point that she arrived. Her small persona, the size and energy of a wasp, buzzed in, full of wrath.

'Webber, what the bloody hell is going on here? Outside, please!'

Meekly, DS Webber followed the wasp out of the room for some serious bollocking. Despite my earlier doubts, I had to feel sorry for him. She would tear strips off him!

'At least you'll come to dinner, Andrea, won't you?' I heard Samuel pester my sister. 'At mine. My mother's cooking. She won't be amused if you don't turn up.'

Andrea agreed to that without any protest. Again I was grateful to Samuel for just being around. He had the knack for making things right.

Andrea confessed to being starved and we decided to make pancakes – our childhood favourite.

Over the pancakes, Andrea asked me a bizarre question even by her standards.

'What do you know about Mum's first love?'

'Dad was Mum's first and last love,' I declared quite definitively, as that was exactly what I wanted to believe.

'Not so. His name was Karl.'

'Karl van Niekerk?' Samuel and I spoke in unison.

'Definitely Karl. Van Niekerk rings a bell, but I wasn't paying attention to his surname. So you know about him?'

'Well, we know him, but not as in ... Anyway, how do you know about him – about him and Mum?'

'I found his letters. Mum stashed them in her junk storage. She must've cared for him at least a little because she kept them.'

I demanded she showed us the letters.

With Samuel peering over my shoulder I read the letters in stunned silence. I was speechless. It had never occurred to me that either Mum or Dad could have had a life before they found each other. I had taken it for granted that they had been together ever since – ever since – ever since they could walk. The letters were an eye-opener. Still, I was finding it hard to accept that there could have been anyone other than Dad in Mum's life. I slipped the last letter back into the envelope and threw the bunch of them on the table.

'Actually,' I pronounced, 'there's nothing there to incriminate Mum.'

'*Incriminate?*'

'You know what I mean!' I waved my arm to appear dismissive. 'It's all him. He goes on and on. Mum says nothing. She didn't reply to any of his letters! For all we know, Karl van Niekerk is a fantasist stalker. I always had my suspicions about him, didn't I, Samuel?'

'Well, you invited him into your house and showed him family albums,' he said unhelpfully.

'You met the man? Wow! Do tell!' Andrea shrilled, all fascination as if this was just some cheap romance novel. It was our mother we were dragging through the mud here!

'There's nothing to tell, Andrea,' I reprimanded her coldly. 'He said he knew Mum, that's all. I was just being polite. He's an old man, you know ... Anyway, I had him under surveillance in connection with a totally unrelated matter—'

'Maybe there is a connection,' Samuel interrupted me, though frankly I had nothing else to add anyway.

'What connection, Samuel?' I groaned, feeling besieged on two fronts.

'If you read his letter carefully, the one,' he shuffled the letters on the pile and took one out, 'where he says,' and Samuel read out,

'But believe me, when you get here, I will explain everything face to face. It isn't simple and I can't do it without looking you in the eye. But rest assured, I have never lied to you. And I won't start now. Just come over and I will tell you the truth. You will understand I couldn't stay in that place any longer.'

'I see . . .' I did see! Of course!

'Karl van Niekerk knows what happened to Helen!'

Andrea looked baffled. 'Who's Helen?'

'Nobody for you to worry about. You've enough trouble on your plate as it is,' I told her.

'We must surrender the letters to the police,' said Samuel.

I paused. They were my mum's private letters. 'We could just tell them. We don't have to show them the letters.'

'The letters are evidence, Maggie.'

'Evidence of what?' Andrea was a nosy little meddler. 'Evidence of what, I'd like to know!'

'Evidence of murder.'

'They don't say he killed anyone.'

'But they do say that he knows who did.'

'He certainly knows something.'

'But who was murdered?'

'His cousin – Helen Weston-Jones. We only just found her body a few months ago, in Bishops Swamp.'

Reluctantly, I agreed to hand the letters over to the police. Clutching the bundle in my hand, I followed Samuel downstairs. DI Marsh was still bollocking Webber, or at least she was talking to him and he was listening. We interrupted.

'Here,' I thrust the letters at Marsh. 'Karl van Niekerk's letters.'

She gazed at me, puzzled.

Sam explained, 'They may be evidence in the investigation into Helen Weston-Jones's murder.'

'Oh?'

'Just read them – you'll see,' I hurried to explain it to her as best I could. Then I added what I really needed to say, 'But disregard anything he writes about my mum. The man is clearly deranged. A stalker. Mum would never have had anything to do with him.'

Chapter Twenty-six

The crowd attending Eugene Kaye's funeral differed from the congregation at Helen Weston-Jones's service. Then the church had been full of blue bloods and minor aristocrats who had never met Helen when she was alive. Now the place was swollen with mere mortals, ordinary plebeians who had known and loved Eugene Kaye. They were here because they felt the pain of losing him, not because it was the done thing. Apart from the family and friends – and that constituted the entire population of Bishops Well – many serving and retired members of the Sexton's Canning police force, dressed in their finery, arrived to bid farewell to Sergeant Kaye, or Sarge Gene as he was known to them. Detective Chief Superintendent Scarfe led the delegation, his polished epaulettes sparkling in the sun. Some of Eugene's ex-colleagues carried the coffin. Behind the pews stood the entire Bishops Well rugby team, complete with their manager, coach, Rhys the barman and assistant coach, the clubhouse caretaker, and all the restaurant and bar employees, ending with Marcus the dishwasher. Everyone wanted to say goodbye to the club treasurer, affectionately known as Uncle Genie. And then there was the brass band taking the roof off with 'Space Oddity', giving Eugene – their once trumpet player – a grand send-off to heaven.

Sam was glad he had booked the clubhouse for the wake. Nobody's lounge would have been big enough to accommodate this number of guests. His mother had wisely engaged the services of a catering company from Salisbury. They had organised a lavish

151

high tea, with salmon and cucumber sandwiches, scones, and cakes. The range of beverages matched the diversity of tastes.

Except for James Weston-Jones, Maggie was supported by every member of Bishops Well AA. They had brought with them various spouses, parents, and girlfriends. Even a couple of local mutts had made it to the wake and were snooping under the tables, begging for scraps, polishing off crumbs on the floor, smelling people's feet, and getting lots of pats on the head. Canine participation in social events was commonplace in Bishops Well, where dogs – immediately after cats – commanded almost divine status. They were adored, they were worshipped, and they were indulged something rotten. There wasn't an establishment in Bishops that did not allow pets inside.

Vera Hopps-Wood had invited Rumpole, her Irish wolfhound. You could tell he was fresh from the dog parlour with his fur untangled and his claws trimmed. She had also ensured that her Right Honourable MP husband, Henry, had abandoned the important business of the State at Westminster in order to be there. He instantly pounced on the unsuspecting Alec Scarfe to lecture him about community policing, as if he had the first idea about it.

Dr Edgar Flynn had brought his mother Lillian and she had smuggled in her latest knitting project in her handbag. As soon as she had finished her macaroon, she had reached for her needles and not stopped since. Will's wife Tracey appeared to take great interest in Lillian's progress. They were chatting avidly although Lillian never took her eyes off her handiwork.

Michael Almond was accompanied by DI Gillian Marsh, who in her turn was accompanied by her enormous Alsatian, Corky. Given her small frame, Gillian devoured an alarmingly large supply of sandwiches – and when those were all gone, moved on to the scones with the efficiency of a powerful vacuum cleaner.

Cherie Hornby was present too. She had remembered to invite members of the teaching fraternity of Bishops Well to hold Maggie's hand. That included Les Foreman plus two other local headteachers and one of their deputies, an English teacher who was recovering from a breakdown (shelf-stacking wasn't for him after all), plus Ivo Murphy and his wife, Megan. Vicar Laurence was entertaining the latter with conversation as she was fairly new to the village and was one of the very few people who had not known Eugene Kaye.

Maggie was in the centre of all this fond support and attention, loved, looked after, and cared for. She, in her turn, was keeping a beady eye on Andrea, even though Andrea had her own bodyguard in the shape of DC Whittaker. He was a large man with a bulbous nose and bushy brows and although he was wearing plain clothes, you could smell he was a copper from a mile away.

Soon Andrea was approached by a man. They hugged and kissed most cordially and seemed to be engrossed in a conversation filled with exclamations and gasps of amazement. Within fifteen minutes, a woman joined them, hooking her arm over his and clinging on to him as if she were laying claim to her precious possession. The man sported a stylish ginger goatee and appeared very uncomfortable wearing a collar and a tie – he was fiddling with his top button and constantly scratching the back of his neck. The woman was more comfortable in her own skin as well as her formal attire, but then women usually are, Sam felt.

Sam was relieved to find his mother delivering one of her know-it-all monologues to a captive audience of Vanessa Scarfe and Vera Hopps-Wood. Vanessa seemed truly enraptured, but Vera concealed a yawn in a glass of wine. Sam noticed a good few of those yawns being drowned in Vera's beverage. The glass was soon empty and Vera vanished in search of a refill. She joined Maggie by the bar. Sam contemplated the possibility of Vera being a bad influence on Maggie as far as alcohol was concerned. Or was it the other way around? After all, Maggie was already nursing her own glass, and it did not contain mere tonic water.

Will was looking relaxed in the company of Dan Nolan and Mary Ruta. Those two were now officially engaged, and there was even talk of an imminent elopement. Sam recalled Maggie telling him that in their younger days Will and Dan had formed a band, Bishop and the Beast. Dan had played the drums and Will was on keyboards. Sam found it near impossible to imagine the upright, sombre Will headbanging and wearing make-up, but now, looking at him laugh and fool around, it no longer seemed beyond the realms of possibility. After all, everyone should have a chance to be young and foolish, including pillars of society such as William Kaye.

Will was tapped on the shoulder by none other than Karl van Niekerk. Introductions, no doubt condolences, and a handshake followed. Karl took Will by the elbow and led him away from Dan and Mary, whispering something into his ear. He was looking down while speaking. Will had to lower his head to hear the old man.

Frankly, Sam was surprised to see Karl on the loose. Judging by the half-baked admissions in his letter, the man should be in police custody answering questions. Sam retraced his steps back to the buffet table to find DI Marsh. She popped a strawberry in her mouth and appeared finally satiated.

'Gillian,' Sam commenced in a non-threatening, casual manner. 'Good to see you mingling with the locals.'

She peered at him with a shadow of suspicion in her quick eyes. 'Well . . . The sacrifices I make in the line of duty,' she said.

'Commendable!' Sam chortled to show his appreciation for this rare display of the woman's good humour. 'Have you lost Michael somewhere?'

'No, he's over there with Edgar Flynn, talking old pottery. And I mean *old*. There are subjects I can't bear to waste my time debating. Old pottery is one of them.'

'Can I get you a drink?'

DI Marsh requested a glass of red wine and they abandoned the buffet to relocate to the bar. Sam handed the drink to her and placed his pint on a coaster. 'So, those letters we gave you – Karl van Niekerk's letters . . . Were they any use?'

'Every bit of evidence is of use.'

'Only I see Karl here, parading around unfazed as if he had nothing to worry about . . .'

DI Marsh put down her glass and leaned towards Sam to speak

154

in a low voice, 'You didn't expect me to arrest the man based on those letters, did you? I thought you were a lawyer. I thought you'd know better.'

'I would've expected you to *interview* the man. I would've expected you to put it to him that you had grounds to believe he may be in possession of information vital to your investigation and that withholding that information would amount to obstructing the police in their inquiries.' Sam rose to the challenge by leaning towards her and parrying her sharp glare with his equally penetrating one.

Gillian Marsh wasn't one for ducking. 'Which I did.'

'And?'

Corky growled, but did not follow it up. His mistress did, 'And, if you must know – though you know damn well that I don't have to tell you anything, but I will because I'm *mingling with the local community* and the Chief Super's watching – so, here it is: we spoke to Mr van Niekerk and he told us exactly what he told me when I'd gone to South Africa to interview him there in the first place. He said Helen had begged him to leave so that she could save her marriage and focus on her baby. He said he hated that *poncy bastard* – his words, not mine – Lord Philip, but he had left her alone with him because she had asked. He'd left, promising never to come back. He kept his word.'

'Was that the revelation he wanted to share with Maggie's mother?'

'It seems so.'

'I don't believe that.'

'Neither do I, but I couldn't quite pull out his nails and ask the question again, could I?'

'So, he didn't make any actual allegation against Lord Philip?'

'No.' Marsh downed her wine and sighed. 'Look, I know how to do my job. If he'd made the slightest insinuation about his lordship, I'd have had his lah-di-dah blue-blooded arse back at the station, answering questions. I don't give a monkey's who he is.'

★

Maggie and Vera joined them at the bar. The two of them were moderately plastered. Sam knew it hadn't been a good idea for Maggie to drink at her father's wake. He had come to know her a little by now and expected that she would fall apart the moment the party was over. At that point, he would have to nurse her broken soul. But it wasn't his place to lecture her about not mixing alcohol and grief.

'Thank you, Samuel,' she drawled into his ear, 'thank you for everything!' And she kissed him. On the cheek.

The kiss was executed in a state of intoxication. He would never be able to hold her to account for that kiss. She probably wouldn't remember it tomorrow.

He said, 'Don't mention it.'

'I won't. My lips are sealed.'

He would love to talk about it some more, actually. A lot more! But now that he had said it and she conceded that it was all in the past, there was no going back to that kiss.

'Have you seen Will?' Tracey entered the bar, looking distracted. 'We really ought to be going. We still have the kids to collect on our way ... I can't find him anywhere!'

Chapter Twenty-seven

'Andrea, remember me? So sorry about your dad. He was a good man.' He spoke in a low baritone. Despite his beard obscuring most of his face, there was something familiar about him. Lines shot out from the corners of his eyes and towards his temples as he grinned at her. His brows were thick and his complexion bore just an insinuation of freckles. Of course she remembered him!

'Matthew!'

She threw herself into his arms. He was a blast from the past – her second-best playmate after Hannah when they were kids, then her pimply teenage boyfriend, then Hannah's ... Then, the radio silence of the past twenty-five years. But this was Matthew and seeing him warmed her from inside.

'You broke my heart, you bastard!' She pushed him away in a playful way and jabbed her finger at his chest. 'You and Hannah!'

'Sorry. It just came out the wrong way ...' He looked genuinely contrite.

'Don't be stupid! It was all child's play. Water under the bridge! I forgave you, anyway ...'

'We were so bloody immature – we should've done it differently ...'

'Forget about it! I did, almost the next day. Honest!' It was true, more or less. It hadn't taken her long to get over Matthew. After that summer, she was off to the all-absorbing vortex of London.

'That's good. I never had a chance to explain ... And then when I saw you at your mum's funeral, I don't know why I hesitated. I didn't have the guts. And when I mustered the courage to talk to you, you disappeared again ... You looked frightfully slim – still do, actually.' His eyes took in her tiny frame, unable to hide his concern. 'I still remember the chubby you, with your round cheeks and puppy fat—'

'Don't you go there! It took me years to shake it off. I want to keep it this way, thank you very much!' She tried to laugh it off, but she had seen the same concern in many people's eyes and it was troubling her. She wanted to shout out to them that she was fine – that she wasn't dying, she was just a bit too busy to take care of herself. But it was on her list.

'I liked you the old way.'

'Not enough, though – you chose Hannah. And she was all legs! I always envied her – well, ever since we became teenagers: me, the ugly duckling, Hannah, the long-limbed Tinkerbell ...'

'But you had the curves, and I wanted them! Hell, did I want your curves!' A well-rounded woman with a rotund midriff and sizeable chest joined them. She hooked her arm over Matthew's. She sported a double chin and cheeks glowing with good humour. Her nose though was still little and upturned. That nose, Andrea remembered fondly, used to be in everybody's business.

'Hannah!'

'Bloody hell, Andrea, I missed you!' Hannah's eyes welled up and she waved her hand to chase the tears away. 'You never came back ' from uni – you just took off without a word. I thought you were dead ... I blamed myself, and Matt—'

'Mainly, she blamed me,' Matthew chuckled.

'True! I was sure you left because of the two of us ... because of us—'

'Don't be silly!' Andrea hugged her oldest friend. She too was close to tears. She had to explain. 'Listen, it was nothing to do with you. I testified at the trial of a very nasty man – an arms dealer. I had to go into hiding. That's what it was.'

'Gosh, that's awful!'

'Yep, it has been – a nightmare ...'

'But you're back now. Is everything back to normal?'

'I don't know. And I don't care! In the end, good things came out of it. I just have to remind myself of the good stuff: I have a family, a beautiful boy – Jack.'

'We must meet them! We'll have to get together. You'll have to tell us all about that arms dealer.' Hannah was already organising a party, her tiny nose twitching. She had always been a party girl. 'Why are they not here with you? Your family, I mean.'

'They're in New Zealand.' Andrea shook her head. 'That's how far I had to go to hide from – from that man.'

'Oh blimey ... When are they coming over?'

'That's the thing – I don't think they can. It's not safe.'

'You don't say! Really?'

'Let's not talk about that! Tell me about you. Hannah, you first!'

Hannah tilted her head and peered – quite unashamedly with love and affection – at Matthew. 'When you know about me, you'll know about Matt.'

'You two? You're actually still together?'

'Married. Twenty-three years and counting. Two girls and a boy. Our oldest, Tasha, is at uni. Emily is sixteen, and in the middle of her GCSEs, as we speak. And Kieran'll be five in October. He almost didn't happen – we thought we were too old ...'

'But we came to our senses. Those doubts it was just a glitch on our conscience.'

'And Matt's dream came true – he has a son at long last.'

'Though he's his mother's little boy.'

'I can't imagine life – our family – without him.'

Andrea felt an acute pain in her chest. She missed Jack. His absence by her side hurt her physically. She had to be with him. Spurred by her longing for her son, she made a decision to book a flight back home – the other home – on Monday.

Hannah was talking in the background – Andrea had missed most of it. She picked up the thread again when Hannah said, 'I wanted you to be my bridesmaid, but I couldn't find you, could I! We looked for you high and low before the wedding.'

'We thought you were hiding from us – deliberately!'

'Giving us the cold shoulder ... Oh well, at least now we know it was nothing to do with us!'

'You should've told us. We'd have dealt with him.'

Hannah was flushed red with laughter, 'Good one, Matt! *Dealt* with the dealer!'

'I've got a better one,' Matthew was clearly beginning to warm up. 'We'd have broken his *arms.*'

Hannah nudged him in the ribs, doubled up in chuckles.

Andrea could not help but laugh with them. 'You two've always been impossible!'

'Speak for yourself,' Matthew replied. 'Remember when you were stuck up that tree behind Mr Wotton's barn?'

'Do you have to remind me?'

'You were hanging between two branches, clinging to the top one for your dear life. Your feet were dangling just five inches above the bottom one, but you wouldn't let go!'

'And you and Hannah were making yourself useful from the ground – debating whose turn it was to go and call for help!'

Hannah nodded. 'Yes, yes, I remember! I didn't want to go. I was shit scared we'd be in trouble for climbing that blinking tree!'

'And I didn't want to go either,' Matthew smirked. 'Well, never before had I had such a detailed view of your knickers. I was quite fascinated ...'

'You swine!' Hannah slapped him on the shoulder.

Matthew went on, undeterred. 'I was sure I was in love with you – or rather with your arse. I said to myself, *I'm gonna marry that girl one day!*'

'And then you married Hannah.'

'My second choice, I'm afraid.' Matthew kissed Hannah on the lips to stop her from protesting.

'I love you people,' Andrea mumbled, blinking away tears of joy. She was happy – she was insanely happy to have rediscovered her old friends.

'Let's have a toast to our reunion!'

*

They relocated to the bar to get champagne. It was Hannah's idea – it was Hannah all over! She had always been over the top, always glitz and glitter, high heels and low-cut tops, setting the world on fire. Andrea was relieved to discover that she had not changed one bit.

Andrea's big happy grin was wiped from her face when she saw Will. He was sitting alone, in the far corner of the bar, clutching a tumbler in his hand. A bottle of vodka was standing next to him. A whole bottle!

Will was not a big drinker. He was almost a teetotaller. When one day he had discovered Maggie and Andrea sharing a joint in their bedroom, he'd had a fit of rage. He hadn't hesitated to exact corporal punishment by way of a slap or two. And although Maggie had had an imprint of his fingers on her cheek, they couldn't complain to Mum and Dad, could they? Maggie had been fifteen, Andrea twelve, and Will – already then he was going on fifty-five. Will had always been a middle-aged man. It most certainly wasn't his style to drink himself under the table on his own, unless he had finally arrived at his mid-life crisis.

Andrea detached herself from her friends and approached her brother. She noticed that he'd already drunk half of the bottle. He was slouched against the tabletop, his elbow sliding on the surface of it, his forearm at an awkward angle and his wrist limp.

'Will . . . are you?' She peered at him helplessly. How could she have let herself forget that this was their dad's funeral? Will remembered. He looked more severely affected than she could imagine. Will was supposed to be the strong one, the sensible one, the one who knew how to handle himself – stiff upper lip and carry on, regardless! 'Are you all right?'

He spared her a bloodshot glance and waved her away. 'Leave me alone . . .' he muttered. 'Piss off . . . I don't give a shit – understand?'

Before Andrea had a chance to challenge his hostility, Tracey shouted towards them from the door, 'Oh, there you are! I've been looking for you everywhere! Did you forget? We've got to be going . . . Will! Come on, let's go!'

She marched in, Maggie and Sam in her wake. Only when they

were close enough to register the half-empty vodka bottle and Will's manic eyes did they stop in their tracks.

'Will?'

'You all right?' Maggie asked.

'I've asked him that already. He told me to—'

'Piss off . . . All of you . . .' Will muttered, swiped his vodka bottle off the bar and tried to get up from the stool. He tripped on something invisible and slumped into Sam's arms. He pushed him away, and staggered.

'Leave me alone . . .'

'He's pissed.' Maggie was incredibly observant.

'You won't be driving anywhere tonight,' Sam told Tracey.' He's in no state . . .'

'Stay with me in the house until he sobers up,' Andrea offered. 'I could do with some company.'

Tracey rubbed her face, lifting her glasses and pressing her fingers into her eyes as if she was trying to rub out the image of her perfectly pickled husband. 'I'll have to go on my own. I must collect the kids from my parents – they're due in school tomorrow. This is so out of character! What the hell is wrong with him?'

Sam said, 'He has lost his father. He's dealing with it the way men do.'

Chapter Twenty-eight

There was a first time for everything in life, even for Will to get wasted. And wasted he was! To the extent that Samuel and Matthew had to lift him to an upright position, hooking Will's arms over their shoulders and, holding him firmly between them, drag him all the way from the clubhouse to my parents' house. None of us had taken a car. There was no need for a car as the clubhouse was within walking distance from the village. Tracey had driven away in the only vehicle we had between us. Will was muttering fiery unpleasantries under his flammable breath along the way. He wasn't cooperating either. His feet bumped and rattled on the cobbled road, refusing or unable to execute basic steps. From time to time he would slip between the two men's fingers and collapse to the ground. The poor lads had to fight him to bring him back up again so that our bizarre procession could continue on its way.

When we finally arrived in the house, it was almost midnight. I directed Samuel and Matthew to Will's old bedroom. Snippets of his rebellious youth featured there proudly in the shape of Black Sabbath posters and some heavy metal paraphernalia, one of which was a plastic but very believable human skull with a collection of half-chewed pens and pencils in it. Samuel and Matthew exchanged meaningful looks before depositing Will on his bed. They sort of let him go and he fell on to the bed with a groan. He lay as he fell, on his back, his arms splayed. Before he closed his eyes, he told us once again to piss off. That was all we got for our trouble.

I apologised to everyone for Will's inexplicably vile attitude and offered them a nightcap. Matthew and Hannah refused. They were in a state of panic. Their fifteen-year-old babysitter might have either departed or brought all of her dodgy friends into the house for a wild party, leaving Kieran locked in his room, crying his eyes out for Mummy. Andrea excused herself, too. She went upstairs to call her family – the midnight hour is spot on for phone calls to New Zealand because of the twelve hours time difference. I was left alone with Samuel.

We sipped our tea in comfortable silence, nodding our heads and sighing heavily. I was thinking that tea was hardly enough to express my gratitude for everything he had done for me. I had to thank him properly, invite him for dinner one day, maybe offer to attend to his garden, which frankly had gone feral since he had taken possession of it.

'Your garden could do with some tidying up,' I suggested, and looking at his face, instantly realised that I hadn't phrased it quite the right way.

'I can't see anything wrong with my garden,' he said, rather defensively.

'Well,' I trod deeper into the hole I had dug for myself. 'It's overgrown with weeds, the hedge is overdue some thorough trimming, and your roses have gone to seed. They need dead-heading, Samuel.'

'They do?' He gazed at me, guilt stamped into his eyes. 'I didn't know. Sorry.'

'What I mean to say,' I began clumsily, 'is that you don't have to be sorry—'

'But I have to be going,' Samuel rose to his feet. 'My mother's probably calling 999 to report me missing. Thanks for the tea.'

'Oh, tea. Of course!' Mine was untouched on the table. I reached for it and for some unknown reason raised it to him in a gesture of raising a toast. 'Thank God for tea! I'll drink to that!' And I drank it in one go.

Samuel smiled awkwardly from the threshold.

'Lock the door, Maggie. Good night.'

My bladder was full. Because of that, I may have squinted in discomfort, which may have come across as scowling. Samuel winced and left. I felt like such an idiot. From wanting to thank the valiant man to forcing him into an apology and a rapid retreat – it was some achievement! I blamed the alcohol. I had to lay off the drink, empty my bladder, go to bed and sleep it off. Tomorrow would bring a new start.

I climbed the steps laboriously to my old childhood bedroom. I was knackered and felt giddy. The emotional stress of the last few weeks was taking its toll on me. Perhaps one too many gin and tonics had played its part too. All I cared for was to crash on my nice soft bed and close my eyes.

The lights were off, but Dad's ghost hovered about, luminescent and agitated. He was worried about Andrea, I could tell. I was worried about Andrea too, but if that wasn't enough, I was worried about Will even more. He seemed to have lost his way. That had taken me aback. I was so very tired. I ignored Dad and crawled into bed.

Andrea's soft whimpering would not let me sleep. She tossed and turned.

'What is it, Andrea? Why aren't you asleep?' I didn't want to sound abrasive, but I probably did.

'It's nothing. Sorry,' she said weakly.

I opened my eyes. 'It's not nothing. Talk to me.'

'I spoke to Jack.'

'That's great!' I rejoiced. 'Isn't it?'

'Well ...' She snuffled. 'And I spoke to Elliot. I told him I was buying my airfare back home on Monday. He didn't sound – I don't know ... He didn't sound excited. In fact, he said we needed to talk – seriously talk about things.'

I agreed with Elliot. 'He probably needs a lot of reassurance from you.'

'Or he wants to end it.'

'Why would he? Don't be daft.'

'You don't understand, Maggie. I can sense it. I know it. His mother hates me. And I can't blame her. She's right, you know? Wherever I go, Maggie, whatever I do, I leave a trail of destruction behind me.'

'You're being overdramatic,' I drawled, feeling the sleep begin to weigh heavily on my eyelids. I allowed myself to close my eyes but resolved to keep my ears wide open.

'I'm not! You've no idea! If it wasn't for me, Dad would still be alive!'

'We had that conversation before – you don't know that, Andrea.'

'I do, I do, I do . . .' she was moaning. 'I can' t– I won't – forgive myself for Dad—'

'Dad's already forgiven you. Anyway, there's nothing to forgive.' My resolve to listen to her was waning. She was flogging the same dead horse of self-recrimination. I really hate repeating myself.

'I killed Dad – with Wayne's hands! I did! And now Elliot doesn't trust me either! I'll never rebuild his trust. I just want to disappear!'

Not again! I thought. She was seriously worrying me. Dad was beside himself, glowing with all his might, wanting me to do something. I dragged myself out of my bed and shuffled to hers.

'Move over,' I told her. She pressed her body against the wall, and I slid in beside her. I wrapped my arms around the very slight body of my little sister. She threw her duvet over me.

'Now,' I whispered, as I had no strength to speak out loud, 'you're not disappearing anywhere. We're going to sleep, and that's final.'

I woke up in the morning with the sun drilling into my eyes, giving me an apocalyptic headache. We had forgotten to draw the curtains in our south-facing window. The sun had managed to rise to the top of the sky – it was late: noon, or even later. Andrea was asleep with her mouth open, breathing in and out softly. I rolled out of bed and tiptoed from the room. I was dehydrated, which, I daresay, is a much more agreeable equivalent to calling it a common hangover. I stumbled downstairs and drunk from the tap in the kitchen. Then I put the kettle on and tossed three teabags into three mugs. While the kettle was crackling joyously, I proceeded to Will's bedroom to raise him from the dead. I was crossing my fingers that he had not thrown up in the night.

He had not, praise be!

But he wasn't in his room, either. That was a tiny bit alarming. Calmly, I told myself he had probably gone to the bathroom. I called out his name. Checked the bathroom – empty. There was a possibility that he had gone to our parents' en suite for a quick shower. I popped over there only to eliminate that possibility. Now, I was beginning to panic. Where was Will?

He was in no state to drive. Anyway, what car would he be driving? Tracey had taken their estate.

I ran upstairs to our bedroom and shook Andrea awake. I explained the situation to her and she gasped, 'God! Not Will, too!'

'What are you saying?'

'Don't tell me that Wayne got to Will too! I would never—'

'No, 'course not!' I repeated half-heartedly, though my heart, in fact, was in my throat. What if she was right? I was tumbling downstairs in yesterday's elegant black linen trouser suit (in which I had slept the night), nearly losing my footing on the landing. Andrea, in her pyjamas, was two steps behind me.

We burst out into the road.

Andrea's minder's car was parked in the lay-by. We hurried towards it. Inside, a policewoman was asleep behind the wheel with DC Whittaker in the passenger seat beside her, his head slumped on her shoulder.

I banged on the window, startling them awake.

'Our brother, Will! He's gone! Have you seen him leave?' *Of course not*, the rational half of my brain was telling me all along, *they had been fast asleep, you idiot!*

They gaped at me blankly.

At last, after a moment of vacant gaping, the policewoman said, 'Calm down, calm down ... I think I saw a taxi pull up ...'

'You *think* you saw it?' Andrea shouted, mainly for the benefit of my left ear which had gone instantly deaf.

'I did. I saw him get in a car. It was a taxi.'

'It wasn't a black BMW by any chance?' As I said that I could feel blood drain from my brain.

'No, no ... It was a silver car – Vauxhall. There's no need to panic. Your brother probably took a taxi to the station.'

'Or he was snatched from under your very noses by John Wayne – or whatever his name is!' I argued hotly.

Andrea gasped again.

'That wouldn't make any sense. Mrs Chapman would be the prime target, not your brother,' DC Whittaker interjected with a word of dubious consolation.

Andrea groaned. I joined her.

'So?' I prompted them.

'We'll run checks with the local taxi companies. Like I said, your brother has probably taken a train home. Why don't you call him?'

Ah, that had not occurred to me until now. I speed-dialled Will's mobile, but hit the brick wall of his short and enigmatic message on his answerphone, *You reached William Kaye. Please leave a message.*

'Will? Call me back! Do you hear me? It's Maggie.'

The next logical step was to call his home number in London. Tracey answered the phone. I had to adopt a calm manner not to alarm her. I said, 'Oh hi, Tracey? Has Will arrived home yet? Just checking.'

'No, not yet,' she replied.

I felt woozy. A cold shiver crept down my spine.

'Is he on his way?' she asked.

'Yes, he ... He must be. He's catching a train home.'

Chapter Twenty-nine

Deirdre Dee knocked on the door and before either Sam or Lord Philip Weston-Jones had a chance to deny her entry she scuttled in, carrying a tray with afternoon tea. She had discovered Alice's Royal Worcester tea set in one of the many unpacked boxes in the garage. That tea set stood proudly on a silver tray, accompanied by fruit scones, strawberry jam, and clotted cream.

'I thought a cup of tea wouldn't go amiss,' Deirdre announced and plonked the tray on top of Lord Philip's Last Will and Testament, which was lying on Samuel's desk.

'Oh, that's very kind,' Lord Philip murmured graciously while Samuel snatched the tray and carried it to the sideboard, muttering his displeasure under his breath.

Lord Philip smiled. 'Will you be taking tea with us, Mrs Dee?'

'Oh no! I wouldn't dream of interrupting the . . . business consultation,' Deirdre declined weakly and looked towards her son for his encouragement to stay, in which case she would gladly join them – her cup and saucer were in fact already on the tray.

But Sam provided no encouragement whatsoever, forcing his mother to retreat. She lamented inwardly at the way her son had turned out. She had not brought him up to be rude. He must have taken after his father in the area of social etiquette. Before closing the study door on her way out, Deirdre added to save face, 'And I'm rather busy in the kitchen. We're expecting guests for supper.'

'Next time,' Lord Philip looked disappointed. That was a small consolation – but still, a consolation nonetheless.

Sam could swear that his mother curtsied before leaving. He had no idea that she would be so star-struck by Lord Philip's lineage. He had never taken her for the groupie type, but then again, her generation had a thing for blue blood. Sam shook his head and stirred his tea. Weston-Jones was scoffing a scone. He had dolloped jam on top of the cream – not the other way around, Sam noted. Mother was bound to ask him later how His Lordship took his scones.

When they finished eating, they returned to the business at hand. Weston-Jones had made a new Will. His old one nominated his younger son Joshua as the heir apparent to the Weston estate and the title that went with it, circumventing the elder son, James. That was unconventional. Traditionally, and that tradition dated back to the times of the Norman conquest, the eldest son would inherit the title and the bulk of the properties while the younger son would join the military or the clergy. It had been a mystery at first, but now Sam was able to put two and two together: Lord Philip had doubted that James was his own flesh and blood. Even after Joshua died, Lord Philip had stubbornly omitted to change his Will in James's favour.

Until now.

Weston-Jones put on his rimless spectacles and read the whole document without haste. He asked a few questions about the annuity for the present Lady Weston-Jones and whether anything could be added to force James to pass the estate intact to his first-born son. Sam explained patiently that such stipulation would have no legal force. Lord Philip was in no position to draft James's Will for him. The proviso in his own testament, for the benefit of his grandson in the event of James's death preceding his own, was the best His Lordship could do to secure the continuity and indivisibility of his estate and title.

Lord Philip nodded thoughtfully. 'I see,' he said. He took a fountain pen out of his jacket breast pocket. 'Shall we ask Mrs Dee to witness it, then? She'd like nothing more, I'm sure.'

Maggie collided with Philip Weston-Jones on the doorstep. She smashed the door into his face and crashed into Samuel's narrow hallway. Lord Philip recovered quickly from the first impact and pushed the door back at Maggie. Soft swearing mingled with profuse apologies, and enquires after their respective wellbeing followed. His Lordship assured Maggie that he was perfectly well. Maggie did the same, unaware of the trickle of blood she mechanically wiped away from her face. A droplet splattered on the floor, and that she saw. She stared at it blankly.

Her sister said, 'You've got a nosebleed, Maggie.'

Deirdre flew out of the kitchen, squealing in agitation. She carried a bag of frozen peas. She plastered it on to the back of Maggie's neck and guided her into the kitchen.

'Sit down, pinch the bridge of your nose, and tip your head forward.'

Sam was too flummoxed to take it all in. He watched wordlessly as the two women fussed over Maggie's nose. He decided to leave them to it and turned his attention to Lord Philip, who blinked at him a couple of times in a bewildered fashion, raised his arm in a farewell salute, and skulked towards his car.

There he bumped into Karl van Niekerk.

It looked like a Mexican standoff, each man glaring hard into each other's eyes, waiting for the other to blink first. What Karl had been doing on the driveway was anyone's guess. Samuel's guess was that he had been following Maggie and Andrea, and that the last person he had expected to see was Philip Weston-Jones.

The two of them stood frozen a couple of metres apart, facing each other in a stony silence until Lord Philip uttered through gritted teeth, 'I told you to never come back!'

Karl van Niekerk said nothing. Instead, he spat at Lord Philip's feet and walked away. Indignant, Lord Philip jumped into his car and drove away with a screech of tyres.

Sam remained out on the porch, wondering if Karl would return – he had obviously been heading this way with some purpose in mind but Karl was gone. Sam went inside.

His mother burst out of the kitchen. She appeared seriously flustered. 'You did tell Maggie six o'clock? Please tell me you did!'

'Yes, I did.'

'The supper's not ready. I'm not ready! It isn't yet five!'

'I've noticed. They're early.'

'Or did you give them the wrong time? No one comes to supper an hour in advance. No one!' Suspicion crept into Deirdre's eyes. She clearly did not know that Maggie wasn't just anyone. Maggie and timekeeping did not get on. She did not possess a single clock that kept the correct time.

'Mother, I said six o'clock – sharp. I remember vividly.'

'So why are they early?'

'Why don't we ask them?'

'That'd be rude!' Deirdre looked appalled. 'What happened to your good manners, Samuel Dee?'

Maggie peered out of the kitchen. Her nose was red, but did not appear misshapen so there was hope it had not been broken. Sam looked at her expectantly. She had popped out just in the nick of time to save him from the third degree.

'Maggie!' he exclaimed. 'Feeling better? Has the nosebleed stopped?'

'The nosebleed? Um . . . Oh yes, that's stopped. It's Will though! I didn't know who to turn to! Will's missing!'

Deirdre returned to the kitchen to continue with her dinner preparations. Maggie and Andrea refused tea, sat in the lounge, and started talking over each other. They weren't making any sense.

'So he definitely took a taxi to the station. DI Marsh called to confirm that—'

'I was sure – still am – Wayne's behind Will's disappearance!'

'But that's where the trail goes cold—'

'That's trademark Wayne . . . People go missing . . . I'll never forgive myself!'

'He bought a ticket to London. The guy in the booth at Sexton's station remembered him—'

'He's using Will to get to me. I know that! I just don't know what he wants me to do! If he harms Will—'

'Oh, Andrea, that's not what the police said! Try to calm down!' Maggie shouted, not very calm herself. Then she lowered her voice to hardly a whisper, 'But, you see, the guy at the station couldn't be sure if Will was alone. Someone, another man, may have been with him—'

'He was forced to get the ticket to London at gunpoint. I know how Wayne operates ... It was to throw the cops off his scent! That's typical Wayne ... Why doesn't he just come for me? It's between me and him! Why won't he face me!'

'Because it's nothing to do with Wayne! Or with you, Andrea!' Maggie snapped at her sister. Then her eyes darted to Sam, and back to Andrea, and to Sam again. Sam knew she wasn't persuaded by her own arguments. He could sense the fear in her voice. Maggie, just like Andrea, dreaded that Will was the next pawn Wayne Kew had taken out in the mad game of chess he was playing against Andrea.

'So why hasn't he made it home?' Andrea pressed on. 'It's been hours since he left Bishops. He's not answering his phone ... Tracey's beside herself with worry ... It is my fault! What have I done!'

Maggie had nothing to say to that. She had run out of steam, fending off Andrea's self-recriminations. She gazed at Sam, hopeless and small, and frightened. He had to do something. Only he didn't know what.

'So ... the police are looking for Will, and they have a clear trail to follow, haven't they?' he asked a leading question in an attempt to offer assurance.

'Yes! But what if they're too late?'

'Just give them time. They'll interview the passengers on that train – see if he actually boarded it, and where he got off. Whether he was alone. There are CCTV cameras on trains. They'll piece it all together. We just have to be patient—'

'But what if—'

'What motive would Wayne Kew have to harm Will?'

'To punish me.'

'Then he would go for someone closer to you: your husband, or your son . . .'

'He doesn't know where to find them.'

'Then he'd focus his efforts on finding them. Or most likely, he'd go directly for you. I honestly don't think he'd bother with Will.'

'You see!' Maggie interjected, 'I told you Samuel would make sense of it all!'

Sam gazed at Maggie with a mixture of affection and surprise. He didn't realise she valued him for his common sense, or anything else for that matter.

Andrea threw a spanner into the works, 'OK, if that's true – if this is nothing to do with Wayne, then where the hell is Will?'

'It's a man thing,' Sam said. 'He's taken some time out.'

'That's what Samuel's father used to do to me all the time!' Deirdre entered the room at just the right time to throw in her twopennyworth. 'Whenever things got a bit complicated – and I'm not talking a life-threatening crisis, or anything too taxing – he'd be out of the door, gone fishing. Literally! Anyway, supper is served.'

Chapter Thirty

Andrea wished she was wrong and the others were right, but wishful thinking wasn't enough to defeat the demons that were whispering in her ear. They were telling her it was her fault. Wayne had caused Dad's heart attack and now he had taken Will. At best it was to use Will as a bargaining chip, at worst it was to harm him as her ultimate punishment. She had little hope. If the former were true, Wayne would have contacted her by now to set out his terms. He was ominously silent.

She had refused point blank to stay at Maggie's. Maggie had to be kept out of it. It had to look like the sisters weren't close. In fact, when leaving Priest's Hole after dinner, Andrea had made a scene. She had yelled at her bewildered sister, telling her to keep her nose out of her life. She had been loud and animated. She had slammed the door in Maggie's face and stormed out. She hoped Wayne had seen it, and believed it – if he was watching.

DI Marsh had told Andrea that all her officers were deployed to look for Will, but there was one sitting in a car two houses down from her parents'. The car was unmarked but she recognised it. It was the same white Ford. Inside was a female figure – DC Macfadyen. She was alone. There used to be two of them, but with the entire Sexton's police force searching for Will, compromises had to be made.

Andrea nodded to DC Macfadyen and the policewoman smiled at her. It was a warm night. Her window was open. The radio was playing Pink's 'What About Us'. Andrea stopped by the car. DC Macfadyen turned the volume down.

'Any news about my brother?'

'Not yet. I'll pop over to let you know as soon as I've got the latest. We're looking for him.'

'Thank you.'

The burden of guilt was weighing heavily on Andrea. She knew she should never have come back, never blown her cover and never have yearned for her past because it would come with a hefty price. She had not found her past – it was long gone anyway – but she had lost Dad, and now Will, and Elliot was on his way out of her life with Jack in tow. She could not let that happen. She had to go home now – to show Wayne that she didn't care about Will, that she was a self-absorbed little girl, the girl Wayne used to know. This was the only way to save her brother. And going home to New Zealand was the only way to salvage her marriage.

She sat at the computer in her parents' lounge, looking for last-minute flights to New Zealand. The cost was no object. The first available flight, connecting through Singapore, was departing from Heathrow at midday on Tuesday. She booked it, paid, and checked in online. She called home, but no one answered. She tried Elliot's mobile only to find that they were on their way to his mother's in Tauranga. They would be having lunch there. He would call her back later in the afternoon, when they got home. He hung up.

Andrea resolved to sit through the night and wait for that call. She poured a glass of water and went upstairs. She packed her suitcase, wondering how on earth she would drag it downstairs. She would have to ask for help – it would have to be one of the officers watching the house outside. They would probably be relieved to see her go.

She showered and sat on her bed. It was early, not yet nine. She would have to keep her mind occupied with something or she would drive herself mad. She remembered Mum's notebook – the troublesome one featuring the notorious Karl. Andrea had put it back in the cubby hole in the eaves. She retrieved the shoebox and took out the notebook. She sat on the floor, her back against the wall, and thumbed through the yellowed pages. Mum's flowery handwriting was like a work of art. Andrea began to read at '10th February'.

I have to write about it, otherwise my head will explode. I do not feel I can talk to anyone. It is too shameful.

My sweetheart has left me.

He went away to live in a place so distant that I cannot imagine it. Sometimes, I suspect it is only a dream: the wild animals, the swimming pools, and the evergreen palm trees. I wake up, look around me and none of it is real. Sometimes I think Africa exists only in books, and Karl only pretended to leave and is now hiding in Sexton's Wood.

I don't understand!

A week ago he just upped and left. We were meeting to go to a dance – our first time out together in public. I wore my best dress under my coat. The chill was pinching my cheeks and I was pleased about that, thinking Karl would like a bit of colour in my face. He always called me his English rose.

He never came. I waited and waited, and then braving the snow I walked all the way to the gates of the Weston estate. Up and down the driveway I paced, but couldn't bring myself to knock on the door and ask for Karl. Mr Gerard, the butler, would be suspicious. He is such a judgemental, old-fashioned man!

I went home and waited for a word from Karl. Nothing.

It has been a week.

If I told anyone, even if I told Lucy and she is after all my best friend, they would laugh at me. They would open my eyes to the truth that Karl van Niekerk was only toying with me and that I am a stupid, stupid girl!

I must forget him. I must!

27th February

Lucy is going to a dance tonight. She has asked me to come with her, in fact she insisted I do. She said Karl van Niekerk was a good for nothing wastrel and I should forget him. She said he was a man of the world and he had taken advantage of my heart. I cried.

Lucy told me to dry my tears so that she could put on some make-up. When she finished she said I looked smashing and I mustn't ruin it with tears. The mourning for Karl was over, she laughed. We were going to have a ball.

I couldn't say no.

I tried very hard not to spoil Lucy's work with tears. Whenever they came, I would blink them away.

Lucy took off with Rod Docherty. Eugene Kaye asked me to dance with him three times. He is a great dancer, smart and confident. He is going to be a policeman, he told me. He was saying lots of things, but I couldn't hear him and my thoughts were somewhere else. In the end, I excused myself and ran away to the toilet. I sobbed violently. My make-up was destroyed. I went home to cry my eyes out in peace. I could not bear being seen crying, not by Lucy, not by anyone. It felt like Karl was dead and I was crying at his funeral.

I was holding my engagement ring from Karl. I put it on and took it off. The diamond sparkled so brightly. It's a South African diamond, the best in the world. We were going to announce our engagement at Easter. I put the ring back in its little velvet box. If only I could put Karl out of my mind just like that.

Still, nothing from him.

10th March

It has been a month since Karl left. There are rumours that he and Helen have eloped together, that they were secret lovers behind Lord Philip's back. Helen is missing too, so it makes sense.

How could I be so blind?

Then again, it cannot be true. It simply can't. Karl proposed to me. We are to be married. We were . . .

Today Mummy told me I should get out more, meet new people. She said she was worried for me, I had turned into a hermit, it wasn't healthy for a young woman like me. She had never before referred to me as a 'woman'. I am twenty-one, I guess that makes me a woman.

No news from Karl.

Snow fell this morning. Quite unexpectedly, though it had been cold for days. It does not often snow in March. The whole world turned white overnight. It was beautiful when I woke up. I opened the curtains and there lay thick snow. Everywhere, even on the bald branches of the chestnut. Rooftops across the whole village, as far as the eye could see, were immaculately white and only the defiant black chimneys puffed out thick, black smoke. I felt so good, so at home, so at peace with the world.

Mummy came in with a mug of cocoa and wished me a happy birthday. She gave me a present from her and Daddy – a pair of white gloves made of lace. So beautiful and delicate!

Lucy of course insisted that we go to a dance to celebrate my birthday. Mummy said Lucy was right, I should go, I should have fun. That was when Mummy said she was worried about me. She also said I would be left on the shelf. It sounded so unlike Mummy. Never before had she been so blunt. She is afraid for me, I know. And she is right to be afraid. I am scared. I don't know how to tell her.

Lucy has a sweetheart, Bert. He isn't a local lad. They are going steady now. Rod Docherty is in a strop – he has always had a soft spot for Lucy. She's getting engaged at Christmas. Bert is saving for an engagement ring. He wants everything done by the book, no cheapskates. I told Mummy. She looked at me and had tears in her eyes. She didn't say as much, but it was there in her eyes: What about you, Irene? I wished I could show her my engagement ring from Karl to put her mind at ease, but then I would have to tell her everything and it would kill her. And it would ruin Daddy.

Easter Sunday

The usual Easter service at St John's. Lucy joined me and a few other girls came too. We stood at the back of the church. It was packed – people were spilling out of the pews and the youth were standing as there was nowhere for us to sit.

Daddy was delivering his sermon, but I wasn't listening. I was very much absorbed in my own thoughts, thinking how I was going to break the news to Mummy and Daddy. How would they take it? Me, the vicar's daughter – such shame!

I was paying little attention to what was going on around me.

And then I felt somebody's eyes on me. I literally felt his eyes on me.

I looked to the left and in a sea of heads, I saw him. Eugene. He was staring at me openly and did not even attempt to avert his eyes when I caught him. I must have blushed for my face felt very hot. I lowered my eyes and wished I could find a hole in which to hide. The words got mixed up in my head and I had to stop singing. I felt such a fool!

Still, it did not end there. I do not know what possessed me but I peeked again, and again he was staring. This time he even smiled at me. It was a somewhat insolent smile – very confident, boastful. I looked away but his face was now before my mind's eye: his cheeky smile and bright eyes, his hair, smooth and shiny with Brylcreem. He had a strong neck and a good pair of wide shoulders under his coat. His coat was dark grey with shiny silver epaulets. He was holding his head up. Everything about Eugene Kaye . . . glittered.

I spent the rest of the service in utter agony, avoiding his eyes and yet being constantly drawn to them. It was torture and boy, was I glad when the service was over.

Then, to my relief, as we began to shuffle towards the exit, I noticed him heading towards me. He was quick and determined to push through, but the crowd was thick and I promptly grabbed Lucy by the elbow and urged her to rush out. We ran to Priest's Hole at top speed!

Nothing escapes Lucy, nothing ever! She giggled all the way and between the giggles told me she had seen me and Eugene exchange glances all through the service, which I denied and tried to explain, but she would not have any of it. She told me – not that I asked, but she just had to say it – that Eugene had been asking after me and that we would make a great couple. I told her she was silly.

I cannot sleep. I keep thinking of Eugene Kaye, and then my thoughts go to Karl, and guilt overwhelms me. I tell myself that Karl is coming back for me, that I have to believe that. I keep repeating that mantra in my head. I wish he could hurry up! And then, I lose the track of Karl and my mind wanders off to Eugene. I cannot understand why my head is filled to the brim with Eugene Kaye.

24th April

Lucy went to a dance with her beau. She looked smashing in her above-the-knee-length dress and her hair cut short into a bob with a heavy fringe. I felt – and probably looked – like such a frump. She had the sense not to ask me to come with her.

But then there was a knock on the door. Daddy answered and I heard another man's voice. Daddy called me to come down.

My heart jumped to my throat. It was Karl! That was my first thought. I dashed downstairs, nearly fell down.

It was Eugene Kaye.

He was dressed to the nines. He looked so handsome that my legs buckled under me. I pulled my threadbare cardigan to my chin. I was ashamed of myself.

Daddy said Eugene had asked if he could take me out. Daddy said he didn't see why not. Mummy came out of the kitchen, looking rapturous.

'What are you waiting for, Irene? Go and get changed!' She waved me upstairs and invited Eugene to come in and wait inside.

I put on my best dress (the one I had worn that night when Karl disappeared) and my new lace gloves.

Lucy was surprised when she saw us arrive at the village hall. She pulled such a funny face that I keeled over laughing. We had an amazing time. Eugene wouldn't let me out of his sight. He walked me home afterwards, and as we stood outside, saying goodbye, he asked me if I would like to step out with him. I said I would like that very much. We kissed.

I now think Karl and Helen have run away together. Everyone thinks that.

A letter from Karl! I was wrong! Everyone was wrong!

I kissed it, danced with it, cuddled it to my heart.

Silly Lucy! I showed her the letter. She told me she was happy for me but I was here, Karl was there, he and I would never be together – it was a silly fantasy. She said she was disappointed in me. She said I had a perfectly wonderful man by my side and he was mad about me – I would be a fool to toss him aside for the phantom of Karl van Niekerk. I couldn't bring myself to explain to her that Karl was a lot more than a memory. After speaking to her, I felt a little like a deflated hot air balloon – I felt like I was falling.

I wrote back to Karl. I told him everything, but I said he had to come back. He wanted me to join him in his African paradise, but I couldn't do that to Mummy and Daddy. To anyone!

I think I had stopped trusting Karl. I could not rely on him and him alone.

I said – in my letter – that I would rather stay here where every place and every person was familiar to me. I was brought up playing hide-and-seek among the tombstones and church pews. I knew every crack in every wall in our house, I knew every path, even those that led nowhere in the woods, I knew every smell, especially in summer when harvest was on and the air was pungent with the scent of fresh hay; I knew every face at the greengrocer's, the post office, in church during the Sunday service, every face was like my own, I knew everything and everyone. I could not leave them.

Then, as I was about to ask him to come back to me, I realised I didn't want him to. As unwise as that was, I didn't want Karl in my life. There was a time when I would have followed him to the ends of this world, but not any more. This is where I belong: with Mummy and Daddy, Lucy and Eugene. And suddenly I was clear that I was in love with Eugene Kaye.

Eugene would never run away. I can trust him.

I screwed my letter into a ball and threw it in the fire. I decided I would speak with Eugene and tell him everything.

1ˢᵗ June

Eugene and I are engaged to be married!

Several pages had been torn out of the notebook. Then came an entry from 15ᵗʰ January the next year.

Grandpa has taken ill. His lungs have always been weak but now he has taken to bed. He is coughing blood and is so thin, so appallingly thin that I can't bear to look at him. His eyes are haunted, his cheeks have sunk so deep into his face that the skin hangs off his cheekbones and jaw to the extent that you could count his teeth — they are near breaking through his skin. He is like a small, skinny boy and yet he is my grandfather and I cannot understand how this can be. It is killing me, but it is killing Mummy even more. She too is a shadow of herself. Two weeks ago she moved out of Priest's Hole to stay with Grandpa in Little Ogburn. She took the spare room next to his bedroom. She wants to be close at hand. She wants to listen to his breathing. It is heartbreaking for her, and for me. The worst thing is that I cannot do anything, not a thing in this world to make it right. Daddy is just about coping without her. His head is buried in the Holy Book day in and out. He's seeking solace from there. He says he is lucky to have me and Eugene around.

There are more letters from Karl. They are addressed to me under my maiden name. Daddy shakes his head sadly when he hands them to me, as if he were saying: 'Write to him. Tell him the truth. Make him stop.' Daddy knows more than he lets on.

I read the first letter over and over again until my eyes bled. He is in such pain! Daddy is right. I have to write to Karl, tell him the truth. But I can't do it. I am paralysed when I think of him. I wish Karl would stop writing. I somehow believe that if he stopped, his pain would stop, too.

20ᵗʰ March

There is no improvement with Grandpa. The doctor said he could not give us any guarantees. Quietly, Mummy went to Sexton's and bought two black dresses, one for her and one for me. She wept as she brought them home. I could not. I do not know how to cry. Tears do not come out. Inside, torrents are pouring out of my heart.

28th June

Today was Grandpa's funeral. Eugene had taken care of all the preparations. Daddy delivered a beautiful sermon. There wasn't a dry eye in the church.

Mummy and I wore the black dresses she had bought for us. Hers was too big. Her face was veiled so that no one would see her sunken, bloodshot eyes. Her hands were very cold and bony. She was clutching my arm as if she were afraid of something. I think I know what frightened her – that I may still leave to be with Karl. I think that she and Daddy started to suspect something when the first letter arrived a year ago. But they have nothing to fear. I wouldn't leave them before – I won't leave them now. Especially now!

I squeezed her hand really, really hard.

12th October

Lucy and Bert are getting married. The date has been set for June next year. I am so happy for her! She is radiant and impossibly joyous. We hugged and kissed, we giggled and splashed out on the biggest two slices of Victoria sponge we could spot at Daphne's. We also had tea.

10th August

Lucy and Bert have gone away to live in Australia. It was always the plan. I will miss her, but she had no choice. Bert took up one of those schemes run by the Australian government. They will get a house and some money to start them off on arrival. Bert has a job. It is a one in a million opportunity for them – here, Lucy has three younger sisters and the whole family are cramped in three small bedrooms. Bert is an orphan, he has been brought up by his auntie, a wealthy woman in *her own right, but Bert does not want to sit and wait for a windfall when she dies. He is ambitious and Lucy thinks the world of him.*

I waved goodbye to them this morning as they boarded the train to Southampton from where they will set sail for Perth. What will I do without Lucy?

12ᵗʰ January

Poor Lucy! She wrote at last. It was a letter of bleak despair. She hates it in Australia. The house they got is nothing more than a barrack, fit for labourers but not for a family. And she is expecting a baby!

They have no money to fund a trip back home. Poor, poor Lucy!

Chin up, I said to her in my letter, you are with the man you love and you are to have his baby, everything else will fall into place, just believe it will! I wrote further about the rainbow after the rain. It was like that for me, I said. Her baby, once born, will change everything for the better. Like it did for me. It will all work out, I said. Have faith!

Maybe that will cheer her up.

There was only one more entry – it was made two days after Maggie was born:

17ᵗʰ August

We have a daughter, Eugene and I. Her name is Margaret – Maggie. She is beautiful. She is ours. She will be her Daddy's little girl.

I look at William. He is already at school. Where did that time go! It feels like only yesterday when I held him in my arms for the first time.

He is fussing around little Maggie. He wants to hold her and I have to explain to him that she would be too heavy for him, that he could drop her and she would cry.

He says, 'I would never! I'm strong! Look, Mummy!' and he flexes imaginary muscles on his skinny arms.

I look into his keen grey eyes and I see Karl. I will have to love this boy twice as hard, for both me and Karl.

Chapter Thirty-one

That was the last entry in the notebook. It ended with Maggie's birth – Andrea hadn't even made it into the world.

She closed the book and put it back in the shoebox. She returned the shoebox to Mum's secret cubby hole. It would stay there for someone else to find. Andrea wasn't comfortable with her newly acquired knowledge. It had the power to destroy what was left of her family: Will, Maggie, and her.

She opened the window and breathed in cool night air. Her head needed to come out of the spin. Family secrets – you heard about them, about other families having them, all those skeletons in their cupboards, but it never applies to you and your own family. Andrea's family, Mum and Dad, Will and Maggie – that was the only true and honest bit of her life. It was something she could always fall back on when everything else failed, when her own mad life took another bad turn. But that illusion had just been shattered.

Dad knew Will wasn't his son. Will had been born four months after Dad and Mum had married. Everyone thought it had been a quick wedding due to Irene expecting Eugene's baby. That wasn't true. The truth was that Dad had saved Mum from disgrace.

Dad had never let out that Will was another man's child. He had treated him the same as his girls, maybe better. Andrea used to resent the things Dad and Will did together to the exclusion of her and Maggie. Rugby, fishing, building pieces of furniture hand in hand. Andrea, too, had wanted to put together a bookshelf, to hammer in a nail, to kick a ball around the pitch, but those privileges had been reserved for the boys. The look on Dad's face was priceless when Will and his Bishops Juniors rugby team had qualified for the county finals. And then there was the other, squinty, hurt look when Will had packed up rugby and taken to heavy metal. Those were the looks only a son's real father could muster. Dad had always been that real father to Will.

Andrea would keep her parents' secret. Nothing good would come from making it known to the world, especially to Will.

She was glad she was leaving in two days' time. She would take that secret with her. Maggie wouldn't drag it out of her. And Maggie could! She was a busybody and she somehow could read Andrea's mind. Andrea could read hers, too. She could tell that deep down, in the heart of her hearts, even though she would never admit it, Maggie blamed her for Dad's death. Maggie was right.

Andrea gazed into the night sky that was full of stars and not quite as black as night should be. She had got used to the southern skies turning off on short notice, the dusk giving way to the night without a fight. Here, the night took its time to crawl out. The dusk ruled supreme for hours. A lone street lamp at the top of the road was spilling an orange tinge on to the hedgerow below it.

Not the slightest movement disturbed the silence. The birds had long since gone to bed. Beneath, DC Macfadyen's car was glowing with a faint bluish light. Andrea couldn't hear any sounds coming from there. DC Macfadyen had said she would come to let her know as soon as Will was found.

A dark slim silhouette appeared at the far end of the road. At first, she could only see his outline and take the measure of his laboured gait. As he came closer, it was just the top of his head, but she recognised Karl van Niekerk. Will's biological father. What was he doing, prowling the night? He seemed to be heading towards the house. An impromptu visit at this hour? Andrea backed into the room. She was thinking fast on her feet: should she let him in and talk to him if he knocked on the door? Should she tell him that she knew?

Almost soundlessly, a car slinked past Van Niekerk. It pulled up by the Wottons' chestnut tree, hiding from sight under the tree's thick canopy. But before it hid, Andrea experienced a moment of déjà vu. It was the black BMW.

She compressed her mouth, not to let out a sound, when a man stepped out of the car and walked briskly towards DC Macfadyen's Ford. When another man emerged, she scampered away from the window. It was Wayne – he looked old, seemingly older than Van Niekerk, perhaps due to his illness – but it was Wayne. No matter how old and ill, Wayne would never be too frail to inflict his revenge.

Her first instinct was to hide under the bed. That was what Hugo had told her to do that night of the cat. *Climb under the bed! Stay there!*

She did.

Flat on her back she was staring at the underbelly of her narrow single bed, the immovable wall to her right. She was trying to steady her breathing. The pounding of her heart was bouncing off the wall and making a loud, drumming noise. Wayne would hear it. The drumming would lead him to her.

There was only a hint of movement downstairs after the front door was kicked in. The two men – maybe there were more than two, she couldn't be sure how many – didn't talk to each other. But they were going from room to room, their footsteps assertive and hurried. Wood creaked on the staircase. Andrea remembered the creaking floorboards of the first floor landing.

She wasn't safe under the bed. Dad had already shown her the only safe hiding place up here in the attic bedroom: the storage cubby hole.

The creaking steps were becoming louder. At least one of the intruders was heading this way.

Andrea rolled from under her bed and on all fours scuttled towards the invisible little door under the slope of the roof. She hooked her finger into the hole where the handle used to be and pulled. It squeaked. She had forgotten about that. Her heart paused in dread. She listened. The steps were very close. She dived into the tight space, pulled the damned squeaky door shut behind her and pushed her eye to the hole.

She could only see the legs up to the man's knees. He walked in without saying anything. He headed for the wardrobe – opened it; old dresses and coats rattled and rippled on their hangers as he searched through them. He took some interest in Andrea's suitcase on the floor – she couldn't be hiding in there, but he kicked the lid open and surveyed its contents. He disappeared for a couple of seconds into the bathroom. Andrea allowed herself a shallow breath.

When he came out of the bathroom, he checked the beds: firstly, Maggie's; then hers. Finally, he lowered himself to the floor slowly and with a groan, as if it was hard on his joints, and looked under the beds. The drumming of Andrea's heart went into a frenzy. She saw his face.

Nothing was left of the handsome, polished Wayne of twenty-five years ago. Gone was his lion's mane of hair. What she had originally taken for shortly cropped greyish hair was in fact his bald scalp, paler than his rubbery yellow face.

She shut her eyes. She couldn't look into that face. She was praying he couldn't see her – hear her – smell her.

Two distinct voices broke out downstairs.

'Who are you? What are you doing here?'

'The police. We're looking for Andrea Kaye.'

'Show me your badge!'

'Sir, you need to leave now.'

'You aren't the police! The police are outside! Who are you!' It was Van Niekerk speaking, his broad South African accent more pronounced because of his agitation.

Wayne was back on his feet. He too was listening.

There was a thud and no more voices. Wayne hurried downstairs.

Shaking, Andrea crawled out of her hiding place. She had left her mobile in her trouser pocket. She prayed it was charged. Her trembling hands found the rectangular cold shape. It was alive! She dialled her emergency number.

Wayne was downstairs. 'What the fuck!' he shouted. Then, almost instantly, he added, 'Torch the fucking place!'

The clone's voice answered the phone on the second ring, 'Yes, Andrea.'

'Hugo? Hugo!' her whisper was urgent and frantic. She hoped he could hear her. 'He's here. Wayne's here. Please come and get me!'

Chapter Thirty-two

The whole world came crashing down on me. To say that I felt disoriented, baffled and just utterly, utterly bereaved would be an understatement. First, Mum. Then, Dad. Now – God forbid – Will. And last night Andrea put the final nail in my coffin. I seemed to have lost my entire family in a blink of an eye.

I don't know what possessed my sister to behave the way she did. She had always been a little unhinged and quite unpredictable, but last night was a shocker. I only asked her to stay the night with me. It was for my sake more than hers. I was petrified. At the rate I was losing my family members, I feared, Andrea would be next. I wanted her nearby. We would talk well into the night, like we used to. No one would hurt us if we stuck together.

But she was having none of it. She screamed at me. She raged and raved. She told me to go to hell and leave her alone. To keep my nose out of her life. Get my own ... And she marched into the sunset.

I don't know if I'll see her again after last night, if she will bother to come and say goodbye before flying off to New Zealand. Frankly, right now, I'm not sure I want to see her. I have spent twenty-odd perfectly satisfactory years without her – I can manage twenty-odd more.

But last night I felt bruised. It hurt – the bit about getting my own life hurt. I sat in Grandpa's old rocking chair, and I rocked, and I contemplated my sister's words. Andrea might have had a turbulent life – unsettled, uncertain and a big fat lie for the best part of it – but she had at least had a life. And a family.

What sort of life did I have? I pondered. I lived in the depths of the Shires, communing with ghosts, digging up old pots, dead-heading roses, eating cake and drinking copious amounts of tea, plus an occasional alcoholic beverage ... On that note, I knocked down a double brandy and took myself to bed.

I slept like a log despite bizarre dreams filled with howling wolves and red skies.

A knock on the door woke me up in the morning. A faint hope crossed my mind that it was Andrea, contrite and apologetic about last night's outburst (for which I was planning to tell her off in no uncertain terms and reserve my forgiveness for later). I rolled off the bed and staggered to the front door.

'Who is it?'

It wasn't Andrea. It was dear old Samuel. 'My mother sent me to invite you for a hearty breakfast. Both of you, of course,' he spoke through the door.

I looked down at the state I was in. I sighed. It would take ages to get this mess ready to face the world. I sighed again. I hoped he could hear it, and understand.

'Has Andrea stayed the night with you?'

'No,' I croaked, 'she went off. She literally went off last night ...'

'Oh dear ... What about you, just you, then?'

'I can't,' I said to the door. 'I'm not hungry. I couldn't hold a conversation with a tree stump, never mind Deirdre – I mean, I want to be alone. Sorry.'

'I see.' The door answered me with Samuel's voice.

I listened with my ear to the talking door and heard Samuel's feet crunch on the gravel as he walked away.

I might have just pushed away the last friend I had left on this planet. I sniffled. Still, this wasn't the time for self-pity. That would have to wait until later and when I was ready I would wallow in it to my heart's content, like a pig in mud, like a dung beetle in ... well, in dung.

For now, I had to shower, get dressed, have a strong cup of coffee and get in touch with DI Marsh to find out about Will. I attended to my morning ablutions in that order.

Drinking my strong coffee, I noted that Deirdre had already emerged into the world, and more particularly entered Samuel's garage where she commenced her battle against unpacked boxes and all manner of junk that Samuel had managed to accumulate in his short, but clearly prolific, habitation of Priest's Hole. Samuel was nowhere to be seen. Strangely though, Alice was hanging out with me, probably out of pity. She was standing next to me, watching her mother-in-law's manoeuvres in the garage.

'Thanks for keeping me company. Everyone else has abandoned me.' I smiled at her.

She didn't answer. She didn't have to. There was another knock on the door and I knew it was Samuel again. Alice hadn't stayed to be nice to me. What was I thinking!

I shouted to the door, 'The key is under the pot, Samuel!'

'Of course it is!' he replied cheerfully and didn't ask me how I knew it was him.

Samuel had come bearing gifts – fresh croissants and an assortment of pastries from Angela Cornish, which she had offered free of charge when he said they were for me. He had concluded that just because I was unable to face his mother didn't necessarily mean that he too would be unwelcome. I couldn't send him away. I may also mention, in the interest of truth and nothing but the truth, that I find the pastries from the 'A Cornish Bakery' hopelessly irresistible. And they were dedicated to me. I made more coffee and we sat down in my lounge devouring buttery croissants et al.

I refused to talk about Andrea – it just wouldn't pass my throat to mentioned that sorry excuse for a sister. To avoid sitting idly and listening to my own jaw chewing the pastries, I asked Samuel about the purpose of Philip Weston-Jones's visit.

'We were ... adjusting his Will.' Samuel wasn't comfortable discussing his clients' business, though I couldn't comprehend why. I am the most discreet neighbour you could ever wish for. I don't blabber – I just want to know everything for my own purposes. I guess Samuel is yet to discover that for himself.

'Adjusting it, huh?' I pursed my lips, but only briefly because the next bite of Danish pastry was heading in the direction of my mouth.

'Yes, we were . . . But there was something interesting I observed after he left.'

'Oh yes?' I said, spluttering a few flecks of almond shavings at Samuel.

He blinked defensively and wiped the shavings from his torso while telling me about Lord Philip and Karl van Niekerk barking at each other in the driveway, almost jumping at each other's throats like a pair of fighting dogs in a ring.

'It's obvious that each suspects the other of Helen's murder, and they don't care about venting their suspicions,' I commented.

'It is clear that they can't bear the sight of each other, yes . . . But it made me think – what Lord Philip said to Van Niekerk . . . His exact words were, *I told you to never come back.*'

'You think there's more to it than just suspicions?'

'I honestly think Lord Philip knows more than he's letting on. But what I can't figure out is why he's not saying it! Why is he covering up for Van Niekerk? They evidently hate each other, so why?'

'Perhaps it's something else? Something unrelated to Helen's death?'

'Hmmm . . . I still think either one of them could lead us to Helen's killer.'

'Come to think about it, Helen's killer may well be dead himself. It happened so long ago! How old would he – or she – be now?'

There was yet another knock on the door. I feared it might be Deirdre. Looking at Samuel's face, he feared the same. But it would be rude not to invite her in. We still had a couple of pastries left and I was as full as a gutter in a downpour.

'I'm coming!' I got up with a groan and limped to the door.

It was Gillian Marsh.

She looked awful! She looked worse now than she had on the

day of Richard Ruta's murder, when she had famously passed out on me. Her face was smeared with tears, still not quite dry. I could swear she was wearing her pyjama top – it had writing on it which said *Sweet Dreams*. Underneath her bra was missing, which was quite obvious. Fortunately, she had bothered to pull on a pair of jeans. Her laces were undone and hung limply around her boots. I had the distinct impression that DI Marsh had come straight from her own bed. I knew this could only mean something dreadful had happened.

'Will!' I shrilled. 'What happened to Will?! You found him, didn't you? Is he—' I battled the final word not to come out. It was a losing battle. 'Is Will dead . . .'

'No, he's alive and well. Can I come in?' She sounded subdued, her voice monotone, as if she were speaking on autopilot. A thought crossed my mind that she was on drugs.

My mind, on the other hand, went into overdrive: it screamed with joy, made itself into a fist and punched the air. Will was *alive and well!*

'Yes, come in, please do. We've fresh pastries from Angela Cornish. I'll make some coffee. Coffee or tea?'

'Coffee is fine.'

She dragged herself to the sitting room and, without acknowledging Samuel, collapsed in my rocking chair. She stared into space. I made the coffee as quickly as I could. The kettle was still warm – I didn't trouble myself with boiling it again. I carried the mug to Gillian.

'Here you are. You must've had a bad night . . . um, judging by . . . um. But I'm so grateful you found him! Where the hell was he? Here, have a bun,' I shoved the cardboard box with what was left of the pastries in front of her nose, 'and tell us everything!'

She didn't take the bun but drank her coffee. 'Yes, your bloody brother,' she started. That didn't sound very promising, but I could forgive her. She had found him alive and well and that was all that mattered, I thought.

'Yes, my *bloody brother*. Has he been in any danger? I hope not. I hope it was just one big misunderstanding, for which we'll have to apologise to the police, of course, for wasting your time. I'm sure! So . . . where did you find him?'

'I'll tell you if you stop talking,' she barked at me. She did have the look of a rabid dog in her swollen eyes – a warning that she refused to be responsible for her next action.

I recoiled into silence.

She put down her empty mug in a gesture of finality. 'Thank you! So, he went to London but never made it home. He booked himself into the first B&B he found and spent the night there. His phone was off. We were able to locate him only when he paid his bill this morning, using his debit card. That's it.' She arched her brows and pulled the sort of face you do when you're talking about something beyond human comprehension.

And it was beyond comprehension. It was totally out of character for Will to behave that way. 'Why would he have done something like that, and not told anyone?'

'Your brother had some soul-searching to do, he tells us.'

I didn't think Will even believed he had a soul. I remembered vividly when he had told Grandpa Bernie that 'his so-called *God*' didn't exist and that all religion was opium for the masses. That was the time when Will had turned his hand to heavy metal. It could have been considered a side effect of puberty, but it had stuck with Will for life. He had not been to church since and got married in a registry office, making Grandpa very, very sad. Had Dad's church funeral sent Will into some downward spiral of finding his immortal soul all of a sudden?

'Oh,' I said.

'Yes, *oh!*' Gillian echoed, malice still twinkling in her eyes. 'Because while the whole of Sexton's CID were looking for your bloody brother, my officer, and my dear, dear friend,' her voice cracked, 'was being butchered in front of your parents' house!'

'W . . . what?' That was Samuel, as I had gone numb.

'Exactly what I said. We were short of men on the ground – because of your missing brother and his bloody soul-searching, and Erin was on her own, watching over your sister—'

It hit me – what she was saying. Andrea! 'Is she ... is she ... is Andrea ... Oh God ...' I was stammering.

But Gillian didn't hear my question. She kept going, 'She shouldn't have been on her own – there should be two officers, that's the rule. Never alone! But she was alone because we were short of men. She was stabbed twice in the chest – stood no chance against her attacker.'

Is Andrea all right? I was only thinking it as I dared not ask that question out loud in the face of DI Marsh being so upset about her officer.

'Is she alive?' Samuel was asking, and I think he meant the policewoman, not Andrea.

'DC Macfadyen's fighting for her life in hospital. The prognosis is very poor. You don't want to know.' DI Marsh relapsed into her prior subdued demeanour. She didn't even wipe away her tears. She took a moment to pull herself together while we waited – me with my heart in my throat, fearing the worst for Andrea, but having no guts to ask, and Samuel.

DI Marsh looked up at me. Her face was now composed. She said in a formal tone of voice, 'I'm here to tell you about your sister.'

I gulped. Samuel grabbed my hand and squeezed it.

'There was a fire at the property – arson started by intruders. Wayne Kew and his men.'

'We heard a fire engine in the night,' Samuel said. I'd heard nothing, I thought, I had slept right through it! I had dreamt of howling wolves and red skies ... But Andrea, I grasped at the straws of logical reason, but if she were dead, I would be seeing her ...

'There's fire damage on the ground floor. One casualty, but it isn't your sister.'

'I knew it wasn't Andrea, I knew that!'

'You won't be able to see her or talk to her, for a while at least – while we're still hunting for Wayne Kew, assuming that he isn't the casualty of the fire. We're yet to identify the body. Your sister suffered some smoke inhalation. We've taken her to a place of safety. She is all right.' There was that look again from Gillian Marsh: anger and resentment.

'I hope DC Macfadyen pulls through.'

'Erin. Her name is Erin.'

Chapter Thirty-three

She was strapped to a narrow metal bed, unable to feel her arms or legs. The ambulance tumbled and veered around sharp corners, throwing the paramedic off balance, but that observation aside, the turbulences had no apparent effect on Andrea. She felt like a dead log. Having removed the oxygen mask from her face, the paramedic sat down and put on his seat belt.

Hugo was in the other seat. She was aware of his presence there. She could not muster enough energy to turn her whole body to search for him.

'Hugo,' she heard herself whisper . . . just. 'Hugo, what day is it? I've a plane to catch.'

'Rest, just rest for now, Andrea. We'll talk later.'

It was instant recognition – the furniture was different, even the wallpaper fresh and new, but it was the same bedroom, the same house where she had been confined for her own safety twenty-five years ago. She was staring at the ceiling – white and clinically sterile. Her eyes travelled to the wall – there was a painting there, a landscape – green and bubbling with trees under a tranquil, baby blue sky fluffed up with candyfloss cloud. She turned her head away from it, and looked at a window. The curtains resembled an ancient Greek toga embroidered with a geometrically shaped gold border running along the hem. They were half open. Outside, the sky was moody. It was impossible to tell how late it was because it was overcast.

Andrea heaved herself up and managed to sit clumsily as if she were learning the motions. She could not remember how she got here; she could not tell how long she had been here. The first thought that came to mind was her flight back to New Zealand: was there still time to catch it? She ought to leave. To go home.

The carpet felt warm and woolly underfoot as if its sole purpose was to give her a sense of tranquillity. She wished she had slammed her feet into shards of broken glass like Hugo had once done – she needed to feel, and to react.

The staircase spiralled downwards. Looking at it she felt dizzy. She climbed it gingerly, clinging on to the rail. There was the tip-tapping sound of a keyboard being punched rapidly. She half-expected to find Hugo in the lounge, the only person her brain was able to place here.

There he was: his back stiffly erect, his eyes looking down at the screen, his knuckled fingers working the keyboard. A mug stood next to him, untouched. The smell of good, rich coffee was pungent.

This scene had been rehearsed in her mind many times over: she would run to him, throw her arms over his manly, unyielding shoulders, and he would – effortlessly lift her up, his hands clasped firmly on her waist; they would laugh and kiss.

'Hugo,' she said. His face shifted towards her. His complexion was darker and rougher than she remembered, his features sharper, his eyes paler – eerily pale. There wasn't a net of wrinkles to make his face more animated, but rather, it seemed the skin had been tightened apart from the heavy folds under his eyes. His hair was thick metal wire. Hugo had aged but had not lost any of his masculinity – if anything, it had matured with him.

'Good morning,' he said lightly. 'Look what you made me do! I haven't done this in years, not since – you, come to think.'

'Sorry. And thank you, I guess. My plane – it's leaving on Tuesday.'

'That's today.'

'Can we still—'

'No, we can't. We don't know what Kew and his men actually know. Kew may still be alive, looking for you.'

'May?'

'We found a body. It's been badly burnt. We're running DNA and dental tests. Patience is the name of this game.'

'You don't understand, Hugo. I have to go. I brought nothing but trouble to ... but mainly, I really have to be with my son, to make sure he's fine.'

'He is.' He closed the lid of his laptop and stood up. 'I will make you coffee. We can talk about it.'

'I don't want to talk!'

He went to the kitchen despite her protestations. She followed him and watched him put the kettle on.

He was speaking without looking at her, 'You can't go now, Andrea. Haven't you heard what I said? Kew and his lot have gone through all your belongings. We can't be sure how much he knows. He might know your address in New Zealand.'

'What?'

'We're doing all the necessary checks. We've got men at Heathrow, their eyes peeled for Kew. We're running all the live CCTV footage at Terminal Four. We have your house and family in New Zealand under surveillance. We don't want to alert them without reason, but it may come to it and if necessary we will have to evacuate them. Like I said, patience.'

'How long?'

'Give us a few days.'

The kettle had boiled and Hugo was putting sugar in the mugs. He remembered how many sugars she took. There was a studied indifference in his actions. He was speaking with cool detachment, 'It may be sooner. For all we know, Kew is already dead.'

'I hope he bloody well is.'

Hugo handed the mug to Andrea. It wobbled in her hand and some of the coffee spilled out. She cursed under her breath and shook her scolded hand. She was angry. 'And why, in the first place, would they've let him out of prison?! The man is a maniac!'

'He has pancreatic cancer.'

'I know, I know … compassionate grounds. But look at the damage he's doing!'

'You've taken the best years of his life from him. He has only months left. He wants to settle scores before he dies—'

'I wish he'd hurry up and die at last! I'd gladly help him.'

Hugo smiled. 'You'd make a good soldier. You act faster than you think.'

'Is that supposed to be a joke?'

'It's supposed to be the truth.' A sparkle of that old mischief of his stole into his face. He was grinning.

'Bah!'

'I missed you.' All of a sudden he was dead serious again. 'God, how much I have missed you!'

'Why did you let me go? You never once tried to find me. I waited and waited … I called that bloody emergency number so many times … I nearly lost my mind! Why, oh why – why did you forsake me!' She tried to be flippant but despite the years gone by, the hurt was still raw. She added in a small voice, 'Why didn't you come with me on that plane?'

'I couldn't. I'm sorry.'

He kneeled, wrapped his arms around her thighs and buried his head in her lap. A sob rippled through his body. She stroked his hair. To her surprise it felt soft, almost silky.

'It's all behind us. Now, it'd be too late for us anyway,' she whispered, more to herself than to him.

He lifted his head and found her hands, and he kissed them. His lips pressed hard. His face was wet with tears. 'If only I was free to go, I would've followed you to the ends of the world.'

Andrea remembered that phrase from Mum's notebook – there had been a time when Mum would have followed Karl to the ends of the world, but that time had passed quickly.

'Let's not dwell on it,' she said. 'It's all in the past. You made a decision and stuck with it – simple.'

'I made a decision to leave. I was packed to go. I had bought a ticket for the same plane you were on.'

'So why . . . what stopped you?'

'Her name is Catherin.'

Chapter Thirty-four

'In the beginning I'd call her Cathy and she liked it, but now she prefers Catherin. She says she doesn't like pet names. She despises affection; affection is too close to pity. She won't bear pity.'

'Who are you talking about?'

'Catherin, my wife. We've been married for thirty-two years.'

'You were married when we—' Andrea cursed her bad luck. Another married man: firstly Wayne, then Hugo.

'Yes, I was. I have her photo. If you'd like to see what she looks like?' He opened his wallet and pulled out a passport-sized colour photograph. He passed it to her without looking at it. 'It's fairly recent, taken about three years ago.'

The woman gazing at her without a smile must have once been beautiful: she had classic, symmetrical features, high cheekbones and a strong jaw, straight nose, and sensually shaped though ghostly pale lips. Her deep-set eyes were grey, large and round. Her eyebrows were pale, almost invisible. Little was to be said of her hair: the colour was a nondescript greying blond. It was brushed away from her face. There was not a trace of make-up to smooth the lines, just the timeless, but somewhat cold beauty. The white shirt she was wearing was buttoned right to the collar. Something was tragically distant and glazed over in her image, in her eyes and in her indifference. She looked drained and tired.

This is the woman Hugo chose over me.

It wasn't that much of a surprise – there was something superior about Catherin, something compelling. Everything made sense at last:

Hugo's last minute change of heart and his long silence ever since that day. He had a life, a life that did not and could not involve Andrea.

She returned the photograph to him. 'She is beautiful.'

'Yes, time doesn't seem to affect her face. But it isn't the face—'

'Stop there. I understand. That's all I needed to know. My question's been answered. It was a long time ago. I was young and naïve. You . . . you forgot yourself for a minute or two. Let's not talk about it.'

'I have to talk about it. I must tell you the whole story. I need you to actually understand why.'

'That sounds a bit patronising.' Her voice dipped to a low, cold monochrome. 'But say what you have to say.'

'I felt incredibly guilty after you left. I was angry with myself because yes, I'd let you down, but even more so because I had let Catherin down. I had come so close to abandoning her and even though I stayed with her I couldn't get over you. We had a terrible few years at first. She suffered. It was unfair on her.'

'I imagine it was,' Andrea sighed. She sipped her coffee. It was cold.

'There have been no more assignments for me, mainly because the Department didn't consider me safe. They sent me for counselling. That solved all my problems!' Hugo laughed.

'I'm sorry.'

'Not half as much as I was . . . The day I was going to join you I packed a few bits and bobs, some old photos and my passport. Catherin was watching me. Those weren't the sort of things you'd take away with you on assignment. Too personal, you see. She knew straightaway what was happening. She used to be in active service – she knew how it worked. She didn't say anything, didn't plead with me to stay. Not a word—'

'She was letting you go, you fool!' Andrea stood up abruptly. Her chair fell back. This conversation was at an end as far as she was concerned.

But not for Hugo. He grabbed her arm. 'Please, hear me out.'

She stayed, but she wouldn't sit back down. She folded her arms on her stomach. It was the body language of someone who didn't plan to stay long.

'Yes, she wanted me to go. She was willing me to leave her. She considered herself a burden that I didn't deserve.'

'A burden?'

'Catherin was shot in Ireland. We were stationed there. The Troubles were just about over, just a random skirmish here and there ... The bullet lodged itself close to her spine. When they operated, things went wrong ... She is paralysed from the waist down. She used to be very physical – her athleticism was one of the qualities that had made her into one of our best. And then there was her Irish Catholic background – she spoke their language, in more than one way. She was an asset in Ulster. A very proud woman, Catherin ... She'd prefer to have been killed. She died inside anyway when she found out she'd never walk again. Now, she's just a shadow of her former self. She has nothing to live for, but you see, she has always wanted me to live my life to the fullest. So, that day she wanted me to go.'

'A noble woman.'

'Oh, yes – always.'

'And she loves you. She'd want you to be happy. She was letting you go! It was her wish ...'

'But I couldn't let her go! Andrea, I am a brutal man, I have killed and I never gave it a second thought. I have few regrets in life. But I'd never forgive myself if I had left Catherin that day. It wasn't because she was crippled. Or because leaving her for a beautiful young girl like you would make me a callous bastard and one day even you'd come to hate me for it.

'It wasn't any of that – it wasn't pity or sense of duty. It was what Catherin and I have ... She took a bullet for me. That bullet in her spine was meant for me. We are bound for life. That bond is stronger than whatever feeling I may harbour for you. Do you understand? Do you really understand?'

Andrea nodded.

'Good!' He pulled her towards him and kissed her forehead. 'Good,' he repeated.

It was dark and the lights weren't on so she couldn't see his face but she heard relief in his voice.

'When I told her yesterday that I was going away to take care of you, she asked, *What took you so long?* She remembered you. She knew how close I'd come to – you know ... She wheeled herself away to her room and stayed there with her back to me when I said goodbye. She didn't want me to see her face. She didn't want to see me.'

'Do you think she may be worried you won't come back?'

'She knows I will. That's what worries her.'

'She loves you.'

'Yes, she does. And what I feel for her is stronger than love. I just don't have a name for it.'

Chapter Thirty-five

I had invited Samuel and Deirdre for dinner to reciprocate their kindness. Since Mum's passing – and her twirling into the afterlife without a second glance in my direction – and then Dad going so suddenly, Samuel had become my knight in shining armour. The image of him wearing armour with a plume of ostrich feathers and riding a frisky stallion made me smile. I hadn't smiled in such a long time. My muscles had forgotten how to go about it.

As was the norm on Thursdays, the Market Square was buzzing with commercial activity. I weaved between the stalls, greeting people, taking in the rich aromas of cooking and spices, and searching for that something special to put on the table tonight. I was spoilt for choice and couldn't quite make up my mind. It was becoming too complicated so I began acquiring all sorts of unrelated produce in the hope that I could later chuck it all into a pot and cross my fingers for an hour while it was stewing.

As I was bagging a cabbage, I was tapped on the shoulder. It was more of a squeeze than a tap. I spun on my heel to find Cherie. She was carrying a big backpack in the military colours of muddy green peppered with yellow blobs. It looked full and heavy.

'Cherie! You going camping?'

'What gave you that idea?'

'The backpack.'

'That's my shopping. I don't do carrier bags, you know. What are you up to?'

'Same as you – shopping.' With my foot I discreetly pushed away my two plastic bags. An eco-warrior, as are most of the staff at Bishops Ace Academy, Cherie wouldn't approve of the amount of plastic my shopping involved. I had been planning to buy bags for life as my tote bag is on its last legs, but our nearest supermarket is in Sexton's Canning and I really had no need to go there (other than to buy the bags, which would be quite ridiculous). Everything else I needed was here in Bishops and could be acquired fresh at the Thursday Market. Luckily, I had my wicker basket in hand laden with natural produce. I elevated it to demonstrate to Cherie my dedication to the cause. She gave it a perfunctory glance.

'Oh my! Are you feeding an army, Maggie?'

'No, but I'm expecting guests for dinner. Samuel and Deirdre.'

'Just the two of them? That's a lot of greens, not that I'm criticising. Healthy eating is my motto too.'

'I'm just not sure what to do with it,' I confessed. 'I'd really, really like to impress them. They've been so good to me of late.'

'If you want to impress them, you won't go wrong with Beef Wellington,' Cherie declared. Being a Napoleonic Wars expert, she was bound to recommend that, wasn't she?

'Doesn't that involve puff pastry? I wouldn't know where to begin with that.'

'Begin with buying a ready-made one.' Cherie shrugged.

I reflected. 'No,' I said at last. 'I think I will just stick with my original plan.'

'I thought you didn't have one.' Cherie cocked her eyebrow. 'Never mind. Must go.'

Once she was gone, I retrieved my plastic bags from under the feet of an unsuspecting man who stumbled over them, and cursed rather unpleasantly. I apologised and returned to my non-existent shopping list. One thing I definitely knew I was buying today was fudge. I had been craving fudge since my life had taken a sharp turn to the bitter side. Jane and Kev Wilcox are the master fudge-makers, famous across the county and beyond. I absolutely worship their Rum & Raisin Fudge Extravaganza. It has everything I love mixed together in perfect proportions.

As I was heading towards their distinct stall with its cream and pink awning, I let my thoughts drift in a different direction: towards Lord Philip's encounter with Karl van Niekerk as relayed to me by Samuel. One of those men was guilty of murder – of that I was certain. Alas, I couldn't tell which. *They* could, but they weren't saying anything.

An intriguing latest development was the sudden vanishing of Karl. Just like all those years ago, he had taken off without warning, and disappeared over the horizon. I had not seen him since Dad's funeral. Samuel had caught a glimpse of him during that hostile encounter with Lord Philip. After that, not a sausage. I had enquired with Terrence Truelove at the Rook's Nest whether Van Niekerk had actually checked out. He hadn't. His bill had not been settled and his belongings were still in his room in the loft. Terrence was not amused. He was threatening to go through Karl's possessions, to sell them for what they were worth and recover his money that way.

I suggested reporting Karl missing to the police. I couldn't help but wonder about the parallels with his disappearance in the sixties. Questions had to be answered rather urgently, I thought. Had he just gone back to South Africa, or was he lying buried somewhere in Sexton's Wood? Would it take another archaeological dig to find his remains, in say another fifty years' time?

I arrived at the fudge counter to be jovially greeted by Jane and Kev. I am after all their most loyal customer. Skinny as a rake, Jane looks like someone who has never even tasted her own fudge, but Kev makes up for it tenfold. He probably lives on fudge. They commiserated with me over the fire at my parents' house and wanted to know every detail – something I was unable to share with them as I was in the dark myself.

'Nothing an insurance payout won't patch up,' I said with forced cheerfulness. Deep down, I felt as if bits of me had burned with the bits of the house. It is – or it was – an original Tudor lodge, Grade II listed with its wonky windows and thatched roof. It was a blessing that the fire had been quickly contained downstairs and hadn't reached the flammable thatch. Andrea, for one, would have been roasted like a leg of lamb on a spit. It was pure luck she had called the emergency services before the fire had even started.

'But it won't be the same as it was,' Jane lamented.

'No,' I agreed, fighting off the trembling of my lower lip.

'Would you like the usual, Maggie?' Kev's voice broke through the thick haze of sadness. He knew what I needed was fudge, not sympathy.

'Yes, please – half a pound of Rum & Raisin Extravaganza.'

Carefully, Kev selected the shapeliest and most raisin-abundant pieces and placed them in a carton. The scales showed well in excess of half a pound, but Kev charged me for half a pound of fudge exactly and told me to enjoy it.

'Oh, I will!' I bade them goodbye and scampered, my spoils safe in my basket.

My shopping basket overflowing with goodies, I decided to stop at the Old Stables for coffee and cake before heading home to cook. I waved to Vanessa and Vera (and Rumpole) who were already there, occupying a table for four. I was fortunate to run into them as the café was full. I headed towards them with my coffee and an almond slice, balancing my tray over other patrons' heads and apologising for random nudges and shoves. While I was extending my heartfelt contrition to one unlucky customer whose coat I seemed to have trampled over, my tray caught another customer in the neck, threatening to decapitate him.

He seized the tray before it did him any real harm. My coffee cup and teaspoon rattled cantankerously in his hands.

'Watch where you're going!'

'I'm ever so sorry—' I gazed, contrite, at the young man who was now in possession of my cake. He was in his very early twenties, slim and gaunt. His olive complexion and large brown eyes signified a Mediterranean connection, but his hair was curly with vivid hints of ginger in it. It was the eyes however that baffled me most. There was an unhealthy sheen to those eyes. My first impression was that he had a fever: his pupils were dilated and red veins splintered the whites of his eyes. But the frenetic sharpness of his gestures pointed to something more sinister – the young man was high, as high as a kite.

'No harm done,' a woman sharing a table with him smiled at me indulgently. She addressed the young man, 'Ollie, be a good boy and give the lady her tray back.'

He did as he was told, shoving the tray at me. Half of my coffee was spilled in the process of the handover.

'Thank you,' I mumbled. 'Sorry, again, I'm sorry.'

'Forget it. My son is a bit touchy. The youngsters these days – a cross every parent has to bear!' She waved a dismissive hand and raised her brow in a display of loving, maternal clemency. I could tell she and he were related even without her saying so. Both had the same Roman noses. She too had a distinct Mediterranean aura about her, reminiscent of Sophia Loren: lustrous black hair rolled into a chic messy bun, sensual lips, and thick, sculpted eyebrows. She oozed riches and authority. Her lipstick was deep red, one of those that don't smear on the edge of a cup. Her expensive bag sat on the edge of the table. I think it was made of some poor alligator or other such scaly creature.

I smiled faintly at her remark and retreated towards my friends' table. I dared not meet the young man's feverish eyes again.

I slumped into a chair. Rumpole rose to his feet like a true gentleman and wagged his tail. I gave him a pat on the head, and relaxed.

'I see you made the acquaintance of Cordelia Conti Lang,' Vera said.

'Who is she?'

'She bought Richard Ruta's mansion, didn't you hear? It had been on the market for hardly a couple of months when she turned up with a cash offer.'

'She bought Forget-Me-Not for cash?'

'Small change for her, darling, small change.'

'Who is she?' I repeated my question.

'Cordelia Conti Lang, the bitcoin queen! Surely, you've heard of her.'

'No, not really. What's *bitcoin*?'

Vera and Vanessa exchanged conspiratorial glances. Vera said simply, 'You need to get out more, Maggie.'

Vanessa however obliged me with an answer. 'It's an Internet currency. She's made a fortune on it.'

'Wow!' That was my closing statement. I had lost interest in the matter. Technology and I don't mix. We are incompatible. And as for currencies, I am very happy with good old sterling, thank you very much. I put aside my soaked tray and wiped the spilled coffee from my saucer with a napkin. I took a sip and instantly felt better. 'I needed that,' I declared. 'The cake looks luscious.' I sank my fork into it.

'Anyway, darling, how are you coping?' Vera turned unexpectedly effusive. She must have suddenly remembered that I was in need of tender loving care. Better late than never, I shrugged inwardly. She leaned over the table and hugged me before air-kissing me on both cheeks.

Vera is at her best when she derides and criticises. She excels at sarcasm but struggles with empathy. I love her nonetheless. We've had some jolly good times over the years, keeping each other company when Henry was away navigating the treacherous currents of Westminster.

'I'm a bit shaken, all things considered,' I admitted, 'but I'll get there in the end.' A stiff upper lip – that's what Dad instilled in all three of us when we were little. *Don't cry or I'll have to give you a reason for it*, he would say. And the threat would work so well that he never had to resort to pulling out his belt.

'And your poor sister – she's been to hell and back. How's she holding up?' Vanessa enquired with her natural warmth.

I snorted, 'You probably know better than I do! All I know is that she's suffered minor smoke inhalation and is being kept in a safe house until they find that Wayne-whatever-his-name-is.'

'Wayne Kew,' Vanessa clarified.

'You see! You're much better informed. Has Alec been saying

anything about Andrea? I just wonder if I'll see her before she goes back to New Zealand.'

'I couldn't tell you. You know how Alec is – even if he knows, he keeps it to himself. But he did mention that Andrea must be pretty important. They're taking good care of her. Apparently, some high-ranking officer's guarding her day and night. A major, I believe he said.'

'A major? Blimey!' Vera was impressed. Unlike me, she had some idea about military ranks.

'That's my sister!' I exclaimed, part proud, part despondent.

'I've heard Will's back?'

'Yes, the police found him in some B&B in London. He was having some me time while the whole of Sexton's CID was looking for him. DI Marsh wasn't amused, but I can see her point. I hope DC Macfadyen pulls through ...'

'Her condition is still critical, I'm sorry to say.' Vanessa laced her fingers as if readying herself for a prayer. 'Erin's such a lovely person. Alec's very fond of her. They all are at the station. Gillian and Mark never leave her bedside. There's always one of them there – they take turns. We all pray she recovers.'

'If it wasn't for my silly brother pulling a disappearing act, she wouldn't have been in that car alone.'

'Please don't blame Will. The police are under-resourced – that's the real reason. Will's probably blaming himself as it is.'

'I wish I knew what he was thinking.'

'You haven't spoken to him?'

'Not yet. As soon as he was found he went home to Tracey and the kids with his tail between his legs. He's got lots of explaining to do. To me, it still feels like my brother is missing. And now, Karl van Niekerk! He's vanished too, I hear. Terrence Truelove was saying—'

Vanessa put down her cup and again interlocked her fingers. 'No, Karl van Niekerk isn't missing. He's been found dead.'

Vera and I just gaped. Not another death in Bishops Well! Our little community was turning into an abattoir.

'Natural causes?' Vera asked. It was a sensible question. After all, Karl van Niekerk was an elderly man.

'I'm afraid not. The victim of that fire in your parents' house, Maggie – Alec and the whole of Sexton's CID were crossing their fingers that it'd be Wayne Kew, but no. The body was identified this morning as Karl van Niekerk.'

Chapter Thirty-six

My Mystery Stew was a success. Samuel had a second helping and Deirdre asked for the recipe. That caused some consternation on my part as I couldn't quite remember what exactly (nor in what precise ratio) I had chucked into the pot. I promised Deirdre I would deliver the recipe tomorrow, thus earning myself time to make it up. I would consult Grandma's handwritten recipe book for ideas as soon I was able to locate it.

Halfway through the stew, I nearly suffered a heart attack. I hadn't noticed when Alice had left the room, giving the floor to some new ghostly arrival on the scene. Because I had missed that, I jumped to my feet in shock when a pale man, looking deceptively like Will, took a seat in a chair at the table.

'Will?!' I was grasping my chest, holding my heart back from breaking through my ribcage. It was racing with insane speed.

'Maggie?' Deirdre and Samuel exclaimed in unison.

For a few traumatised seconds, I stood riveted to the floor, trying to recover my breath and my wits. I knew of course that I wasn't looking at a living man, so the logical conclusion would be that Will was dead. That was what had thrown me off balance on his arrival. But then, on closer inspection of the apparition, I began to see irreconcilable differences: this man was shorter and more wiry than Will, and he wore outdated clothes that Will wouldn't be seen in, dead or alive. Although there were strong traces of Will in his features, he was not Will at all. He just resembled him to a fault.

'What is it, Maggie? Is it Alice?' Samuel's eyes darted between me and the empty chair (occupied by the intruder).

'I haven't got a clue,' I said. 'It's someone . . . I . . . Alice is gone . . . There is a man here. I never met him in my life, at least I don't think I did, but for a second . . . God, I thought it was Will!' The last word came out as a whimper.

'It's your nerves. You've been on edge for weeks . . .' Samuel approached me, placed his hand reassuringly on my back and made me sit down.

Deirdre looked alarmed. 'What man? And why, in God's name, are you talking about Alice?'

Before we had a chance to explain (and that would have been a challenge – Deirdre may be getting on but she's as sharp as a razor and doesn't suffer fools gladly), we were saved by a knock on the door.

Now, that *was* Will – in person and very much alive, though not looking his best.

'Will! Here you are at last!' I was relieved. I threw myself into his arms whether he found that acceptable or not.

Deirdre had followed me to the door for some reason. She said, 'Will Kaye, of course. Maggie foretold your arrival a few minutes ago. How uncanny!'

Everything became clear when Will sat down with us and started talking. Without offering any apologies or explanations for his disappearing act, he said that he had come from Sexton's Canning, where he had just given a full statement to the police. He popped over before going back to London because he wanted to 'put me in the picture before I found out through different channels', by which he probably meant our infallible Bishops Well grapevine.

Will looked rotten: unshaven and dishevelled, drained of colour and hunched. He wasn't himself.

'I took a bit of time off to think about this – to decide what to do.'

'Tell me about it! Everyone was looking for you! We feared that devil had abducted you. At least you were found in one piece. That's all that matters.' I felt eerily calm now that I could see him, as if a

217

big wave had crashed into me but now it was retreating slowly with the ebbing tide. All was well.

'But what were you thinking about?' Deirdre wanted to know. It was a rational enquiry, but I wasn't sure Will would take to it kindly. He could be one prickly character when he put his mind to it.

Indeed, he glared at Deirdre.

'It's Deirdre, Samuel's mother. Surely, you remember her!'

'Yes, sorry.' He got his bearings – and manners – back.

'So, what were you thinking about? What was the thinking that you couldn't do at home, or at least without warning us that you needed to go away?'

'It smacks of a mid-life crisis if you ask me.' Deirdre interjected again. This time it was Samuel who shot her a warning glance.

Will hardly heard her. He was looking at me in the most unsettling way – something between sorrow and defiance. At last he said, 'I didn't want to believe him, but I couldn't argue with the evidence – Mum wrote to him before she passed away. She told him the truth. Dad is not my ... father. We all thought I was simply conceived the wrong side of the blanket, but it's much worse than that. Karl van Niekerk was my biological father.'

I could see plainly now where the resemblance came from. The spirit who had heralded Will's arrival was Karl. Will had Karl's eyes and the squarish shape of his face, and his nose, and ... everything else.

'Yes,' I whispered, 'I can see that. You two look so alike ... I don't know how I didn't see this earlier.'

'He told me everything after Dad's funeral. He took me to one side, said he was Mum's old friend – could we go for a walk and talk? We crossed the fields behind Mr Wotton's paddock, and went into Sexton's Wood. Mum and Karl used to meet there, he said. He showed me the place—' Will's voice cracked a little on the last sentence. It had to be hard for him to say it. Even I found it somehow immoral, almost incestuous. To think that Mum—

'In his defence – in Mum's defence – it was before she met Dad.' Will seemed to read my thoughts.

'So, when Karl suddenly left the country, your mother found herself pregnant and at a loss,' Samuel speculated. 'Eugene rode to the rescue ...'

'Yes. Karl didn't know she was expecting. He was hoping she'd join him in South Africa, but instead, she married Dad and he became my father, in every way.'

'That was what you needed to get your head around?'

'That, and more.'

'There's more?' I thought finding out that your father wasn't really your father would be more than enough to mull over in the solitude of a shabby B&B. It was a shock to me. It had to be a catastrophe to Will. He and Dad had been ... well, like father and son! Will's entire world – which was a very orderly and secure place – must have been shattered. He had so many pieces to pick up and put back together! I went to him and hugged him. He was rigid with discomfort.

'It's not the end of the world,' I reassured him. 'You're still my big brother. You were just lucky to have two dads.'

'Lucky?' Will snorted. He isn't an adventurous man. He likes clarity. Having two fathers must have muddied the waters for him big time.

'I bet you could do with a stiff brandy,' I proffered helpfully.

'Yeah. Just one. I don't want a repeat of last Saturday.'

The three of us had brandy. Deirdre opted for sherry. Luckily, I had a bottle of that too. I also presented everyone with a piece of Rum & Raisin Extravaganza. Even Will had one.

Samuel said, 'That other bit Karl told you about – was that to do with Helen's death?'

'Yes,' Will nodded. We turned – all ears. 'He said he wanted the truth to be out – he wanted to start *our relationship*,' Will drew inverted commas in mid-air, 'on the right footing: no secrets, no lies. He said he'd wanted to tell Mum all along, only she had never replied to his letters. Not until, that is, when she wrote to him about me, and that was just a few months ago.'

'So,' I prompted him, 'did he confess?'

'Was it him or Lord Philip?' Sam asked.

'My money is on—' I started.

'It was both of them and neither of them. Complicated. They had a row, and a fist fight. Philip was making accusations against Helen. Nasty accusations that James wasn't his child. He wanted to know who the father was. He told Helen to go and be with him – her "negro lover", and to take "the bastard" with her. He demanded that Karl dealt with it. Helen was beside herself, desperate. She was crying – just crying – she couldn't even bring herself to deny it. Of course, Karl stood up for her. There was a scuffle. It came to a fist fight between Philip and Karl. Helen stepped in to separate them, shouting that she would leave, telling them to stop. One of them – and they accused each other – one of them hit her. She flew backwards and hit the back of her head on the grate of the fireplace.

'They tried but they couldn't bring her back. They panicked. Well, Karl panicked. Philip was more . . . organised. He told Karl to go away, to disappear and never come back. He threatened him – told him he had the best lawyers that money could buy, and they'd put the whole blame on Karl, and make it stick. Karl had no money for lawyers. He knew he stood no chance against a mighty lord of the realm. Philip gave him money for a new start abroad. He said he'd take care of everything – he'd convince people that it was an accident. It was either that or both of them would end up on trial for manslaughter, and Karl would lose.

'Even though Karl knew he wouldn't get away with it if he stayed to face justice, he bargained with Philip, and Philip made promises. He gave Karl his word that Helen would have a proper burial and that he would bring up James as his son and heir. There was nothing better that Karl could achieve by staying. And on top of that, he could do with the money. It was a large sum. He and Mum were engaged. The money would be a start. It was enough to buy a place in South Africa. He said to me he had regretted that decision ever since – he had lost Mum, he'd never got to know me, and his life had been a mess. And to top it all, Lord Philip had broken his promise – lost his nerve and decided to conceal his wife's death. Karl had thought Helen would get a decent burial. When he found out that her body had been dumped in the swamp, he was livid. He came to confront Philip about it.

'But primarily, he came back for me. He wanted to meet me and to explain everything. He wanted to straighten everything up. With everyone, he said, including Dad.'

'Dad?'

'Yes. That's the other thing. He went to see Dad – to introduce himself, to thank him for being a father to me – all that. It was meant to be a peace offering.'

'I bet there was more to it than just gratitude,' I had already pieced the puzzle together. Karl had to be the anonymous caller who had reported Dad's heart attack. Karl had caused it. I just needed Will to confirm it for me.

'Yes, there was more. Karl insisted he wanted to meet me and tell me who he was. Dad objected. He got angry. His heart gave out – it happened fast. Karl said he'd called an ambulance, then he'd tried CPR. He trained to be a paramedic at college, so he knew when . . . when it was over.'

'And he just walked away, like he had done to Helen. Charming!' I sneered. Yes, I was angry – bloody livid! What he did wasn't right – it wasn't how things were done here. 'He was a coward. A coward! You hear me?!' I was glaring right at him – at his ghostly apparition. Oh yes, he knew! He knew I was talking to him.

'He was,' Will nodded. 'I couldn't condone it, or forgive him. I didn't want to acknowledge him as my father – I wouldn't give him the satisfaction. But . . . I don't know . . . He begged me to give him a chance. I had to take myself out of the situation and think about it. I was confused . . . ashamed. I still am.'

'Whatever he did is no reflection on you.' It was Deirdre. 'It's nurture that matters more in the end, and your father brought you up to be a fine man. Trust an old woman – I know a fine man when I see one.'

A little tear rolled out and trickled down Will's cheek. I was quick to offer him another piece of fudge. Meantime, Karl had vanished – probably for the third and last time. A niggle of suspicion entered my mind: what if Karl went chasing after Mum? Dad would have a big battle on his hands. But he would fight Karl to the death – or rather, beyond it. Then again, all that unnecessary macho fisticuffs! Mum had already made her choice once. She had chosen Dad. And she would choose him all over again.

I swallowed my doubts and washed them down with another brandy.

After we waved goodbye to Deirdre and Samuel, we went back to the sitting room to confer about our little sister. Will told me that even DI Marsh didn't know where Andrea was. He had asked her and all she could tell him was that Andrea was in good hands. Whose hands? Well, that was classified. The hunt for Wayne Kew was still on. We had to be patient. I had almost abandoned hope that I would see Andrea before they bundled her away to New Zealand, or some other remote destination in the Antipodes.

Will looked spent. I made up the bed for him in the spare room and gave him some hot milk with honey to help him sleep. As for myself, the box of Rum & Raisin Extravaganza would have to do. I took the box to bed with me.

Chapter Thirty-seven

Andrea woke up, put on her dressing gown, and went downstairs in search of a bite to eat. Hugo was already up, looking bright eyed and bushy tailed, pottering around with a kitchen spatula. The aroma of morning coffee mingled with the smell of smoked bacon.

'Good morning, madam! Full English breakfast is being served. We've got sausages, eggs – fried, not scrambled – mushrooms, bacon of course, and tomatoes. Did I miss anything? Ah, toast!' He plucked two slices out of the toaster and dropped another two into it. He performed a tennis backhand volley with his spatula and executed a tidy bow.

'You're in a good mood!' She grabbed a mug and poured herself coffee. With all his secrets and regrets out in the open, he was a changed man. This was the old Hugo from when she had first clapped her eyes on him: carefree and just plain funny.

'I've my reasons to be. Sit down. Grub's up!' He served the breakfast with panache, a tea towel draped over his arm and a jolly 'Bon appetit!' rolling off his tongue with a put-on French accent.

'Thank you. So what's the good news? If it isn't top secret, of course.'

'The New Zealand police have reported no suspicious developments, strange characters, or anything untoward around your neighbourhood. They've had the place under surveillance for a while. Border Control officials gave us a full list of arrivals in recent months, since your mother's funeral, and we had all passengers vetted. No links to Kew. He's still on the loose somewhere in the UK, but we are reasonably assured that he doesn't know your address, your identity, or anything about your family in Auckland.'

'Thank God! So, I can go home?'

'That's the best thing you can do. We'll have you on the plane by tomorrow evening. You just need to call your husband, let him know you're on your way.'

Andrea squealed with delight. 'You've no idea how happy you've just made me! I could kiss you!'

'Why don't you?' He peered at her with the old spark of mischief in his eye.

'We best don't go there,' she laughed. 'Not again!'

'You're right there. It only took us twenty-five years to clear the air after our last kiss.'

They laughed, and he told her silly jokes that made her laugh even more.

'Do you remember that special place you took me before you left?' he asked, his face suddenly serious. 'That secluded glade, your secret hideaway in the woods?'

Of course she remembered. 'The place where you said you could die a happy man?'

'Yeah,' he smiled ruefully, 'a perfect place to die in. You think a lot about dying when you're in the firing line, soldiering, not knowing when your time is coming . . . I'll have you know I haven't thought of dying in ages. I must be getting old!'

'You? Never!'

'Anyway, I went looking for it. Several times. I couldn't find the blasted place. I meandered, got lost a few times, landed in a bog of some kind . . . It was gone! Do you think it's gone? Overgrown with new trees and so on . . .'

'No, it's still there. I went there the other day, to remember—'

'That's where we—'

'Yes, we did.'

'But we won't do it again.'

'No, we won't.'

'Still, I'd love to visit it again. One last time, before you go.'

'I'll take you there.'

They drove by the house without stopping. This escapade, like the previous one, hadn't been authorised by Hugo's superiors, but that didn't stop him. The leopard didn't change his spots.

When she saw the house, Andrea wasn't sure it was such a good idea. The downstairs windows and the front door were boarded up. Smoky black discolouration on the walls testified to the recent fire. She shuddered – she could have died in there. Someone had.

'Did they identify the body?' she asked Hugo.

'Oh, I didn't tell you, did I? They're ninety-nine per cent sure it was an old man by the name of Karl van Niekerk. He's missing. They're just running DNA tests to confirm that.'

'Yes . . .' She remembered seeing Van Niekerk head in the direction of the house. She had contemplated confronting him about his relationship with Mum and about Will's parentage. It was too late. The truth would probably never surface, and that, she thought, was for the best.

Hugo pulled up in the same lay-by where her minders used to park their unmarked police cars. Now the lay-by was empty. They stepped over a stile to cross a low fence and followed a narrow path overgrown by high grass. A splatter of bright yellow buttercups enlivened the dense greenery of the field. Everything swayed in a gentle breeze. A bizarre thought crossed Andrea's mind: it was certainly a perfect day and a perfect place to die.

'Are you sure you can find the place?' Hugo asked.

'How can I not?' She beamed at him. 'Just follow the leader.'

The footpath dipped into the wood.

On his way back from the Deeds Office in Sexton's Canning, Sam decided to take the scenic route passing by Maggie's parents' house to check that his instructions had been complied with. He was glad to see that the property was secured, the windows boarded up, and the police tape removed. It looked like neither Maggie nor Will would have the inclination or – in Maggie's case – the business acumen to deal with the insurance claim and organising the restoration work. This was a listed building and things would get complicated with the local authority sticking its nose into the remedial works every step of the way. According to Eugene's Will, the house was bequeathed to the three siblings in equal shares. That complicated matters even further. As it was, Andrea was nowhere to be found and would perhaps remain un-contactable in the future. Nothing could be done without her consent.

As Sam approached in his Jag, he saw two unfamiliar cars. One was a Ranger Rover and it was already parked opposite the house. The other pulled up behind. It was a black BMW. A slim, hunched man got out of the car. He was scanning the fields beyond the chestnut tree, his hand sheltering his eyes from the sun. He then leaned back into the car to fetch something from the glove compartment, shut the door, and set off into the field.

Sam was intrigued. He pulled up behind the BMW and turned off the engine. He tracked the man's trajectory. On the edge of the wood he saw two figures: a larger male and a small female. He didn't know the man, but he recognised the woman. It was Andrea.

It seemed like she was leading the way, going voluntarily. The two of them did not appear to be in a particular hurry and they didn't look worried – just a couple of ramblers ambling into the wood. Nevertheless, Sam didn't feel comfortable leaving them to it and driving off. The man who was following them had made him anxious. There was something about him – an agitated stride and intensity bubbling in his body language. Who was he? Could he possibly be Wayne Kew? And what was Andrea doing in Bishops? The last Sam had heard was that she had been taken away to a safe house.

Out of curiosity, Sam also decided to take a walk in the woods.

'You know these woods inside out,' Hugo was impressed.

Andrea laughed. 'I literally lived here as a child. All of us kids used to roam the woods, build dens and fires and just get up to no good.'

'You haven't changed, then!'

'Careful!' she warned him mockingly.

They negotiated their way through a dense and prickly thicket to emerge into a bright and open glade – Andrea's secret retreat. It was untouched. The grass stood tall and undisturbed, seemingly never trodden on. It was uncannily silent, as if they were in a bubble.

'You found it!' Hugo looked elated, and it didn't seem like he was teasing her.

'I never lost it.'

'Our special place . . .' He reached to her, took her hands into his and lifted them to his lips. A flutter of emotion buzzed in her stomach. The memories of their love affair flooded her every conscious thought. They were so real and so fresh in her mind that it seemed like it had only happened yesterday.

The sharp sound of a snapped twig, followed closely by another one, burst the bubble. Deer, she thought, or a badger. Had they disturbed an animal? She felt Hugo's lips on her hand, passionate and warm. There was another noise: a much louder and sharper crack. Hugo's lips slackened. His hands released hers. He slumped to the ground.

'It was only a matter of time, love.' Wayne's eyes drilled hard into her. A cold wave of different memories washed over her: the black African night, the deserted car park, the three bodies falling down.

This time she could not run. There was no way out. She wouldn't get away, but she wouldn't go without a fight either. She wasn't scared. She was angry. This would be her last stand. With the deafening, piercing wail of a mortally wounded animal, Andrea charged at her enemy. That took him by surprise. Their bodies collided before he could cock his gun. The impact knocked the gun out of his hand. It went flying behind him. Her teeth sunk into his cheek. She drew blood. He howled. With the last ounce of strength in his disease-ravaged body, he grabbed her by the hair and pulled her off. He tossed her to the ground and pounced on her. He pushed his knees into her arms, pinning them down. She was incapacitated. He formed a tight fist and aimed at her temple as she glared right at him, panting with hopeless fury.

'You stupid bitch! You thought you could get away from—'

A second shot resonated. An exit wound opened in Kew's forehead. Instead of his fist, blood and brain matter spluttered at Andrea's face. Finally, his bulk fell limp on to her. Stillness and silence followed. Whoever had shot Wayne was standing somewhere there holding his breath.

She couldn't work it out. It couldn't be Hugo. He was lying lifeless next to her. The shot had come from behind Wayne.

At last, some movement: the rustle of grass, steps . . .

'Andrea!' Someone – a man – shoved Wayne's body off her and leaned over her. His hot and rapid breath hit her face. 'Are you all right? Can you hear me?'

She realised who it was.

'Samuel? I'm fine. What about Hugo?'

He turned to Hugo, pressed his ear to his mouth and listened.

'It doesn't look good, he's lost a lot of blood, but I can feel his breath on my face. I'm calling an ambulance.' She heard him talk to an operator, trying to explain how to find them, failing, then agreeing to come out of the wood and meet the ambulance on the road.

He was going to abandon her here!

She experienced a moment of sheer panic. 'And Wayne? Is he dead? Is he really . . . Don't leave me alone with him!'

Sam peered at her strangely. He squeezed her hand. 'He's dead. The bullet went through his head.' He gazed, baffled, at Wayne's body, and then at the gun still smoking in his hand.

He added, with utter disbelief, 'I killed a man.'

Chapter Thirty-eight

Didn't I say that Samuel Dee was a knight in shining armour? Wasn't I right! He is now my greatest hero, beating Che Guevara, Nelson Mandela, and even David Attenborough by a country mile. He is more than a hero – he is the bee's knees. And I am proud to call him my neighbour.

The man had killed for me.

Well, OK, it was for my sister, to save her scrawny backside from certain death, but really – indirectly – it was for me. Or because of me. Because we were neighbours and friends, and because he was a hero – *my* hero. If Alice wasn't constantly hanging around, breathing – metaphorically of course – down his neck, I would probably be madly in love with him. As things stood, I just loved him to bits – platonically, of course. One day, I told myself, a time would come when I would get a chance to repay the favour, and kill for him – perhaps. Or maybe something less drastic.

Five days after the shooting in Sexton's Wood, I was going on a chauffeuring errand. First, I had to collect Andrea's family from the airport, and then Andrea herself from the hospital. They were coming to stay at my place for a couple of weeks. Will and Tracey were expected to join us in the evening.

I went to the garage to fetch my trusty Hyundai. I had to plough through an accumulation of junk piled up there since the Jurassic era. I don't use my car often and when I do it seems to be buried in objects which I no longer have use for in the house, like jars and bottles, blankets part-digested by moths, and broken pieces of furniture. I managed to uncover my vehicle and reverse it from the garage without a major incident. I then knocked on Samuel's door. He opened it fairly quickly, considering that he still looked deeply traumatised and not quite himself in a pair of stretched boxers and a white vest.

'Hi, Samuel!' I beamed at him.

He seemed alarmed. 'This is early ... What happened?'

It was indeed the crack of dawn, which I forgot to mention, but the plane was landing at 8:15 at Heathrow and we still had a three-hour drive ahead of us. I say *we*, because I was just about to ask Samuel to come with me.

'Get ready, Samuel. I'm driving you to London. We're picking up Elliot and Jack from the airport.'

He must have just awoken as he gazed at me puzzled. 'And who are these people?'

'Andrea's family, of course! We'll take them to the hospital. No – not because they need a hospital, but because we need to collect Andrea from there. Then we're back home. It shouldn't take us longer than, well ...'

'A whole day?'

'More or less.'

'And I'm coming on this merry trip because?'

'Oh, don't you know? Because you're our hero! They want to meet you – they want to thank you!'

'It's fine. They can thank me when they get here.'

'Um ... I need you to navigate. I don't trust that satnav woman – she's too good to be true ...'

'It's not her fault you can't tell your right from your left, Maggie.'

'Still, I don't like her tone. She's a patronising cow.'

Sam scrutinised my trusty little Hyundai with a very critical eye. Then he scrutinised me, and finally he said, 'I'll go as long as you aren't driving. And not in that. Give me five minutes to change. We'll take my car.'

★

I am allergic to maze-like buildings, full of tunnels and doors leading to more tunnels, and to crowds. Heathrow isn't a place for me. I was already feeling flushed and flustered, the mass of people throbbing around me and the lack of windows leaving me disoriented. We – Samuel, actually – found the correct gate at the correct terminal and watched the wave of new arrivals pushing towards us. It was at this point that I realised I didn't know what Elliot and Jack looked like. Every time Andrea had tried to show me their photos, her blasted phone was out of battery.

I should have thought of it earlier and made a sign out of an old box of cornflakes with their names printed on it. I began to panic. I was going to miss them altogether – they would walk past us, and I wouldn't know them from Adam (or from Andrea, to be precise!). I squeezed Samuel's arm, and confessed.

'You don't know what they look like?' he shouted over the cacophony of airport greetings.

'That's what I said … If we could make a sign …'

'Ha!'

I had an idea. 'Have you got your hanky?' I knew Samuel to always carry a handkerchief. And he didn't let me down today – he had one. He handed it to me compassionately, probably thinking that I needed to wipe my tears.

I snatched it and spread it on the floor. In large capital letters I wrote ELLIOT & JACK CHAPMAN using a purple glitter lipstick that I discovered in the depths of my handbag (origin unknown – it wasn't my colour). I lifted my banner in the air and waved it over my head.

Samuel gazed at me doubtfully. 'You look like you're surrendering.'

'I most certainly am not!' I retorted and decided to wave the banner harder and chant 'CHAP-MAN-CHAP-MAN-CHAP-MAN …'

Samuel, I noticed, had moved a couple of steps away from me. But a boy thrust a finger in my direction and pulled his father's sleeve, shouting, 'That's our name, Daddy! Over there! That crazy lady over there!'

The man peered at me from under the brim of his ridiculous hat, typical of men from Down Under who are into cattle farming. He tipped the hat to me. 'Maggie?' He sounded a bit guarded and a bit apprehensive. Obviously, I didn't inspire much confidence in him.

'Elliot! Jack! How lovely to meet you at last!' To counter his suspicions, I went for the effusive and wholehearted approach. I embraced Elliot first, then Jack. He was a delightful young man, and had a touch of Dad in his features. I bit my lip to stop myself from weeping with joy.

'I'm Sam, Maggie's neighbour.' Samuel shook Elliot's hand in a man-to-man, no-nonsense fashion.

'This is the man who saved your mummy's life,' I told Jack.

'He shot that gangster dead?'

'Yep!'

'Wow!' Jack was hypnotised. He was staring at Samuel, his mouth gaping open.

'He can tell you all about it on our way back to Bishops. It'll be a long drive.'

Elliot shook Samuel's hand again, this time with reverence and gratitude, 'Thank you.'

'It's nothing.' Samuel is so self-effacing that sometimes I feel he deserves a slap.

'It wasn't nothing!' I said. 'It was what you call *heroism*.'

I didn't explain why Andrea was in hospital. It hadn't been clear at first, what with all the adrenaline pumping and real casualties dead on the ground, but Andrea had a bullet in her shoulder just to the side of her collarbone. It was the same bullet that had gone through Wayne Kew's head, and lodged itself in her upper chest, just a centimetre above her left lung. There'd been blood all over her. Little did she realise that not all of it was Wayne's. She had felt no pain. Only when the paramedics had taken a look at her had they realised that she, too, was wounded.

The bullet had not caused any real damage other than the superficial tissue penetration and a grazed bone, so it was successfully removed during a two-hour-long surgery. And now Andrea was as good as new, ready to go home and release the bed for another patient who needed it more.

On our arrival, we found her sitting in a chair, dressed and packed, her arm in a sling.

'Aren't you lucky, sis?' I enthused.

'To be still alive? You bet!' she replied, beaming.

'That too. But to have all those men falling over you!'

She stiffened a bit, and so did Elliot. 'What do you mean, Maggie?'

'Well, isn't that obvious? Wayne must've still been carrying a torch for you. Why else would he have taken a bullet for you?' I elucidated, feeling that somehow I was treading into dangerous waters. Yet, I trod deeper, 'In his head, as it happens.'

'Oh, that!' She recovered her wits, and smiled again. 'I don't think he did it out of choice.'

'I'll take a bullet for you, Mum!' Jack declared.

'You'll do no such thing,' Andrea wagged her finger at him. 'Don't let Auntie Maggie mess with your head. Come here, and give your mother a cuddle.'

He pounced on her. They hugged and cuddled, and there was simply no telling one from the other in their bundle.

Elliot had given them as much time and space as they needed. He then went to Andrea, pulled her into his arms, and said in a breaking voice, 'You gave us such a fright!'

'Sorry.'

I think she meant it. She was welling up, poor thing. And so was I. I'm not one to defend my wayward sister – she's nothing but trouble – but she'd had an unfair share of bad luck and deserved a break. Just to catch her breath before she would do something stupid again. Because she would. That's why Dad was still hovering about her. He wasn't going to leave – he would have to be her guardian angel for the rest of her life. I bet he was dying – oops! – to pass on

233

to the other side and join Mum, especially because Karl van Niekerk was already there, worming his way into Mum's favours, but Dad had put fatherhood first.

I winked at him and I swear – I could almost swear – that he winked back.

Andrea kissed Elliot while still embracing Jack who was firmly attached to her leg, holding on for dear life to his mum. My heart was melting at an alarming rate.

'Is that it? No more skeletons in your closet? Nothing more under the carpet?' Elliot asked.

'That's it.'

I begged to differ. Knowing Andrea, there was an army of skeletons in her handbag alone. But I wasn't going to spoil the moment. Andrea was very capable of doing that all by herself.

'Before we go,' she said to prove my point. 'I want to see Hugo.'

'Hugo? That man—' Elliot went visibly pale. His jaw tightened and he didn't finish his sentence.

'That man who looked after me, protected me, almost died because of me,' Andrea finished it for him.

'Yes, of course – that man.'

We all flocked to see Hugo. His recovery had been a bit slower than Andrea's due to the fact that his injury was much more serious. The bullet had gone into his left lung, which had collapsed as a result. He was however going to pull through.

In his private room we found a woman in a wheelchair, keeping him company. He had been asleep but as we stormed in, he opened his eyes. The woman in the wheelchair fixed her eyes on Andrea. It was a stern look. She had wonderfully blue but cold eyes. That look stopped Andrea in her tracks. She even appeared to retreat back into the corridor, except that we all stood behind her so she was trapped with the woman.

'I just ... I'm leaving today. I just came to say thanks to ... to Hugo,' Andrea mumbled.

Hugo gave her a faint smile. 'Don't mention it.'

'So that's her?' The woman asked him.

He nodded, with a sort of contrite squint.

Again the woman's gaze descended on Andrea. 'We meet at last. Not that I ever wanted to meet you.'

'I'm sorry about . . . everything. I—I'm sorry—' Andrea continued mumbling.

'I'm sure you are. Don't be. You're just one of those perfect victims – people like Hugo need people like you so that they can perform their heroics.'

The three of them were looking at each other, intensity cutting the space between them like a knife. Many unspoken sentiments – not all of them good – were shooting across their triangle. The rest of us stood there like lemons, yearning for the final goodbye.

'I'll be off, then.' Andrea put us out of our misery in the end.

I had no doubt that she was the cause of all that discomfort and resentment, but I would be damned if I would ask her what that was all about, especially in front of Jack and Elliot. That skeleton was best left buried deeply in Andrea's conscience.

'Who's that lady in the wheelchair?' Jack had no such reservations.

'Oh, that? Well, that was Mrs Aniston – Hugo's wife.'

Of course, I thought bitterly. Dad's spirit looked put out too.

There was another person we had to visit on our way out – DC Macfadyen. She was still in a critical condition and the prognosis wasn't promising. We found her room. She was breathing through a tube and was in an induced coma, oblivious to the goings-on around her. Gillian Marsh was present in the room with a book on her lap. She closed it when we arrived.

'I was reading to Erin. Doctor's orders. Though I don't think she can hear me . . .'

'Oh, she can! She definitely can.' I could see DC Macfadyen's spiritual presence floating nearby, looking positively gobsmacked. The poor woman! There she was – her physical body, that is – lying lifeless and assisted by machines with all its bodily functions, while her soul hovered aimlessly, unsure whether it should stay or go now. The fact that her spirit had already evacuated her body wasn't a promising development. I feared she was on her way out.

'Keep talking to her,' I instructed Gillian. 'She's listening, and she needs lots of reassurance to feel welcome back in life.'

Back at home I ordered a takeaway pizza deal and put my feet up. I wasn't going to cook – I was knackered. I sent Andrea, Elliot, and Jack upstairs to unpack their bags and refresh. Jack did not make it back downstairs despite the promise of a pizza hanging fat and juicy in the air – he had passed out on the bed. Apparently, he hadn't slept a wink on either of the two planes they'd had to take to get here. He had been too excited at the prospect of being with Mum. But now he had seen her at last and found her alive and well, he had relaxed and gone to sleep, bless him!

I asked Samuel to fetch Deirdre – we had excess pizza on our hands due to Jack capitulating to tiredness. Deirdre, Will, and Tracey, and the pizza delivery boy on a scooter, all arrived simultaneously at my doorstep. After a series of warm introductions, we scattered ourselves around the sitting room with slices of pizza on paper napkins. I was determined not to have to do any washing up. We drank lemon squash and remembered the good old times. I felt fuzzy inside, so fuzzy that I retrieved my box of Rum & Raisin Extravaganza from my bedroom and shared the remaining pieces with my guests. There were ten perfect little cubes of fudge in the box, so I ended up having the final three just to finish the lot and be done with it. Starting tomorrow, I would think of shedding some unwanted pounds.

It was someone – Samuel, I believe – who raised the question of what we wanted to happen to our parents' house. We had inherited it jointly and this was our chance to make a joint decision about its future. Did we want to restore and sell it? Did we prefer to sell it as it was without investing in it? Or perhaps our desire was to keep it for whatever mysterious reason. Yes, it was Samuel – none of us would have thought of such triviality on such a rare day where the three of us sat together in one room.

I stole a glance at Dad, who was in the room with us, looking rather emotional for a ghost. His impression was blurry and a bit erratic in appearance. I could tell he was worried. That house was the last place on this planet where Andrea, Will, and I could come together for old times' sake. Without it, we would scatter like leaves in the wind never to be blown in the same direction again. Andrea would fly off to the Antipodes, Will back to London and his important job, and I ... Well, I had Priest's Hole to keep going. Old houses were needy – they forever demanded their owners' undivided attention. And they knew how to throw a hissy fit with burst pipes or leaky roofs. But we couldn't abandon our family home. I gave Dad the thumbs up to keep his spirits up.

'We can't be selling the house,' I declared.

'Dad would turn in his grave if we did,' Andrea supported me.

Will had no choice. 'We'll keep the house, but there's work to be done and I'm not—'

'Samuel?' I gazed pleadingly at my neighbour.

He rode to my rescue without delay. 'I'll get some quotes and get on with making an insurance claim. As it happens, I have a bit of time on my hands.'

'We'll come as often as we can.' Andrea looked at Elliot, who smiled. 'Summer holidays, maybe Christmas. We've some catching up to do.'

'There'll be no excuses at Christmas time – that's a given.'

'Our kids will get to know each other – they're about the same age,' Tracey chipped in.

'Christmas is great,' Will said, 'but the house will stand empty for the rest of the year – with the exception of Andrea's summer visits. Don't get me wrong, but somehow I don't think they'll be that frequent – going by your track record.'

Andrea hung her head.

'It's not healthy for a house to stand still,' I concurred with Will.

Everyone looked at me pointedly, as if to say that all houses stood still and that's precisely what they did. I sighed. 'I didn't mean *standing still* as in *standing still*.'

'Of course not,' Samuel feigned his agreement.

'What I meant was, well . . . it isn't good for a house not to have a purpose. And I know houses house people – primarily . . .' I could just hear Dad chortling in the background. 'But the house has to bubble with life and be filled with people.'

'I wish we could move back here,' Andrea looked despondent. She peered at her husband and there was some unspoken exchange between them. She nodded, resigned. 'But our life is in New Zealand – our friends, Elliot's family, Jack's granny and his rugby team . . .'

It hurt me just a little – just a tiny prick to my heart – to realise that Andrea would be going away again. I had somehow, unwisely imagined that once the dust had settled she would return to Bishops and everything would go back to how it used to be. But I had to admit that, just like houses, life didn't stand still. I glanced at Dad – he was still jittery and apprehensive. I wished he was here in body and mind, sharing his Solomon's wisdom with us. And then, he told me! I can't explain how he said it and how I was able to hear it. In fact, I don't think I heard it at all – I just knew!

'We're going to turn it into a lodge! It used to be a lodge in the olden times, it can be a lodge again. Maybe even a B&B! How hard can it be to grill a few sausages and scramble an egg?'

'I'm not sure . . .' Will and his reservations! The man had no sense of adventure! 'We'd have to employ someone to run it – it'd be a costly enterprise . . .'

'No, we wouldn't! I'm going to run the place. I'll run it personally,' I announced without a scrap of prior thought going into my announcement. The thought occurred a second later: I might struggle on my own. I gazed hopefully at Samuel, the bee's knees, and added hastily, 'And I'm sure Samuel will help with the books and legal stuff, and—' I stopped there though inwardly I was thinking of just about everything except for gardening. I could do the garden, no problem.

'That'd be a welcome distraction for Samuel,' Deirdre backed me up. 'He needs to get out more – and to get a life!'

Samuel appeared briefly perplexed. His fate was being decided for him and on his behalf, without his consent. It would only be polite to provide it. He smiled and said, 'Why not?'

Chapter Thirty-nine

It was bucketing down. The complete crew of the Bishops Well Archaeological Association stood gathered in the swamp, water dripping from their noses, rain bombarding their drawn hoods, and mud spluttering around them like mini grenade explosions. We were on the other side of the Easter holidays, full of chocolate eggs and calories. We had newborn energy to spend.

Cherie and Maggie had jointly removed what was left of the police tape restricting access to the dig. The excavation holes made in the autumn were fast filling with water, its level rising with alarming speed. This place wasn't called a swamp for no reason, Sam reflected philosophically, and curled his cold, wet fingers around the handle of his trowel.

He exchanged a heavy sigh with James, who was standing next to him. He and his family had returned to Bishops for Easter, shortly after Lord Philip had been released without charge, the CPS having concluded that he had no case to answer and it wouldn't be in the public interest to pursue an old gentleman for a crime that may have been committed by another. The fact that he was a member of the House of Lords played its part too. James had forgiven him, after months of tortuous soul-searching.

Edgar Flynn looked eager to dig. There was a keen spark in his eye, undampened by the weather. The man was impervious to the elements, Sam mused, or he simply had no life to go back to at home. Just like Sam.

The newest AA member, Ivo Murphy, also appeared enthusiastic.

He had even dragged his wife Megan with him, to introduce her to the motley crew of Bishops' amateur archaeologists. She seemed to have taken to Vanessa Scarfe, but then who wouldn't – Vanessa was the sweetest, cuddliest woman in town, with a heart of gold. She had instantly taken Megan under her wing.

Vera kept to herself. Suspicious by nature, she took her time to warm up to any newcomers in Bishops Well, but once she had, she would be all theirs. Vera was rather slow on the uptake. Rumpole had arrived with her to assist with the works in his special canine way. But discouraged by the downpour, he had hurriedly trotted away and was circling the woods, looking for a place to shelter.

They were watching Vicar Laurence bless the place. Maggie had come up with the idea and they all reluctantly agreed. She had got it into her head that there might be more unhappy souls haunting the site, dying to be put to rest.

Vicar Laurence – himself looking none too pleased about the adverse weather conditions – mumbled a few rushed prayers, turned to the gathering of nutters and declared the place to be comprehensively exorcised. Not quite exorcised but it was words to that effect, illegible as they were drowned in the incessant murmur and hiss of the rain.

At long last, trowels and pickaxes in hand, the archaeologists resumed their excavations.

Author's Note

In the second instalment of The Shires Mysteries Maggie's wayward sister returns to Bishop's Well after her two-decade exile in the Southern Hemisphere. The homely, idyllic setting of The Shires is pitted against the exotic but perilous Southern Africa and the beautiful but distant New Zealand.

Like Andrea, I spent twenty years down under. Unlike Andrea, I wasn't hiding from a murderous mobster, but merely studying, working, partying and exploring those far-flung worlds in all their alien and absorbing glory. I collected many memories along the way. Later I would be able to incorporate them into my writings and be certain of their authenticity.

Andrea's experience of life down under is based on my own, and a few anecdotes described in the book really did happened. I will never forget the celebrations that followed South Africa defeating New Zealand at Ellis Park, Johannesburg, to take the Rugby World Cup in 1995. Drunken revelries carried on for days (and nights), and indeed I had the absolute honour of bumping into Francois Pienaar in one of Rosebank's nightclubs and having his autograph scribbled on my forearm. Although South Africa is a huge country with a troubled history, at the time when I lived there Nelson Mandela was president and it seemed like a cosy little corner with the friendliest, most fun-loving people you could ever wish to meet.

Of course, my rugby loyalties were severely tested when I settled in New Zealand because in New Zealand rugby isn't just a sport – it's a religion, and the All Blacks are gods. I had to hang on for dear life to my fond memories of Francois Pienaar's autograph on my forearm so that I wouldn't be swayed to the Other Side by the irresistible charm of Jonah Lomu.

As much as South Africa is a place to be merry, New Zealand, in my experience, would be a perfect hidey-hole – the best imaginable witness protection stronghold. It lies in the Antipodes and so it takes a while to get there, even by plane. It is sparsely populated with its sheep population outnumbering humans by five to one. Privacy is fiercely respected and everybody minds their own business. Before moving to the small town of Pukekohe (located just a stone's throw away from Frodo's hobbit hole), I lived in a house in Auckland overlooking an estuary dotted with mangroves under the unbelievably blue sky – a house just like Andrea's. And if that wasn't picturesque enough, I would often travel to Taupo to commune with one of the most hypnotising lakes on this planet …

But beautiful as those other worlds may be, I will have to insist that, in the end, all roads lead to The Shires, and particularly to the sleepy, quaint town of Bishop's Well.

Discover more gripping novels by Anna Legat . . .

Join Maggie Kaye and Sam Dee on their next adventure in . . .

All is not well in the village. The local meadows have been the pride of Bishops Well for hundreds of years, but now they are facing the sharp blades of developers. The landowner is a rich and reclusive author who is happy to see them destroyed, but the villagers – including Sam Dee and Maggie Kaye – are fighting back.

Until, that is, someone decides to silence one of their number permanently.

As Maggie and Sam soon discover, there is more than a quick buck to be made in the developers' plans. There are age-old secrets and personal vendettas that could have deadly repercussions in Bishops Well today.

With Sam's legal expertise and Maggie's . . . well, Maggie-ness, they delve into the past, determined to unearth the truth. And, as sparks begin to fly, could there finally be something more between this sleuthing duo?

Available to order

ACCENT

Go back to the beginning in . . .

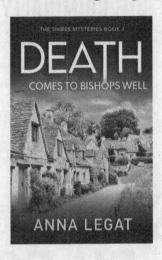

When Sam Dee moves to the beautiful Wiltshire village of Bishops Well,
he expects a quiet life of country walks and pub lunches. OK, so his new
neighbour, Maggie Kaye, is a little peculiar, but she's very nice – and
his old pal Richard Ruta lives just down the road.

But when Richard throws one of his famous parties, things take a sinister
turn. Sam, Maggie and the rest of the guests are dumbfounded when Richard
falls down dead. A horrible tragedy – or a cunningly planned murder?

With a village full of suspects – and plenty of dark secrets – just who
exactly would want to bump off their host? Is there a connection
to another mysterious death, nearly twenty years before?

Armed with her local knowledge, Maggie – with Sam's reluctant but
indispensable help – is soon on the case. But when the body count
starts to rise, will sleepy Bishops Well ever be the same again?

Available to order

THRILLINGLY GOOD BOOKS
FROM CRIMINALLY
GOOD WRITERS

CRIME FILES BRINGS YOU THE LATEST RELEASES FROM
TOP CRIME AND THRILLER AUTHORS.

SIGN UP ONLINE FOR OUR MONTHLY NEWSLETTER AND BE THE FIRST
TO KNOW ABOUT OUR COMPETITIONS, NEW BOOKS AND MORE.